SEVEN WONDERS

LOST IN BABYLON

PETER LERANGIS

HarperCollins *Children's Books*

First published in the USA by HarperCollins *Publishers Inc* in 2013
First published in Great Britain by HarperCollins *Children's Books* in 2013
HarperCollins *Children's Books* is a division of HarperCollins*Publishers* Ltd,
77-85 Fulham Palace Road, Hammersmith, London, W6 8JB.

The HarperCollins website address is
www.harpercollins.co.uk

1

Copyright © HarperCollins*Publishers* 2013

ISBN 978-0-00-751505-9

Printed and bound in Great Britain by Clays Ltd, St Ives plc

FOR MY AMAZING FRIENDS
AT THE NATIONAL BOOK STORE AND MPH,
AND THE GREAT READERS THEY SERVE ON
THE OTHER SIDE OF THE WORLD.

CHAPTER ONE

DEATH. TOAST.

BY THE THIRD day back from Greece, I no longer smelled of griffin drool. But I still had bruises caused by a bad-tempered bronze statue, a peeling sunburn from a trip around the Mediterranean on a flying ball, and a time bomb inside my body.

And now I was speeding through the jungle in a Jeep next to a three-hundred-pound giant who took great joy in driving into potholes.

"Keep your eyes on the road, Torquin!" I shouted as my head hit the ceiling.

"Eyes in face, not on road," replied Torquin.

In the backseat, Aly Black and Cass Williams cried out in pain. But we all knew we had to hang on. Time was short.

1

We had to find Marco.

Oh, about that time bomb. It's not an actual physical explosive. I have this gene that basically cuts off a person's life at age fourteen. It's called G7W and all of us have it—not only me but Marco Ramsay, Aly, and Cass. Fortunately there's a cure. Unfortunately it has seven ingredients that are almost impossible to find. And Marco had flown off with the first one.

Which was why we were stuck in that sweaty Jeep on a crazy rescue mission.

"This ride is bad enough. Don't pick the skin off your face, Jack!" said Aly from the backseat. "It's disgusting!" She pushed aside a lock of pink hair from her forehead. I don't know where she gets hair dye on this crazy island, but one of these days I'll ask her. Cass sat next to her, his eyes closed and his head resting against the seat back. His hair is normally curly and brown, but today it looked like squid-ink spaghetti, all blackened and stringy.

Cass had had a much worse time with the griffin than any of us.

I stared at the shred of skin between my fingers. I hadn't even known I was picking it. "Sorry."

"Frame it," Torquin said distractedly.

His eyes were trained on a dashboard GPS device that showed a map of the Atlantic Ocean. Across the top were the words RAMSAY TRACKER. Under it, no signal at all. Zip.

We each had a tracker surgically implanted inside us, but Marco's was broken.

"Wait. Frame a piece of *sunburned skin*?" asked Aly.

"Collect. Make collage." If I didn't know Torquin, I would think he had misunderstood Aly's question. I mean, the four of us kids are misfits, but Torquin is in a class by himself. He's about seven and a half feet tall in bare feet. And he is *always* in bare feet. (Honestly, no shoe could possibly contain those two whoppers.) What he lacks in conversation skills he makes up for in weirdness. "I give you some of mine. Remind me."

Aly's face grew practically ash white. "Remind me not to remind you."

"I wish I only had a sunburn," Cass moaned.

"You don't have to come with us this time, you know," Aly said.

Cass frowned without opening his eyes. "I'm a little tired, but I had my treatment and it worked. We have to find Marco. We're a family."

Aly and I exchanged a glance. Cass had been flown across an ocean by a griffin, who then prepped him for lunch. Plus he was recovering from a so-called treatment, and *that* wasn't easy.

We'd all had treatments. We needed them to survive. They held off our symptoms temporarily so we can go on this crazy quest to find a permanent cure. In fact, the Karai

Institute's first job is to help us cope with the effects of the G7W.

Not to brag or anything, but having G7W means you're descended from the royal family of the ancient kingdom of Atlantis. Which is probably the coolest thing about incredibly ordinary, shockingly talent-free me, aka Jack McKinley. On the positive side, G7W takes the things you're already good at—like sports for Marco, computer geekiness for Aly, and photographic memory for Cass—and turns those qualities into superpowers.

On the negative side, the cure involves finding the stolen Loculi of Atlantis, which were hidden centuries ago in the Seven Wonders of the Ancient World.

And if that wasn't hard enough: six of those Wonders don't exist anymore.

A Loculus, by the way, is a fancy Atlantean word for "orb with cool magic power." And we did find one. The story involves a hole in time and space (which I made by accident), a griffin (disgusting half eagle, half lion that came through the hole), a trip to Rhodes (where said griffin tried to lunch on Cass), some crazy monks (Greek), and the Colossus of Rhodes (which came to life and tried to kill us). There's more to it, but all you need to know is that I was the one who let the griffin through, so the whole thing was basically my fault.

"Hey . . ." Aly said, looking at me through squinty eyes.

4

I turned away. "Hey what?"

"I know what you're thinking, Jack," she said. "And stop it. You are not responsible for what happened to Cass."

Honestly, I think that girl reads minds as a hobby.

"Torquin responsible!" Torquin bellowed. He pounded the steering wheel, which made the whole vehicle jump into the air like a rusty, oil-leaking wallaby. "Got arrested. Left you alone. Could not help Cass. Could not stop Marco from flying away with Loculus. Arrrrgh!"

Cass moaned again. "Oh, my neelps."

"Um, Torquin?" Aly said. "Easy on the steering wheel, okay?"

"What is neelps?" Torquin asked.

"Spleen," I explained. "You have to spell it backward."

Luckily the Jeep reached the end of the winding jungle path and burst onto the tarmac of a small landing field. We were finally at our destination. Before us, gleaming on the pavement, was a sleek, retrofitted military stealth jet.

Torquin braked the Jeep to a squealing stop, doing a perfect one-eighty. Two people were inspecting the plane. One of them was a pony-tailed guy with half-glasses. The other was a girl with tats and black lip gloss, who looked a little like my last au pair, Vanessa, only deader. I vaguely remembered meeting both of these people in our cafeteria, the Comestibule.

"Elddif," Cass said groggily. "Anavrin . . ."

5

The girl looked alarmed. "He's lost the ability to speak English?"

"No, he's speaking his favorite language," Aly replied. "Backwardish. It's a form of English. That's how we know he's feeling better."

"Those two people . . ." Cass muttered. "Those are their names."

I sounded out the words in my head, imagined their spelling, and then mentally rearranged the letters back to front. "I think he means Fiddle and Nirvana."

"Ah." Fiddle looked toward us with a tight smile. "I have been rushing this baby into service. Her name is Slippy, she's my pride and joy, and she will hit Mach three if you push her."

Nirvana drummed her long, black-painted nails on the jet's wall. "A vessel that breaks the sound barrier deserves a great sound system. I loaded it up with mp3s."

Fiddle pulled her hand away. "Please. It's a new paint job."

"Sorry, Picasso," she replied. "Anyway, there's some slasher rock . . . emo . . . techno . . . death metal. Hey, since you're going back to the States, might as well play the tunes that remind you of home."

Going back.

I tried to stop shaking. People back home would be looking for us 24/7—families, police, government. Home meant detection. Re-capture. Not returning to the island.

6

Not having treatments. Not having time to collect the cure. Death.

But without Marco's Loculus, we were toast.

Death. Toast. The story of our lives.

But with no signal from Marco, what else could we do? Searching for him at his home just seemed like the best guess.

As we stepped out of the Jeep, Torquin let loose a burp that made the ground rumble.

"Four point five on the Richter scale," said Nirvana. "Impressive."

"Are you sure you want to do this, guys?" Fiddle asked.

"Have to," Torquin said. "Orders from Professor Bhegad."

"Wh-why do you ask?" Cass said to Fiddle.

He shrugged. "You guys each have a tracker surgically implanted inside you, right?"

Cass looked at him warily. "Right. But Marco's is busted."

"I helped design the tracker," Fiddle said. "It's state of the art. Unbustable. Doesn't it seem weird to you that his stopped working—just coincidentally, after he disappeared?"

"What are you implying?" I asked.

Aly stepped toward him. "There's no such thing as unbustable. You guys designed a faulty machine."

"Prove it," Fiddle said.

"Did you know the tracker signal is vulnerable to trace radiation from four elements?" Aly asked.

Fiddle scoffed. "Such as?"

"Iridium, for one," Aly said. "Stops the transmissions cold."

"So what?" Fiddle says. "Do you know how rare iridium is?"

"I can pinpoint more flaws," Aly said. "Admit it. You messed up."

Nirvana pumped a pale fist in the air. "You go, girl."

Fiddle dusted a clod of dirt off the stepladder. "Have fun in Ohio," he said. "But don't expect me at your funeral."

CHAPTER TWO

"THE MISTAKE"

"I SET YOUR dog on fire and wipe the floor with rags made of the memories of everything I ever did with yooooouu . . . !"

As Nirvana's mix blared over the speaker, Torquin's lips curled into a shape resembling an upside-down horseshoe. "Not music. Noise."

Actually, I kind of liked it. Okay, I left out some of the choice words in the quote above, but still. It was funny in a messed-up way. The tune was taking my mind off the fact that I was a gazillion feet over the Atlantic, the plane's speed was pushing me back into my seat, and my stomach was about to explode out my mouth.

I looked at Aly. Her skin was flattening back over her cheekbones as if it were being kneaded by fingers. I couldn't help cracking up.

Aly's eyes shone with panic. "What's so funny?"

"You look about ninety-five years old," I replied.

"You sound about five," she said. "After this is over, remind me to teach you some social skills."

Glurp.

I turned away, awash in dorkitude. Maybe that was my great G7W talent, the superhuman ability to always say the wrong thing. Especially around Aly. Maybe it's because she's so confident. Maybe it's because I'm the only Select who has no reason to have been Selected.

Jack "The Mistake" McKinley.

Fight it, dude. I turned to the window, where a cluster of buildings was racing by below us. It was kind of a shock to see Manhattan go by so fast. A minute later the sight was replaced by the checkerboard farmland of what must have been Pennsylvania.

As we plunged into thick clouds, I closed my eyes. I tried to think positively. We would find Marco. He would thank us for coming, apologize, and hop on the plane.

Right. And the world would start revolving the other direction.

Marco was stubborn. He was also totally convinced he was (a) always right and (b) immortal. Plus, if he was home, telling the story of our abduction, there would be paparazzi and TV news reporters waiting at the airport. Milk cartons with our images in every supermarket. WANTED posters hanging in post offices.

How could we possibly rescue him? Torquin was supposed to protect us in case of an emergency, but that didn't give me confidence.

The events of the last few days raced in my head: Marco falling into the volcano in a battle with an ancient beast. Our search that found him miraculously alive in the spray of a healing waterfall. The ancient pit with seven empty hemispheres glowing in the dark—the Heptakiklos.

If only I'd ignored it. If only I hadn't pulled the broken shard from the center. Then the griffin wouldn't have escaped, we wouldn't have had to race off to find it without adequate training, and Marco wouldn't have had the chance to escape—

"You're doing it again," Aly said.

I snapped back to attention. "Doing what?"

"Blaming yourself for the griffin," Aly replied. "I can tell."

"It crushed Professor Bhegad," I said. "It took Cass over an ocean and nearly killed him—"

"Griffins were bred to protect the Loculi," Aly reminded me. "This one led us to the Colossus of Rhodes. *You* caused that to happen, Jack! We'll get the Loculus back. Marco will listen to us." She shrugged. "Then maybe you can let six more griffins through. They'll lead us to the other Loculi. To protect us, I can help the KI develop . . . I don't know, a repellant."

"A griffin repellant?" Cass said.

Aly shrugged. "There are bug repellants, shark repellants, so why not? I'll learn about them and tinker with the formula."

Tinker. That was what Bhegad called Aly. We each had a nickname—*Tinker, Tailor, Soldier, Sailor.* Aly was the Tinker who could fix anything, Marco the Soldier because of his strength and bravery, Cass the Sailor for his awesome navigational ability. Me? *You're the Tailor because you put it all together*, Bhegad had said. But I wasn't putting anything together now, except pessimism.

"DIIIIIIIE!"

Nirvana's sudden shriek made us all spin around. Torquin bounced upward and banged his head on the ceiling. "What happened?" I asked.

"The end of the song," Nirvana said. "I love that part."

"Anything good?" Torquin said, scrolling through the tunes. "Any Disney?"

Cass was staring out the window, down toward a fretwork of roads and open land. "We're almost there. This is Youngstown, Ohio . . . I think."

"You *think*?" Aly said. "That doesn't sound like you."

"I—I don't recognize the street pattern . . ." Cass said, shaking his head. "I should know this. I'm drawing a blank. I think something's wrong with my . . . whatever."

"Your ability to memorize every street in every place in the world?" Aly put her arm around him. "You're nervous about Marco, that's all."

"Right . . . right . . ." Cass drummed his fingers on the armrest. "You sometimes make mistakes, right, Ally?"

Aly nodded. "Rarely, but yes. I'm human. We all are."

"The weird thing is," Cass said, "there's only one part of Marco that *isn't* human—the tracker. And those things don't just fail—unless something really unusual happens to the carrier."

"Like . . . ?" I said tentatively.

Cass's eyes started to moisten. "Like the thing none of us is talking about. Like if the tracker was destroyed."

"It's inside his body," Aly said. "He can't destroy it."

"Right. Unless . . ." Cass said.

We all fell silent. The plane began to descend. No one finished the sentence, but we all knew the words.

Unless Marco was dead.

CHAPTER THREE

INCIDENT IN OHIO

"HEY!" AS CASS turned and jogged up the street toward me, I whipped my two hands behind my back.

"So, are we there?" I asked nonchalantly.

Cass looked at me curiously. "What are you doing?"

"Scratching," I replied. "A lottery card. Which I found."

"And how will you collect if you win?" He burst out laughing. "Come on. The house is just ahead. Number forty-five Walnut Street. The green porch."

I'm not sure why I didn't tell him the truth—that I'd found a piece of burned wood and a gum wrapper on the ground, and now I was using them to write my dad. Maybe because it was a dumber idea than entering a lottery. But I couldn't help it. All I could think about was Dad. That he was just one state away.

I shoved the note into my back pocket. We jogged up the road to Torquin and Aly, who were in the entrance to a little cul-de-sac in the middle of Lemuel, Ohio. Torquin had parked our rented Toyota Corolla in a secluded wooded area down the block, to avoid being seen. As I joined Cass and Aly, we stood there, staring at the house like three ice sculptures.

Torquin waddled ahead, oblivious.

"I can't do this . . ." Aly said.

I nodded. I felt scared, homesick, worried, and nine thousand percent convinced we should have let Bhegad send another team to do this. Anyone but us.

The house had a small lawn, trimmed with brick.

Its porch screen had been ripped in two places and carefully repaired. A little dormer window peeked from the roof, and a worn front stoop held a rusted watering can. It didn't look like my house, but somehow my heart was beating to the rhythm of homesickness.

A kid with an overstuffed backpack was shambling toward a house across the street, where his mom was opening a screen door. It brought back memories of my own mom, before she'd gone off on a voyage and never returned. Of my dad, who met me at school for a year after Mom's death, not wanting to let me out of his sight. Was Dad home now?

"Come!" Torquin barked over his shoulder. "No time to daydream!"

He was already lumbering up the walkway, his bare feet *thwapping* on the gray-green stones. Cass, Aly, and I fell in behind him.

Before he could ring the bell, I heard the snap of a door latch. The front door opened, revealing the silhouette of a guy with massive shoulders. As he stepped forward I stifled a gasp. His features were dark and piercing, the corners of his mouth turned up—all of it just like Marco. But his face was etched deeply, his hair flecked with gray, and his eyes so sad and hollow I felt like I could see right through them.

He glanced down at Torquin's feet and then back up. "Can I help you?"

"Looking for Marco," Torquin said.

"Uh-huh." The man nodded wearily. "You and everyone else. Thanks for your concern, but sorry."

He turned back inside, pulling the door shut, but Torquin stopped it with his forearm.

"Excuse me?" The man turned slowly, his eyes narrowing.

I quickly stepped in front of him. "I'm a friend of Marco's," I said. "And I was wondering—"

"Then how come I don't recognize you?" Mr. Ramsay asked suspiciously.

"From . . . travel soccer," I said, reciting the line we had prepared for just this occasion. "Please. I'm just concerned, that's all. This is my uncle, Thomas. And two other soccer players, Cindy and Dave. We heard a rumor that Marco might be in the area. We wondered if he came home."

"The last time we saw him, he was at Lemuel General after collapsing during a basketball game," Mr. Ramsay said. "Then . . . gone without a trace. Like he ran away from everything. Since then we've heard nothing but rumors. If we believed them all, he's been in New York, Ashtabula, Kuala Lumpur, Singapore, Manila, and Ponca City. Look!" He grabbed a basket of snapshots off a nearby table and thrust it toward me.

"I—I don't understand," I said, sifting through pixelated, blurry shots of jockish-looking teens who were definitely not Marco. "Why would people lie about seeing him?"

"People want the reward," Mr. Ramsay replied wearily. "One hundred thousand bucks for information leading to

Marco's return. It's supposed to help. Instead, we're just bombarded by emails, letters, visitors. All junk. So take my advice, kid, don't trust rumors."

As Marco's dad took the basket back and returned it to the table, two people emerged from inside the house—a trim, red-haired woman and a girl in sweats. The woman's slate-blue eyes were full of fear. The girl looked angry. They were both focused on Torquin. "I'm . . . Marco's mother," the woman said. "And this is his sister. What's going on? If this is another scam, I'm calling the police."

"They're just kids, Emily," Marco's dad said reassuringly. "You guys have to understand what we're going through. Today it was a repair guy. Flashed some kind of ID card, said he was going to inspect the boiler. Instead he snooped through our house."

"Bloggers, crime buffs," Mrs. Ramsay said. "It's like a game to them. Who can find the most dirt, post the most photos. They have no idea what it is . . . to lose . . ." Her voice cracked, and both her husband and daughter put arms around her shoulders.

Torquin's phone chirped, and he backed away down the stoop. Aly and Cass instinctively followed. Which left me with the three Ramsays, huddled together in the semidarkness of their living room.

The feeling was too familiar. After my mom died, Dad and I hardly ever left each other's sides, but each of us was alone, locked in misery. Our faces must have looked a lot like the Ramsays'.

I was dying to tell them what had really happened to Marco, the whole story of the Karai Institute. Of their son's incredible heroism saving our lives, of the fact that he could swoosh a shot now from clear across a campus lawn.

But I also knew what it was like to lose a family member. And if Cass was right, if Marco's tracker silence meant he was dead, I couldn't get their hopes up.

"We . . . we'll keep looking," I said lamely.

As I began backing away, I felt Torquin's beefy hand on my shoulder, pulling me down the stairs. His face, which wasn't easy to read, looked concerned. "Thank you!" he shouted. "Have to go!"

I stumbled after Torquin, Cass, and Aly. Soon we were all running down the street toward our rented car, top speed. I had never seen Torquin move so fast.

"What's up?" Cass demanded.

"Got . . . message," Torquin said, panting heavily as he pulled open the driver's side door. "Marco found. Get in. Now."

"Wait—they found him?" Aly blurted. "Where?"

Torquin handed the phone to her. Cass and I came up behind, looking over her shoulder as we walked:

TRACKER ACTIVE AGAIN. RAMSAY NOT IN OHIO.
STRONG SIGNAL FROM LATITUDE 32.5417° N,
LONGITUDE 44.4233° E

"Where's that?" I asked.

"It can't be . . ." Cass shook his head.

"Cass, just tell us!" Aly said.

"Marco," Cass replied, "is in Iraq."

"What?" I cried out.

But the other three were already at the car, climbing in.

Quickly, while they weren't looking, I pulled out my note to Dad. And I tossed it down a storm drain.

CHAPTER FOUR

EGARIM

THE CHOPPER BLADES were so loud, I thought they'd shake my brains out through my ears. *"Are you sure you read the tracker right?"* I shouted toward the front seats.

Professor Bhegad didn't even turn around. He hadn't heard a word.

We'd met him and Fiddle at the airport in Irbīl, Iraq. They'd flown separately from the Karai Institute when Marco's signal was finally picked up. Now the whole gang— Bhegad, Torquin, Fiddle, Nirvana, Cass, Aly, and I—was crammed into the front seat of a chopper winging over the Syrian Desert. Our shadow crossed a vast expanse of sand, dotted by bushes and fretted by long black pipelines.

The cabin was stifling hot, and sweat coursed down my

21

face. Cass, Aly, and I huddled together in the backseat. On the long flight from Ohio, we'd had plenty of time to talk. But the whole thing seemed even more confusing than ever. "I still can't understand why he would come here!" I said. "If I were him, I'd go home. No-brainer. I mean, we all want to see our families again, right?"

I could practically feel Cass flinch. He had bounced from foster home to foster home; he didn't have a family to go back to. Unless you counted his parents, who were in prison and hadn't seen him since he was a baby. "Sorry, I shouldn't have said that . . ." I said.

"It's okay, Jack 'Foot-in-Mouth' McKinley," Cass replied with a wan smile. "I know what you mean. Actually, I'm happy Marco is alive. I just was wondering the same thing you were—why *Iraq*? What's there?"

Professor Bhegad slowly turned, adjusting the heavy glasses that slid down his sweating nose. "It's not what is there, but what *was* there," he said. "Iraq was the site of Ancient Babylon."

Cass's eyes widened. "Duh. The site of one of the Seven Wonders—the Hanging Gardens!"

"He decided to go on a rogue mission to find a Loculus all by himself?" Aly said. "Without my tech skills, or Cass's human GPS? If I were Marco, I'd want to do this as a foursome! All of our lives are at stake. Going solo makes no sense. Even to an egotist like Marco."

22

"Unless," I said, "he *isn't* trying to go solo."

"What do you mean?" Cass asked.

"I mean, he may not know that his tracker is busted," I said. "Maybe, when he left Rhodes, he figured we'd pick up the signal and follow him. Maybe he just wanted to force things, to speed the mission up."

Aly raised an eyebrow. "How do we know he didn't disable and re-enable it on purpose?"

"You'd have to be a genius to do that!" I said.

"I could do it," Aly said.

"That's my point!" I replied.

Aly folded her arms and stared out the window. Cass shrugged.

Now Professor Bhegad was shouting, his face pressed to the window. "The Tigris and Euphrates Rivers! We are approaching the Fertile Crescent!"

I gazed down. I knew that Ancient Babylon was the center of a bigger kingdom called Babylonia. And that was part of a larger area known as Mesopotamia, which was Greek for "between two rivers." Now we could see them, winding through the desert, lined with thickets and scrubby trees that looked from above like long green mustaches. Everywhere else was dusty, yellow, and dry. The area sure didn't look fertile to me.

I squinted at the distant ruins. A stone wall snaked around the area. Inside were mounds of rubble and flattened,

23

roped-off areas that must have been archaeological digs. Gazing through a set of binoculars, Bhegad pointed out a small skyline of low buildings near a gate in the wall. Some were flat-roofed and some peaked. "Those are restorations of the ancient city," he said with a disapproving cluck of the tongue. "Crude, crude workmanship . . ."

"Where were the Hanging Gardens?" Aly called out.

"No one knows," Bhegad answered. "Babylon was destroyed by an earthquake in two hundred B.C. or thereabouts. The rivers have changed courses since then. The Gardens may have sunk under the Euphrates or may have been pulverized in the earthquake. Some say it may not have ever existed. But those people are fools."

"I hope it's Door Number Two," Aly said. "Pulverized. Turned to dust. Just like the Colossus was. At least we'll have a chance for two out of seven Loculi."

"More than twenty-eight percent," Cass piped up.

I looked at the tracker panel on the cockpit. Marco's signal was near the Euphrates River, not quite as far as the ruins. As Fiddle descended, we could see a team of guards outside the archaeological site, looking at us with binoculars.

"Wave! Hi!" Nirvana said. "They're expecting us. They're convinced this is a major educational archaeological project."

"How did you arrange all this?" Cass asked.

"I was a professor of archaeology in another life," Bhegad

replied. "My name still carries some weight. One of my former students helps run the site here. He also happens to be a satellite member of the Karai Institute."

Fiddle descended slowly and touched down. He cut the engine, threw open the hatch, and let us out.

The sun was brutal, the land parched and flat. The dusty soil itself seemed to be gathering up the heat and radiating it upward through our soles. In the distance to our right, I could see a bus rolling slowly toward the ancient site. Tour groups made their way slowly among the ruins, like ants among pebbles. In between, the sandy soil seemed to give way to an amazingly huge lake.

"Do you see what I see?" Aly said.

Cass nodded. "Egarim," he said. "Don't get too excited."

"Translate, please," I said.

"Mirage," Cass replied. "The soil is full of silicate particles. The same stuff glass is made of. When it's so bright and hot like this, the sunlight reflects off all those particles. At a sideways angle, it looks like a big, shining mass— which resembles water!"

"Thank you, Mr. Einstein," I said, scanning the horizon. Directly ahead of us, across the yellow-brown desert, was a line of low pine trees that stretched in either direction. The heat-shimmer coming up from the ground made the trees look as if they were rippling in an invisible current. "That's where Marco's signal is coming from. The Euphrates."

Marco was so close!

I checked over my shoulder. Torquin and Nirvana were struggling to lift Professor Bhegad out of the chopper and put him in a wheelchair.

"This is going to take forever," Aly said. She darted toward Torquin, pulled the tracking-signal detector from his gadget belt, and bolted toward the river. "Come on, let's start!"

"Hey!" Torquin cried out in surprise.

"Let them go, we have our hands full here!" Nirvana said.

Our footsteps made clouds of yellowish dust as we ran. Closer to the river, the ground was choked with scrubby grass and knots of small bushes. We stopped at the thicket of pine trees that stretched in both directions.

The ground sloped sharply downward. Below us, the Euphrates slashed a thick silver-blue S like a curved mirror through the countryside. To the north it wound around a distant settlement, then headed off toward mountains blurred by fog. To the south it passed by the Babylonian ruins before disappearing into the flatness. I scanned the riverbank, looking for signs of Marco.

"I don't see him," Aly said.

I held up the tracker. Our blue dot locator and Marco's green one had merged. "He's here somewhere."

"Yo, Ocram!" Cass shouted. "Come out, come out, wherever you are!"

26

Rolling her eyes, Aly began walking down the slope toward the river. "He might be hiding. If he's playing a prank, I will personally dunk him in the water."

"Unless he throws you in first," I said.

I glanced quickly back over my shoulder to check on the others. Nirvana was struggling to push Professor Bhegad's wheelchair across the rocky soil. He bounced a lot, complaining all the way. Torquin had taken off his studded leather belt and was trying to wrap it around Bhegad like a seat belt, causing his own pants to droop slowly downward.

I started through the brush. It was dense and maybe three to five feet high, making it hard to see. As we moved forward, we kept calling Marco's name.

We stopped at the edge of a rocky ridge. None of us had seen this from the distance. It plunged straight downward, maybe twenty feet, to the river below. "Oh, great," Aly said.

I looked north and south. In both directions, the ridge angled downward until it eventually met the riverbed. "We'll be okay if we go sideways," I said.

I went to the edge and looked over. I eyed the tangle of trees, roots, and bushes along the steep drop. Since Marco had taught us to rock climb, steep embankments didn't scare me as much as they used to. This looked way easier than climbing Mount Onyx.

"Maybe there's a shortcut," I said. Quickly I stepped over the edge, digging my toes into a sturdy root. I turned so my chest would be facing the cliff. Holding on to a branch, I descended another step.

"Whoa, Jack, don't," Cass said.

I laughed. "This is ea—"

My foot slipped. My chin hit the dirt. I slid downward, grasping frantically. My fingers closed around branches and vines. I pulled out about a dozen, and a dozen more slipped through my hand. I felt my foot hit a root and I caromed outward, landing at the bottom, hard on my back.

Aly's face was going in and out of focus. I could have sworn she was trying to hold back a smile. "Are you hurt?"

"Just resting," I lied.

"I think I'll look for a path," Cass called down.

I closed my eyes and lay still, my breath buzzsawing in my chest. I heard a dull moan, and I figured it must have been my own voice.

But when I heard it again, my eyes blinked open.

I sat up. Aly and Cass were just below the crest of the ridge, trying to make their way down. They were both shouting. But my eyes were focused on a thick, brownish-green bush, maybe ten yards away.

A pair of shoes jutted from underneath.

CHAPTER FIVE

TOGETHER,
WE FELL INTO DARKNESS

NEW BALANCE BASKETBALL shoes. Size gazillion wide.
With feet in them.

I ran to them, grabbed the ankles, and pulled. The legs
slid out—Ohio State Buckeye sweatpants—and then a
ripped-up KI polo shirt.

From above, Fiddle shouted at me to give him CPR.
How did you do CPR? I wished I'd taken a course. All I
could think about were scenes in TV shows—one person
blowing air into another's lungs.

As I lowered my mouth carefully, his eyes flickered
open from a deep sleep. "Jack? Hey, bro. I didn't know you
cared."

I sprang back. "What the—how—you were—we
thought—" I stammered.

29

"Spit it out," Marco said, sitting up. "I've got time. I've been waiting for you. It gets boring here all alone."

He was fine. Resting in the shade, that's all! I helped him up and bear-hugged him. "Wooooo-hooo!"

Footsteps pounded the dirt behind me. Aly and Cass ran down a path from the lower side of the ridge. They had taken the long way around.

"Dudes!" Marco yelled. "And dudette."

As they jumped on him, laughing, and squealing with relief, I stepped back. My initial joy was wearing off as quickly as it had come. Our reaction seemed somehow wrong.

I watched his face, all pleased with himself, all happy-go-lucky returning hero. Everything we'd been through, all the hardship in Rhodes, the abandonment, the awful visit to Ohio—it all began to settle over me like a coat of warm tar. I flashed back to the last time I saw him, in a room at a hotel in Rhodes. With Cass lying unconscious on a bed.

He'd skipped out on us. As if flying off with our only chance of survival was some kind of game. He hadn't cared about anyone at the Karai Institute. Or how many lives he'd turned upside down.

"Brother Jack?" Marco said curiously, staring out at me from the hugfest. "'Sup? You need a bathroom?"

I shook my head. "I need an explanation. Like, when did you come up with the idea to find a Loculus by yourself?

Just, whoosh, hey, I'll go to Iraq and be a hero?"

"I can explain," Marco said.

"Do you have any idea what we've been through?" I barked. "We just got back from Ohio."

"Wait. Did you—go to my house?" he asked, his eyes widening.

I explained everything—our trip to Lemuel, the visit to the house, the expressions on his mom and dad and sister's faces. I could see Marco's eyes slowly redden. "I . . . I can't believe this . . ." he murmured.

"Jack, maybe we can talk about this later," Aly urged.

But Marco was sinking against the trunk of a pine tree, massaging his forehead. "I—I never wanted to go home. I remember how painful it was for Aly when she tried to call her mom." He took a deep breath. "Why did you go there? Why didn't you just follow my signal here? That's what I thought you'd do."

"Your tracker malfunctioned," I said. "It was off for a couple of days."

"Really?" Marco cocked his head. "So you risked everything and went to the States? For me? Wow. I guess you're right, I do owe you an explanation . . ."

"We're all ears," Aly said. "Start from Rhodes."

"Yeah . . . that hotel room . . ." Marco said. "It was hot, the TV shows were all in Greek, Cass was asleep. All I wanted to do was take a break. You know, hop on the old

31

Loculus, maybe scare a few goats and come right back—"

"Goats?" I said. "Cass was in a coma!"

"Dumbest thing I ever did. I know," Marco said. "I'm a moron. I admit it. But it gets worse. So I'm flying around, and I get distracted by this little island called Nísyros. Looks like a volcano from the air, hot girls on the beach, you know. I swoop in close, make people scream. Fun times. Only when I get back, Cass isn't in the room anymore. I panic. But you guys are probably already flying away. I figure, great, you've abandoned me."

"Did you actually say 'hot girls'?" Aly said, her face curdling with disdain.

"So I figure I'll race you back," Marco went on. "But how do I get back to the island of the KI Geeks? It's halfway between nowhere and the Bermuda Triangle. And then I hear something. This voice. And here's where it gets complicated. And awesome." He paused, looking around.

"Ahoy, there!" came Professor Bhegad's voice. Fiddle was pushing him down a sandy path, about forty yards away.

"*He's* here?" Marco said, looking confused. "Wait. Four Karai peeps?"

"This is a big deal—*that's* why they're here!" Aly said. "You could have died, Marco. Or been abducted by the Massa. Besides, aren't you due for a treatment?"

"I don't need treatments," Marco said, his voice rushed and agitated.

"This is no joke, Marco, you could die," Cass reminded him.

"We need to take you back," Aly said, glancing around. "Where's the flight Loculus?"

"I had to hide it. People here saw me flying. There was a crowd with cameras." Marco reached out, gathered us into a huddle, and spoke fast. "I screwed up and I owe you all big-time. But I'll make it worthwhile, I promise. Look, there's some stuff I have to show you, okay? I've been here awhile, and I've found out some amazing things. Like . . . hold for it . . . Loculus Number Two."

My jaw dropped. "You found it already?"

"Not exactly, but I know where it is. Interested? I thought so." Marco began running toward the river, and of course we followed.

He paused by the bank. Heat shimmered off the water and dragonflies flitted along the surface. Near the opposite bank, a boat floated around a bend with two people lying lazily, their fishing rods slack. "It's there," Marco said.

"In that boat?" Cass said.

"No, *there*—in the water," Marco replied. "You're Selects, just like me. Can't you *feel* it? You know, that weird music thing that Jack talks about?"

Aly scrunched her eyes. "No . . ."

The music.

I'd felt it in the center of Mount Onyx, when I found

the Heptakiklos. It wasn't a song, really, not even a sound that you heard through your ears. It was a kind of full-body thrum, as if my nerves themselves were being played by invisible fingers like a harp.

Somehow, I was always the one who felt this most intensely. But right now it was only a suggestion, barely a tickle. It surprised me that Marco felt it, too.

Marco smiled. "No offense, Brother Jack, but you're not the only one who senses this stuff. It's in there, guaranteed. The closer you get, the more you feel it."

"You went into the water to find it?" Cass asked.

Marco nodded. His face was glowing with excitement. "Yup. I haven't located it yet, but what I found down there will blow your mind. For real. I'm not even going to try to explain. Trust me. You have to see it."

Cass's blotchy face was turning a uniform shade of white. "I—I'm happy to wait here. Swimming and I don't really get along."

"I'll hold on to you, brother," Marco said, taking his arm.

Professor Bhegad's voice shouted from behind us: "My boy—come here, this wheelchair doesn't do well on wet sand!" He was close to the bottom now. His wheelchair wasn't liking the dry sand, either.

Cass struggled to wrench himself away. "We can't just jump in, Marco! We have to clear this. You may be cool about breaking the rules, but you know the KI."

"Why are you worried about them?" Marco asked.

"Uh, maybe because they're the ones in charge of our lives?" Aly said.

Marco groaned. "They'll require a chaperone, or an official KI submarine, whatever. That'll take the fun out of it. We'll do this fast, I promise. You will thank me!"

I stepped closer to the water. Toward the sound. *An hour ago we had no Loculi, and now we have a chance at two. Two of seven.*

But I stopped short. Bhegad was shouting now. Freaking out. Completely confused by what was going on. Why we were standing by the bank of a river, looking like we were about to go for a swim? Were we nuts?

I stepped back, shaking my head. We needed the KI's support. Marco's flight was a huge complication. A good plan was better than chaos. Just because the Song of the Heptakiklos beckoned, I didn't mean we had to listen right this instant. "Just give me a couple of seconds, Marco," I said.

As I turned toward Bhegad and the others, I felt a vise-like hand land on my shoulder. And I was flying back toward the water.

"Banzaaiiiiii!" Marco had us all in his grip, our feet off the ground. *"Take a deep breath, hang on—and most of all, trust me!"*

We had no choice. Together, we fell into the darkness of the Euphrates.

CHAPTER SIX

PEACEFUL

MUCK. GRAY-GREEN, THICK, weed-choked muck.

No wonder Marco couldn't find the second Loculus.
You couldn't see three feet in front of your nose.

As I swam, trying to keep up with him, noodle-like
shapes slimed my face. Marco was holding tight to Cass.
The fluorescent strip on Cass's backpack flashed occa-
sionally in the dim ribbons of light that somehow broke
through the water. I was getting colder by the second. With
my clothes and shoes, I felt heavy like a whale.

Down . . . down . . . how far was this thing? It was practically black now. The light was way too far over our heads.

*As far down as you go, you will need an equal amount of
air to swim back up.* It's what I learned in summer camp.
I learned to sense when I was half spent. And I was way

past that. Already my head felt light and my heart seemed about to explode.

Marco wasn't slowing a bit. Aly banged me on the shoulder. She was gesturing, urging me to go back up with her. I knew she was right. Marco was going to kill us. How far were we supposed to go? What exactly were we going to see—and where?

Ahead of me, Marco had stopped swimming. He still held tight to Cass, who was now hanging limply in the water. The two of them were silhouetted by a weird, dull yellow glow below them.

As I swam toward them, I realized I was gaining speed. *An undertow.*

I tried to pull back but I couldn't. The glow was intensifying, looming closer. It was a circle of bright tiles with a center of solid black. In front of me, Marco seemed to be changing shape—blowing out to an amorphous humanoid blob, then shrinking to clam-size.

What's going on?

My head snapped back, and suddenly I was surging into the black hole as if sprung by a giant rubber band.

As I passed through the hole, it let out a deep, threatening buzz. A halo of green-white light shot sparks from its circumference into my body. My mouth opened into an involuntary scream. I collided with Marco and Cass, but they felt porous, as if our molecules were joining, passing through one another. My left leg smacked against something hard, and I bounced away.

I was spinning with impossible speed, as if my head were in ten places at once. And then I felt myself catapulted forward, and I thought my limbs would separate into different directions.

But they didn't. I flattened out, decelerating. The water's temperature abruptly dropped, and so did its texture. All at once it had become clear and cool—and I was whole again. Solid. But the change had unsettled every biological function inside me. My brain registered relief, but my lungs were in chaos. As if someone had reached inside and squeezed them with a steel fist.

Aly . . . Marco . . . Cass. I spotted them all in my peripheral vision, rising. But Cass's legs hung like tentacles, undulating with each of Marco's powerful thrusts. Those two would reach the surface first. I pushed with all remaining strength, fighting to stay conscious. Aiming toward a dull, flat-gray surface glow above us.

My arms slowed . . . then stopped.

I felt myself traveling to a dream world of bright sun and cool breezes. I was floating over a field of waving grass, where a white-robed shape stood from a circle embedded in the ground.

As she turned, I could see the seven Loculi, glowing, revolving. They seemed to blend together, so their shapes merged into a kind of circular cloud.

The Dream.

No. I don't want it now. Because I'm not asleep. Because if I have the Dream now, it might be because I'm dead.

"I knew you would come."

The voice was unfamiliar, yet I felt it was a part of me. I knew instantly who the figure was. She turned slowly. Her eyes were the color of a clear tropical ocean, her face gentle and kind, ringed with a floating mane of glorious red hair.

Her name was Qalani.

Whenever I'd seen her, it had been in a ring of explosions, some kind of strange flashback to the destruction of Atlantis. In the Dream, I came close to death but always woke up.

Here, she had come to meet me. As always, her face looked familiar. She resembled my mom, Anne McKinley—and now, deep under the Euphrates, it was more than a resemblance. It was a beckoning, a welcoming.

"Hi, Mom," I said.

"I've been waiting," she said with a knowing smile. "Welcome to have you back."

I couldn't help grinning. Our old family saying! I'd blurted it out to Dad once, when he returned from a business trip to Manila. From then on, we always used it as our own private joke.

I felt strangely peaceful as she reached toward me. I would be fine. I would finally be meeting her, in a better place.

Her hand gripped my shoulder, and darkness quickly closed in.

CHAPTER SEVEN

FRESH AND DEWY

"GAAAH!" MY FACE broke through the water's surface. Air rushed into my mouth like a solid projectile. I sucked in huge gulps.

She was gone.

"Mo-o-om!" I shouted.

"No! Marco!" a voice shouted back.

I blinked water from my eyes. I could see Marco rising and falling on a wild current. He let go of me, swimming toward Aly, pushing her toward the bank. I could see her struggling to stand, grabbing onto Cass's arm.

I was too far into the middle, the deeper water. I struggled to push myself high enough above the surface for a proper breath. As I went under again, I fought to stay conscious.

"Hang on, brother!" Marco shouted.

His fingers locked around my arm. He was swimming beside me, pulling us both toward the bank. His arms dug hard into the frothing current. Aly and Cass were struggling onto the shore, staring over their shoulders at me in horror.

Marco and I bounced downstream in a helpless zigzag. We careened around a jutting rock that rose up between us, forcing Marco to let go of me. Directly in our path was a downed tree. I kicked hard and up, opened my arms, and let it hit me full force in the chest. My legs swept under the wood as I held tight.

"Marco!" I yelled.

"Here!" Marco clung to the tree about three feet to my left, closer to the riverbank. We both hung there, catching our breaths. "How's your grip, Brother Jack? Steady?"

I nodded. "I think . . . I can make my way to the shore!"

"Good—see you there!" Marco swung up onto the wood, stood carefully, and scampered toward the shore like an Olympic gymnast. Jumping onto the bank, he began calling for Aly and Cass.

I yanked myself onto the fallen tree. Lying there, I felt my chest beating against the slippery wood. I didn't dare try to stand. Slowly I reached out toward the shore, gripping farther along the branch. In this way I managed to shimmy along at a snail's pace until I finally reached the bank and flopped onto the mud.

Farther upstream, Aly had made it to solid ground. Marco was back in the river, helping Cass out of the water. I struggled to my feet. My legs ached and rain pelted my face, but I hobbled toward them as fast as I could in the soggy soil.

A total freak rainstorm. One moment, hot and dry air. The next, *this*. Was this normal in the desert?

What was going on here?

"Jack!" Aly threw her arms around me as I arrived. Her face was warm against my neck. I think she was crying.

"Behave, you two," Marco said.

I pulled away, feeling the blood rush to my face. "What just happened?" I said.

Cass was staring across the river, looked dazed. "Okay, we jumped into the river. We hit a rough patch. We came out the other end. So . . . we should be staring across the river, at the place we left from, right?"

"Left," Marco said. "Right."

"So where is everything?" he asked. "Where are Torquin, Bhegad, Nirvana? They should have made it down here by now."

Aly and I followed Cass's glance. "Looks like we were carried pretty far downstream," I said.

"Yeah, like a zillion miles away," I said.

"That," Cass said, "would be geographically elbissopmi."

"How do you *do* that?" Aly said.

A dense cloud cover made it hard to see north and south, but I could see no sign of human life—no settlements, no Babylonian ruins, no KI people. Just swollen river in either direction.

"We can't waste time—come on!" Marco was already heading up the slope into a thick pine grove.

Cass, Aly, and I shared a wary glance. "Marco, you're not telling us something," I said. "What just happened?"

Marco scampered through the trees without an answer, as if our near drowning, our battering against the rocks, had never happened. Cass looked at him in disbelief. "He can't be serious."

"Chill is not in that boy's vocabulary," Aly said.

We followed behind as fast as we could. My legs were bruised and my head bloody. My arms felt as if I'd been bench-pressing a rhinoceros. The slope wasn't too steep, really, but in our condition it felt like Mount Everest. We caught up with Marco at the edge of the pine trees. Here, everything seemed a little more familiar. Just beyond the grove I could see a vast plain of dirt to the horizon. The clouds were lifting, the water-soaked ground quickly drying. Scrubby bushes dotted the landscape, which was crisscrossed by a network of wide paths cut through the plain.

"Check it out," Marco said, gesturing to the left.

A giant rainbow arched through the sky, sloping downward into a city of low, square, yellow-brown buildings—thousands of them, most with crown-like sand-castle roofs. The city rose on a gentle hill, and if I wasn't mistaken, I thought I could see another wall deeper inside the city. The outer wall contained a mammoth arched gate of cobalt-blue tiles. In the center of the city was a towering building shaped like a layer cake. Its sides were ornately carved, its windows spiraling up to a tapered peak. The city's outer wall was surrounded by a moat, which seemed to draw water from the Euphrates. Closer to us, outside the city limits, were farms where oxen trudged slowly, plowing the fields.

"Either I'm dreaming," Aly said, "or no one ever told us there was a phenomenally accurate ancient Babylonian theme park on the other side of the river."

"I don't remember seeing this from the air," I said, turning to Cass. "How about you, Mr. GPS—any ideas?"

Cass shook his head, baffled. "Sorry. Clueless."

"It's not a theme park," Marco said, ducking back into the trees. "And it's not the other side of the river. Follow me, and keep yourselves hidden by the trees as long as possible."

"Marco," Aly said, "what do you know that you're not telling us?"

"Trust me," Marco said. "To quote Alfred Einstein: 'a follower tells, but a leader shows.'"

He slipped back into the trees, heading in the direction of the city. Aly, Cass, and I fell in behind him. "It's *Albert*

Einstein," Aly corrected him. "And I don't believe he ever said that."

"Maybe it was George Washington," Marco said.

We trudged through the brush. The river roared to our right. Roared? Okay, it was swollen by the rain—but how long could it have rained, five minutes?

The tree cover seemed a lot denser than I'd remembered seeing it from the other side. It partially obscured our view of the city, save for a few glimpses of distant yellowish walls.

As the rain clouds burned away, the temperature climbed. We may have walked for ten minutes or an hour, but it felt like ten days. My body still felt creaky from our little swim adventure. All I wanted to do was lie down. I could tell Cass and Aly were hurting, too. Only Marco still seemed fresh and dewy. "How far are we going?" I called ahead.

"Ask George Washington," Aly mumbled.

Marco took a sharp turn and stopped short at the edge of the trees. He peered around a trunk, signaling us to come close. With a flourish, he gestured to his left. "Abracadabra, dudes."

I looked toward the city and felt my jaw drop. The tree cover completely ended here. Up close, I could see that the city spilled directly to the banks of the Euphrates.

Marco was climbing a pine tree and urged us to do the same. The branches hadn't been trimmed, so it was easy to get maybe fifteen feet or so above the ground.

From this vantage point we could see over the outer wall and into the city. It was no theme park. Way too vast for that. It wasn't a city, either. Not like the ones I knew—no power wires, no cell towers, no cars. The roads leading into the city were hard-packed dirt. On one of them trudged a group of bearded men in white robes and sandals, leading swaybacked mules laden with canvas bags. They were heading toward a bridge that led over the moat and into the city gate. From the lookout towers, guards watched them approach. I craned my neck to see what the place was like inside, but the walls were too high.

"These people are about as low-tech as it gets," Cass said. "Like, from another century."

I felt a chill in spite of the hot sun. "From another millennium," I added.

"M-M-Marco . . . ?" Aly said. "You have some 'splainin' to do."

Marco shook his head in wonder. "Okay. I'm as baffled as you are. Lost in the Land of the Big Duh. No idea where we are or how we got here. I wanted to show you, partly because I couldn't believe it was real. But you see it, right? I'm not crazy, am I? Because I was having my doubts."

A rhythmic whacking noise nearly made me slip off my branch. We all scrambled down the trees. A little kid's voice was coming nearer, singing in some strange language.

Instinctively we drew closer together.

Strolling up the path toward us was a dark-haired boy of about six, wearing a plain brown toga and holding a gnarled stick. As he sang, he whacked a hollow, dead tree in rhythm, his eyes wandering idly.

He stopped cold when he saw us.

"Keep singing, little dude," Marco said. "I like that. Kind of a reggae thing."

The boy glanced from our faces to our clothes. He dropped his stick and darted back toward the main road. We must have seemed pretty strange to him, because he began shouting anxiously in a language none of us knew.

At the road, a caravan of camels turned lazily toward him. A man with graying hair was at the head of the caravan, leaning on a stick and talking to a city guard dressed in leather armor, who had strolled out to meet him. Both of them turned toward us.

The guard had a thick black beard and shoulders the size of a bull. Narrowing his eyes, he began walking our way, a spear balanced in his hand. He shouted to us with odd, guttural words.

"What's he saying?" Aly asked.

"'Does this toga make me look fat?' How should I know?" Cass said.

"We're not in Kansas anymore, Fido," Marco said. "I say we book it."

47

He pushed us toward the river. We began running into the woods, down the slope, tripping over bushes and roots. I felt like I was re-banging every bruise I had. Marco was the first to reach the river banks. Cass was close behind, looking fearfully over his shoulder.

"He'll give up," Marco whispered. "He has no reason to be mad at us, just probably thinks we're dressed weird. We hide for a few minutes and wait for Spartacus and Camel Guy to go away. Then when things are quieter, we go find the Hanging Gardens."

"Um, by the way, it's Toto," Aly whispered.

"What?" Marco snapped.

"We're not in Kansas anymore, *Toto*," Aly said. "Not *Fido*. It's a line from *The Wizard of Oz*."

As we crouched behind some bushes, Marco's eyes grew wide. I looked in the direction of his glance. Over the tops of the trees, a solid black band shimmered across the sky. It wasn't a cloud cover exactly, but more like a distant gigantic cape.

"And, um . . . that thing?" Marco said. "That's maybe the wizard's curtain?"

I stood and ran to higher ground, to a place where I could see the city. I spotted the guard again and ducked behind a tree. But he wasn't concerned about us anymore. The guard, the camel driver, the boy, and a couple of other men were hurriedly herding the camels toward the bridge.

"I don't like this," Cass said as he caught up to where I was standing. "Let's get out of here before a tornado strikes. We need to get Professor Bhegad. He'll know what to do."

"No way, bro," Marco protested. "It's just weather. We need to move forward. And I have about a million things I have to tell you."

In the distance an animal roared. Birds flew frantically overhead, and a series of crazy, high-pitched screeches pierced the air. This place was giving me the creeps. "Tell us on the other side," I said, heading back down.

Aly, Cass, and I bolted for the river. It was three against one.

"Wusses. All of you," Marco said. And with a disgusted sigh, he followed us back in to the river.

CHAPTER EIGHT

IT'S ALIII-IVE!

"LOOK! IT'S MOVING! It's aliii-ive! It's alive, it's alive, it's aliiiive!"

It was Aly's voice. That much I knew. And I had a vague idea why she was sounding so dorky.

I tried to open my eyes but the sun was searing hot. My muscles ached and my clothes were still wet. I blinked and forced myself to squint upward. Marco, Aly, and Cass were leaning over me, panting and wet. Behind them, the cliff rose into the harsh, unforgiving sun.

"Don't tell me," I said. "It's a line from a movie."

Aly beamed. "Sorry. I can't help it. I'm so relieved. The original *Frankenstein*. Colin Clive."

"Welcome to the living," Marco said, helping me up off

the sand. "The original *Seven Wonders Story.* Marco Ramsay."

The landscape whirled as I struggled upward. I looked warily up the slope. "What happened to Ali Baba and the camels?"

"Gone," Marco replied, his eyes dancing with excitement. "We are back to the same spot where we left in the first place. And are you noticing something else? Look around. Look closely."

I saw the worn path to the top of the ridge. I saw the gray river, placid under the rising sun. "Wait," I said. "When we left, the sun was almost over our heads. Now it's lower."

"Bingo!" Marco said.

"From *Bingo*," Cass murmured. "Starring Bingo."

"Meaning what, Marco?" Aly said. "I'm supposed to be the smart one. What do you understand that I don't?"

"Hey!" A distant, high-pitched voice made us all turn sharply. Nirvana was sprinting up the beach in loud Hawaiian shorts, a KISS T-shirt, and aviator sunglasses. *"Oh . . . my . . . Gandalf!"* she screamed. "Where have you guys been?"

Marco spun around. "Underwater. 'Sup, Dawg? Where's Bhegad?"

Nirvana slapped him in the face, hard.

"Ow," Marco said. "Happy to see you, too."

"We thought you were dead!" Nirvana replied. "After you jumped? I nearly had a heart attack! Bhegad and Fiddle and the Hulk—they're all in each other's faces. 'How could

51

you let this happen?' 'How could *you*?' 'How could *you*?'
Blah blah blah. Fiddle's insisting we call nine-one-one,
Bhegad says we can't, Torquin's just going postal, and I'm
Will you guys just take a pill? So we all jump in the river to
look for you, except for Bhegad, who's so mad he's practically doing wheelies. Finally we give up. All we can do is
wait. Soon we assume you all drowned. Torquin is crying.
Yes, tears from a stone. It does happen. Fiddle is like, 'Time
to break up the KI and look for a new job!' Bhegad insists
we set up camp. Maybe you'll come back. Or we'll find the
bodies. So we've been sitting here for two days eating beef
jerky and—"

"Wait," I said, sitting up. "Two days?"

"Torquin was crying?" Cass said.

Over Nirvana's shoulder, I could see Fiddle pushing
Professor Bhegad toward us. Torquin was waddling along
beside them, his beefy face twisted into a pained expression that looked like indigestion but probably was concern.
About twenty feet behind them was a camp-type setup—
three big tents, a grill, and a few boxes of supplies.

When had they set that up?

"By the Great Qalani!" the old man cried, holding his
arms wide. "You're—okay!"

No one of us knew quite what to do. Professor Bhegad
wasn't exactly a huggy kind of guy. So I stuck out my
hand. He shook it so hard I thought my fingers would fall

52

off. "What happened?" he asked, his eyes darting toward Marco. "If I weren't so relieved, I'd be furious!"

Marco's face was flushed. He blinked his eyes. "My bad, P. Beg . . . shouldn't have run off like that . . . whoa . . . spins . . . mind if I sit? I think I swallowed too much river water."

"Torquin, bring him to the tent. Now!" Bhegad snapped. "Summon every doctor we have."

Marco frowned, drawing himself up to full height with a cocky smile. "Hey, don't get your knickers in a twist, P. Beg. I'm good."

But he didn't look good. His color was way off. I glanced at Aly, but she was intent on her watch. "Um, guys? What time is it? And what day?"

Fiddle gave her a curious look, then checked his watch. "Ten-forty-two A.M. Saturday."

"My watch says six thirty-nine, Thursday," Aly said.

"We fix," Torquin said. "Busted watches a KI specialty."

"It's still working, and it's waterproof," Aly said. "Look, the second hand is moving. We left at 6:02, our time here in Iraq, and we were back by 6:29. Exactly twenty-seven minutes by my watch. But here—actually in this place—almost two days passed for you!"

"One day and sixteen hours, and forty minutes," Cass said. "Well, maybe sixteen and a half, if you count discussion time before we actually dove."

"Aly, this does not make sense," I said.

"And anything else about this adventure does?" Aly's face was pale, her eyes focused on Professor Bhegad.

But the professor was rolling forward, intent on Marco. "Did no one hear me?" he said. "Bring that child to the tent, Torquin—now!"

Marco waved Torquin away. But he was staggering backward. His smile abruptly dropped.

And then, so did his body.

As we watched in horror, Marco thumped to the sand, writhing in agony.

CHAPTER NINE

A QUESTION OF TIME

"IF YOU SAY, 'It's alive,' I will pound you," Marco said.

His eyes flickered. Professor Bhegad exhaled with relief. Behind him, Fiddle let out a whoop of joy. "You are a strong boy," Bhegad said. "I wasn't sure the treatment would take."

"I didn't think I needed treatments," Marco replied. A rueful smile creased his face as he looked up at Aly, Cass, and me. "So much for Marco the Immortal."

Cass leaned down and gave him a hug. "Brother M, we like you just the way you are."

"Sounds like a song," said Nirvana, who was clutching Fiddle's and Torquin's arms.

I glanced at Aly and noticed she was tearing up. I sidled close to her. I kind of wanted to put my arm around her, but I wasn't sure if that would be too weird. She gave me a look, frowned, and angled away. "My eyes . . ." she said. "Must have gotten some sand in them. . . ."

"Aly was telling me about your adventure," Bhegad said to Marco. "The Loculus seeming to call from the river . . . the weather change . . . the city on the other side. It sounds like one of your dreams."

"Dreams don't change the passage of time, Professor Bhegad," Aly said.

"It was real, dude," Marco said. "Like some overgrown Disney set. This big old city with dirt roads and no cars and people dressed in togas, and some big old pointy buildings."

Fiddle nodded. "Hm. Ziggurats . . ."

"Nope," Marco said. "No smoking."

"Not cigarettes, *ziggurats*—tiered structures, places of worship." Bhegad scratched his head, suddenly deep in thought. "And the rest of you—you all confirm Marco's observation?"

Nirvana threw up her arms. "When Aly talks about it, you assume it's a dream. But when Marco says it, you take it seriously. A little gender bias, maybe?"

"My apologies, old habits learned at Yale," Bhegad said. "I take all of you seriously. Even though you do seem to be talking about a trip into the past—which couldn't be, pardon the expression, anything more than a fairy tale."

"So let's apply some science." Aly sank to the ground

and began making calculations in the sand with her finger. "Okay. Twenty-seven minutes there, about a day and sixteen-and-a-half hours here. That's this many hours . . ."

THERE: 27 MIN

HERE: 1 DAY + 16½ HOURS

. . . OR 40½ HOURS

"Twenty-seven minutes there equals forty-and-a-half hours here?" I asked.

"How many minutes would that be?" she said. "Sixty minutes in an hour, so multiply by sixty . . ."

$$\begin{array}{r} 40.5 \text{ hrs} \\ \times\ 60 \text{ mins} \\ \hline 2{,}430 \text{ mins} \end{array}$$

Aly's fingers were flying. "So twenty-seven minutes passed while we were there. But twenty-four-hundred thirty minutes passed here. What's the ratio?"

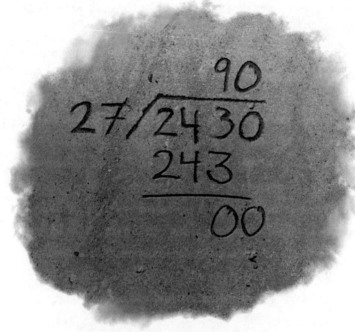

"Ninety!" Aly's eyes were blazing. "It means we went to a place where time travels ninety times slower than it does here."

Fiddle looked impressed. "You go, girl."

"*Whaaat?* That's impossible!" Cass shook his head in disbelief, then glanced at Professor Bhegad uncertainly. "Isn't it?"

I desperately tried to remember something weird I once learned. "In science class . . . when I wasn't sleeping . . . my teacher was talking about this famous theory. She said to imagine you were in a speeding train made of glass, and you threw a ball up three feet and then caught it. To you, the ball's going up and down three feet. But to someone outside the train, looking through those glass walls . . ."

"The ball moves in the direction of the train, so it travels many more than three feet—not just up and down, but forward," Professor Bhegad said. "Yes, yes, this is the theory of special relativity . . ."

"She said *time* could be like that," I went on. "So, like, if you were in a spaceship, and you went really fast, close to the speed of light, you'd come back and everyone on earth would be a lot older. Because, to them, time is like that ball. It goes faster when it's just up and down instead of all stretched out."

"So you're thinking you guys were like the spaceship?" Nirvana said. "And that place we found—it's like some parallel world going slower, alongside our world?"

"But if we both exist at the same time, why aren't we seeing them?" Marco said. "They should be on the other side of the river, only moving really slow a-a-a-a-a-n-n-n-d speeeeeeeeaki-i-i-i-ing l-i-i-i-ke thi-i-i-i-s . . ."

"We have five senses and that's all," Aly said. "We can see, hear, touch, smell, taste. Maybe when you bend time like that, the rules are different. You can't experience the other world, at least with regular old physical senses."

"But you—you all managed to traverse the two worlds," Bhegad said, "by means of some—"

"Portal," Fiddle piped up.

"It looked like a tire," Marco said. "Only nicer. With cool caps."

Bhegad let out a shriek. "Oh! This is extraordinary. Revolutionary. I must think about this. I've been postulating the existence of wormholes all my life."

Torquin raised a skeptical eyebrow. "Pustulate not necessary. See wormholes every day!"

"A wormhole in *time*," Bhegad said. "It's where time and space fold in on themselves. So the normal rules don't apply. The question is, what rules *do* apply? These children may very well have traveled cross-dimensionally. They saw a world that occupies *this space*, this same part of the earth where we now stand. How does one do this? The only way is by traveling through some dimensional flux point. In other words, one needs to find a disruption in the forces of gravity, magnetism, light, atomic attraction."

"Like the portal in Mount Onyx," I said, "where the griffin came through."

"Exactly," Professor Bhegad said. "Do you realize what you were playing with? What dangers you risked? According to the laws of physics, your bodies could have been turned inside out . . . vaporized!"

I shrugged. "Well, I'm feeling pretty good."

"You told me you could *feel* the Loculus, Jack," Bhegad said. "The way you felt the Heptakiklos in the volcano."

"I felt it, too," Marco said. "We're Select, yo. We get all wiggy when we're near this stuff. It's a G7W thing."

"Which means, unfortunately, you will have to return . . ." Bhegad stated, his voice drifting off as he sank into thought.

"Yeah, and this time without the twenty-first-century clothes, which make us stick out," Marco said. "I say we hit the nearest costume shop, buy some stylish togas, and go back for the prize."

"Not togas," Aly said. "Tunics."

Professor Bhegad shook his head. "Absolutely not. This is not to be rushed into. We must return to our original plan, to finish your training. Recent events—the vromaski, the griffin—they forced our hand. Made us rush. They thrust you into an adventure for which you were not adequately prepared . . ."

"Old school . . . old school . . ." Marco chanted.

"Call it what you wish, but I call it prudent," Professor Bhegad shot back. "Everything you've done—Loculus flying, wormhole traveling—is unprecedented in human history. We need to study the flight Loculus. Consult our top scientists about further wormhole visits. Assess risk. If and when you go back through the portal, we must have a plan—safety protocols, contingencies, strategies, precise timing to your treatment schedule. Now, turn me around

61

so we can get started."

Fiddle threw us a shrug and then began turning the old man back toward the tents.

"Yo, P. Beg—wait!" Marco said.

Professor Bhegad stopped and looked over his shoulder. "And that's another thing, my boy—it's Professor Bhegad. Sorry, but you will not be calling the shots anymore. From here on, you are on a tight leash."

"Um, about that flight Loculus?" Marco said. "Sorry, but you can't study it."

Professor Bhegad narrowed his eyes. "You said you hid it, right?"

"Uh, yeah, but—" Marco began.

"Then retrieve it!" Bhegad snapped.

Marco rubbed the back of his neck, looking out toward the water. "The thing is—I hid it . . . *there*."

"In the water?" Nirvana asked.

"No," Marco replied. "Over in the other place."

Bhegad slumped. "Well, this makes the job a bit more complicated, doesn't it? I suppose you do have to go sooner rather than later. Prepared or not. Perhaps I will have to send the able-bodied Fiddle along to help you."

"Or Torquin," Torquin grunted indignantly, "who is able-bodied . . . er."

Fiddle groaned. "This is not in my job description. Or Tork's. We were told one Loculus in each of the Seven

Wonders. Not in some fantasy time warp—in the real world."

"The second Loculus, dear Fiddle," Bhegad said, "is indeed in one of the Wonders."

"Right—so we should be digging, not spinning sci-fi stories," Fiddle said. "You see those ruins down the river—*that's* where the Hanging Gardens were!"

"But our Select have gone to where the Hanging Gardens *are*." Bhegad gestured toward the water, his eyes shining. "I believe they have found the ancient city of Babylon."

CHAPTER TEN

ARABIC OR ARAMAIC?

"LEATHER BACKPACKS WITH hidden compartments?" Professor Bhegad asked, reading off a list of supplies. "Leather sandals?"

"Check," said Nirvana. "Soaked in the river and dried out, for that ancient worn-in look. And you have no idea how hard it was to find size thirteen double E, for Mr. Hoopster."

"Sorry," Marco said sheepishly. "Big feet mean a big heart."

"Oh, please," Fiddle said with a groan.

"Tunics?" Bhegad pressed onward. "Hair dye to cover up the lambdas? Can't let the Babylonians see them, you know. Their time frame is close to the time of the destruction of Atlantis, almost three millennia ago. The symbol might mean something to them."

"Do a pirouette, guys," Nirvana said.

We turned slowly, showing Bhegad the dye job Nirvana had done to the backs of our heads. "It was a little hard to match the colors," Nirvana said. "Especially with Jack. There's all this red streaked in with the mousy brown, and I had to—"

"If I need further information, I'll ask!" Bhegad snapped.

"Well, *excuuuuuse me* for talking." Nirvana folded her arms and plopped down on the floor of the tent, not far from where I was studying.

We were feverishly trying to learn as much as we could about Babylon and the Hanging Gardens. Professor Bhegad had been tense and demanding over the last couple of days. "Ramsay!" he barked. "Why were the Gardens built?"

"Uh . . . I know this . . . because the king dude wanted to make his wife happy," Marco said. "She was from a place with mountains and stuff. So the king was like, 'Hey babe, I'll build you a whole mountain right here in the desert, with flowers and cool plants.'"

"Williams!" Bhegad barked. "Tell me the name of the, er, king dude—as you so piquantly call it—who built the Hanging Gardens. Also, the name of the last king of Babylon."

"Um . . ." Cass said, sweat pouring down his forehead. "Uh . . ."

65

"Nebuchadnezzar the Second and Nabonidus!" Bhegad closed his eyes and removed his glasses, slowly massaging his forehead with his free hand. "This is hopeless . . ."

Cass shook his head. He looked like he was about to cry. "I should have known that. I'm losing it."

"You're not losing it, Cass," I said.

"I am," he replied. "Seriously. Something is wrong with me. Maybe my gene is mutating. This could really mess all of us up—"

"I will give you a chance to redeem yourself, Williams," Bhegad said. "Give me the names the Babylonians actually called Nebuchadnezzar and Nabonidus. Come now, dig deep!"

Cass spun around. "What? I didn't hear that—"

"Nabu-Kudurri-Usur and Nabu-na'id!" Bhegad said. "Don't forget that! How about Nabu-na'id's evil son? Marco, you take a turn!"

"Nabonudist Junior?" Marco said.

"Belshazzar!" Bhegad cried out in frustration. "Or Bel-Sharu-Usur! Hasn't anyone been paying attention?"

"Give us a break, Professor, these are hard to remember!" Aly protested.

"You need to know these people *cold*—what if you meet them?" Bhegad said. "Black—what was the main language spoken?"

"Arabic?" Aly said.

Bhegad wiped his forehead. "Aramaic—*Aramaic*! Along

with many other languages. Many nationalities lived in Babylon, each with a different language—Anatolians, Egyptians, Greeks, Judaeans, Persians, Syrians. The great central temple of Etemenanki was also known as the . . . ?"

"Tower of Lebab—aka Babel!" Cass blurted out. "Which is where we get the term *babble*! Because people gathered around it and talked and prayed a lot."

"Cass will fit right in," Marco said, "speaking Backwardish."

Bhegad tapped the table impatiently. "Next I quiz you on the numerical system." He plopped down a sheet of paper with all kinds of gobbledygook scribbled on it:

$$\text{Y} = 1 \qquad \text{YY} = 2$$

$$\text{Y\!\!\!\!Y} = 4 \qquad \langle = 10$$

$$\langle\!\langle = 20 \qquad \text{Y} \quad \text{Y} = 60+1$$

"Memorize these numbers," Bhegad said. "Remember, our columns are ones, tens, hundreds, et cetera. Theirs were one, sixty, thirty-six hundred, et cetera."

"Can you go slowly," Marco said. "Like we have normal intelligence?"

"Those, my boy," Bhegad said, pronouncing each word exaggeratedly, "may perhaps resemble bird prints to you, but they're numbers. Start from that fact . . . and *read*! We will have a moment of silence while you attempt to learn. And I attempt to settle my roiling stomach."

As Fiddle pulled him back toward a table where his medicines were set up, I slid down to the ground with a book in hand, next to a pouting Nirvana. "Dang, what did he eat for breakfast?" she mumbled.

"He's just worried, that's all," I said. "About us being in a wormhole."

Across the tent, Cass and Aly huddled over a tablet, studying research documents the professor had downloaded—histories, ancient–language study manuals, reports on social behavior norms. "Okay, so the upper class dudes were *awilum*," Cass was saying, "the lower class was *mushkenum*, and the slaves were . . ."

"*Wardum*," Aly replied. "Like *wards* of the state. You can remember it that way."

"Mud-raw backward," Cass said. "That's easier."

"What? Mud-raw?" Marco slapped the table. "This is

ridiculous. Yo, P. Beg, this isn't Princeton. We can't learn the entire history of Babylon in two days. We're not going there to live. Let's just pop over and bring this thing back."

I thought Professor Bhegad would freak. For a moment his face went beet red. Then he sighed, removing his glasses and wiping his forehead. "You know, in the *Mahabharata*, the Hindus wrote of a king who made a rather quick journey to heaven. When he returned the world had aged many years, people were feeble and small. Their brains had rotted away."

"So wait, we're like that king?" Marco said. "And you're the world?"

"It's a metaphor," Bhegad said.

"I never metaphor I didn't like," Marco said, "but dude, your brain won't rot away. It's preserved in awesome."

"I may be dead by the time you return. I am concerned about the passage of time. And I do have a plan." Bhegad looked each of us in the eye, one by one. "I am giving you forty-eight hours. That will be six months for us. We will continue to maintain a camp here and wait patiently for the five of you. If you are as marvelous as we think you are, that will be enough time to find both Loculi. When the time is up, no matter what happens, you will return. If you need another voyage, we will plan it then. Understood?"

"Wait—you said the five of us," I said warily. "Fiddle is coming?"

"No, you need protection, first and foremost," Professor

Bhegad looked at Torquin. "Don't lose them this time, my barefooted friend. And keep yourself out of jail."

* * *

"Step . . . step . . . step . . . step . . ."

Torquin called out marching orders like a drill sergeant. He had tied us together at the waist with long lengths of rope, which dragged on the sand between us as we walked. We were lined up left to right—Marco, Aly, Torquin, Cass, and me.

"Is this necessary?" Aly asked as we reached water's edge.

"Safety," Torquin said. "I lose you, I lose job."

I glanced over my shoulder. Professor Bhegad, Nirvana, and Fiddle were waiting and watching, near a big, domed tent.

"Who wants to go first?" I asked.

With a sly grin, Marco lunged for the water like a sprinter. His rope pulled Aly forward, then Torquin, Cass, and me. Torquin bellowed something I can't repeat.

I felt myself go under, floundering helplessly. Being tied to Torquin wasn't a help. His flailing arms smacked against me like boards.

Don't fight the water. It's your friend. That was Mom's voice—from way back during my first, terrifying swim lesson at the Y. I could barely remember what she sounded like, but I felt her words giving me strength. I let my muscles slacken. I let Marco's body pull me. And then I swam in his direction.

Soon I was passing Torquin. The rope's slack was long enough so I could open up some distance. I could see Aly's feet just ahead of me, kicking hard. Her rope was nearly taut to Torquin. She was holding tight to Cass, who chopped the water as best as he could.

There. The circle of tiles, just below us. The strange music began seeping into my brain.

This is going to hurt. Don't fight it.

I braced myself. I let my body go. I felt the sudden expanding and contracting. Like I was going to explode.

It hurt just as much, felt just as inhuman. But it was the second time, and I was more ready than I expected. I blasted through the other side of the circle, my lungs nearly bursting, my body looser and prepared for the cold.

I was not, however, prepared to be yanked backward.

My rope was taut.

Torquin.

Was this some kind of joke? Was he stuck?

I turned. Torquin had not emerged. It was as if he were pulling me back through. Over my shoulder, I could see Cass and Aly trying to swim away, also pulling at the rope in vain.

It was like a tug of war between two dimensions.

Marco swam next to me and grabbed onto the rope. Fumbling in his pack, he took out a pocket knife. He slashed once . . . twice . . .

The rope snaked outward. It snapped back into the portal.

We tumbled backward. The portal glowed, but its center was pitch black. The frayed ends of the rope disappeared into the darkness.

Where was Torquin? Marco began swimming toward the portal with one arm, waving us up toward the surface with the other. My concern for Torquin's life lost out to sheer panic. I didn't have long before my breath would run out. None of us did.

I turned and kicked hard. Aly was pumping toward the surface. I grabbed onto Cass's length of rope and held tight, pulling him along.

Cass and I exploded through the surface, gasping and coughing. I looked around desperately, expecting to crash into a boulder. But the river was calmer than the last time. "Where's . . . Aly . . . Marco?" Cass gulped.

A shock of dyed red hair burst through to the sunlight. Aly looked like she could barely breathe. She was sinking under. I had to help. "Can you make it to the river bank on your own?" I asked Cass.

"No!" he said.

Yeeeeahhhhh! cried a voice closer to the shore. Marco was thrusting upward, shaking his head, blinking his eyes. In a nanosecond, he was swimming toward Aly. "Go to shore!" he cried out to us. "Did Torquin come through?"

"I don't think so!" I said.

With powerful strokes, Marco swam Aly to the shallows,

where she was able to stand. Then he plunged back the way he'd come. "We have to find him!" he cried out. "I'll be right back!"

As he disappeared under the surface, Cass and I swam toward Aly. We were in a different part of the river from last time. Shallower. It didn't hurt that the bad weather had stopped, and the current was calmer.

We reached the sandy soil and flopped next to Aly, exhausted. "Next time . . ." she panted, "we bring . . . water wings."

Gasping for breath, we waited, staring at the river for Marco. Just as I was contemplating a jump back in to find him, his head broke through. We stood eagerly as he swam to shore. Trudging up to the bank, he shook his head, his lips drawn tight. "Couldn't do it . . ." he said. "Went right up to the portal . . . tried to look through . . . considered going back . . ." In frustration, he smacked his right fist into his left palm.

"You did your best, Marco," Aly said. "Even you need to breathe."

"I—I failed," Marco said. "I didn't get him."

He pushed his way through us and slumped down onto the sandy soil. Cass sat next to him, putting a skinny arm around his broad shoulder. "I know how you feel, brother Marco," he said.

"Maybe Torquin got stuck in the portal," Aly suggested.

Marco shook his head. "We could fit an ox team through that thing."

"He might have gotten cold feet at the last minute," Cass said, "and gone back."

We all nodded, but frankly that didn't sound like Torquin. Fear wasn't in his toolkit. He was a good swimmer. And he had lungs the size of a truck engine. All I could think about were Professor Bhegad's words: *What rules do apply, in a world that one must experience cross-dimensionally?*

"Maybe he *couldn't* get through," I said quietly. "Maybe we're the only ones who can. I mean, let's face it, we each do have something he doesn't have."

"A vocabulary of more than fifty words?" Cass said with a wan smile. Under the circumstances, his joke landed flat.

"The gene," I said. "G7W. He's not a Select."

"You think the portal recognizes a *gene*?" Aly asked.

"Think of the weird things that have happened to us," I said. "The waterfall that healed Marco's body. The Heptakiklos that called to me. The fact that I could pull out a shard and let a griffin through, when others had tried but couldn't. All these things happened near a flux area, too. The gene gives us special abilities. Maybe jumping through the portal is one of them."

Cass nodded. "So while we passed through, Torquin just . . . hit a wall. Which means he may be back with Professor Bhegad, safe and sound."

"Right," I said.

"Right," Aly agreed.

We all stared silently at the gently rolling Euphrates, wanting to believe what we'd just agreed on. Hoping our beefy, laconic guardian was all right. Knowing in our hearts and minds that no matter his outcome, one thing was clear.

We were on our own.

CHAPTER ELEVEN

MATTER AND ANTIMATTER

"GOTCHA!" MARCO GRABBED my hand as I leaped over a narrow trench. It carried water from the Euphrates, up through the pine grove and into the farms for irrigation. I was the last one over.

Cass was crouched low, stroking a palm-sized green lizard in his hand. "Hey, look! It's not afraid of me!"

Aly crouched beside him. "She's cute. She can be our mascot. Let's call her Lucy."

Cass cocked his head. "Leonard. I'm getting more of a *he*-vibe."

"Uh, dudes?" Marco looked exasperated. "I'm getting a go-vibe. Come on."

Cass gently put Leonard in his backpack. We continued

walking toward the city, hidden by the trees. It was the height of the day and the sun beat mercilessly. Through the branches I glanced at the farm. Carts rested on the side of yellow mud-brick buildings. I figured the farmers must have been napping.

Cass sniffed the air. "Barley. That's what they're growing."

"How do you know?" Marco asked. "Were you raised on a farm?"

"No." Cass's face clouded. "Well, sort of. I lived on one for a couple of years. An aunt and uncle. Didn't work out too well."

"Sorry to hear it," Marco said.

Cass nodded. "No worries. Really."

As they walked on ahead, I glanced at Aly. Questioning Cass about his childhood was never a good idea. "I'm worried about Cass," she confided, lowering her voice. "He thinks his powers are dwindling. And he's so sensitive about everything. Especially his past."

"At least he's got us. We're his family now," I said. "That should give him strength."

Aly let out a little snort. "That's a scary thought. Four kids who might not live to see fourteen. We're about as dysfunctional as it gets."

Ahead of us, Marco had put an arm around Cass's shoulder. He was telling some story, making Cass laugh. "Look," I said, gesturing with my chin. "Dysfunctional, maybe, but don't they look like a big brother and little brother?"

Aly's worried expression turned into a smile. "Yeah."

As we neared the edge of the pine grove, we were all dripping sweat. Cass and Marco had pulled ahead, and they were now crouched by a pine tree at the edge of the grove. We gathered next to them. No one had noticed us. No one was near. So we could take in a long, clear view of the city.

Babylon sprawled out from both sides of the river. Its wall was surrounded by a moat, channeled from the river itself. A great arched gate, leading into a tunnel, breached the wall far to our left. Outside that gate, a crowd had gathered at the moat's edge. They were almost all men. Their tunics had more folds than ours, with thicker material bordered in a bright color.

"We didn't get the garb right," Aly said.

"We look like the poor relatives," Cass remarked.

"It is what it is," Marco said. "Let's walk like we belong."

As we stepped out from the trees, I noticed that Cass was chewing gum. "Spit that out!" I said. "You weren't supposed to bring stuff like that."

"But it's just gum," Cass protested.

"Hasn't been invented yet," Aly said. "We don't want to look unusual."

Cass reluctantly spat a huge wad of gum into the bushes. "In two thousand years, some archaeologist is going to find that and decide that the Babylonians invented gum," he muttered. "You making me spit that out may have changed the future."

We all followed Marco out of the trees and onto the desert soil. As we approached the city wall, the crowd grew loud and raucous. They'd formed a semicircle with their backs to us, shouting and laughing. Some of them scooped rocks off the ground. Three men stood guard, facing outward, looking blankly off in to the distance. They wore brocaded tunics with bronze breastplates and feathered helmets. They looked powerful and bored.

"Behold Babylon," Marco whispered.

"Just past Lindenhurst," Cass whispered back. "That's the Long Island Railroad. Babylon line. Massapequa, Massapequa Park, Amityville, Copiague, Lindenhurst, and Babylon. I can do them backward if—"

A horrible scream interrupted Cass. It came from the center of the crowd, and a second later, the men all roared with approval. Instinctively we stopped. We were about sixty or seventy yards away, I figured, but no one was paying us any mind. I could see a couple of boys racing toward the crowd with armfuls of stones. As the people ran to grab some, a gap opened in the semicircle. Now I could see what was inside—or *who*. It was a small, wiry man in a ragged tunic with a thick purple border. He was cowering on the ground, covering his head with his hands and bleeding.

The color drained from Aly's face. "They're stoning him. We have to do something!"

"No, because then they'll stone us," Cass said, "and we'll be dead before we're born."

Staggering to his feet, the bloodied man shouted something to the crowd. Then he took a step backward, yelped, and disappeared—downward, into the moat.

I heard a splash. Another scream, worse than any we'd heard so far. The crowd was standing over the moat, peering down. Some bellowed with laughter, continuing to throw rocks into the water. Some turned away, looking ill.

From behind us I heard the sound of wheels crunching through soil. The men in the mob began turning toward the sound, falling silent. A few dropped to their knees. We did the same.

A four-wheeled chariot rolled into sight along the packed-dirt road. It was pulled by four men in loincloths, and the driver wore a maroon-colored cloak. Behind him, on a cushioned throne, sat a withered-looking man dressed in a brocaded robe. He wore a fancy helmet encrusted with jewels, which made his thin face and pointed beard look ludicrous.

As the chariot neared the moat, the crowd and the guards bowed to the ground. The slaves trotted the vehicle over the bridge, the king glancing briefly down into the water as he passed.

If he saw anything horrifying, it didn't register on his face. He yawned, leaned back into his seat, and waved lazily to the crowds who dared not look at him.

"Is that King Nascar Buzzer?" Marco asked.

"Nebuchadnezzar," I said. "Maybe."

"I don't think so," Aly said. "I think it's Nabu-na'id. I did some calculations. This ripping apart of time had to start somewhere. Before the split, our time and Ancient Babylon time were in sync. And I figure that was around the sixth century B.C. Which is about the time that the Hanging Gardens were destroyed. During the reign of Nabu-na'id. Also known as Nabonidus."

"Okay, maybe this is a dumb question, but why are there ruins?" Marco said. "If Babylon time-shifted, wouldn't the whole city have just disappeared? So what are those rocks we see back in the twenty-first century?"

"It must be like matter and antimatter," Aly said. "The two parallel worlds existed together. Babylon continued to exist at regular speed *and* at one-ninetieth speed. And we are the only ones who can see both of them."

As the king disappeared through the gate, a guard rushed out toward us. He shouted back over his shoulder, and another two followed.

Soon six of them were racing our way. "Look unthreatening," Marco said.

"We're *kids*," Aly replied.

81

"I think I'm going to throw up," Cass said, his entire body shaking.

"Confidence is key," Marco said. He smiled at the approaching soldiers, waving. "Yo, sweet tunics, guys! We're looking for Babylon?"

The guards surrounded us, glaring, six spears pointed at our chests.

CHAPTER TWELVE

DEEP DOODOO

I DIDN'T NEED to understand Aramaic to know we were in deep doodoo.

The guards' leader was maybe seven feet tall. An evil, gap-toothed smile shone through a black beard as thick as steel wool. He jabbered orders to us, waited while we stared uncomprehendingly, then jabbered something else. "I think he's trying out different languages," Aly murmured, "to figure out which one we speak."

"When does he get to English?" Marco asked.

Trembling, Cass lifted his hands over his head. "We. Come. In. Peace!"

The men raised their spears, tips to Cass's face.

"Never mind," he squeaked.

The leader gestured toward the city, growling. We

83

walked, our hands quivering fearfully over our heads. As we reached the bridge over the moat, I peered downward. The moat's water churned with the action of long, leathery snouts. It was muddy and blood-red.

"C-c-crocodiles," Cass said.

I closed my eyes and breathed hard, thinking of the man who had jumped in. "What kind of place is this, anyway?" I murmured.

"Definitely not Disney World," Marco replied.

The city's outer wall towered over us. The entrance gate was more like a long entrance chamber, tiled with bright blue brick. Every few feet there was a carved relief of an animal—oxen, horses, and a fantastical beast that looked like a four-legged lizard. As we trudged through the tunnel, people backed away, staring. On the other side, we emerged onto a narrow dirt street lined with simple mud-brick buildings. Next to one building, a man sheared a sheep while a boy giggled and held tufts to his chin, baahing.

The guards pushed us to move fast. The city was vast, the streets narrow. As we walked silently on pebbly soil, I could feel the glare of eyes from windows all around us. After about fifteen minutes, I could feel myself slowing down in the noonday sun. The heat was unbearable, the closely packed mud-brick houses seeming to trap it and radiate it back into our faces. We stopped to drink from a barrel, and a carriage trundled by, pulled by a wiry slave and carrying a round-faced man with a big belly. From here, I could see another high wall, leading to some inner part of the city. The great tower was beyond that. "Is that the Tower of Babel?" I asked.

"Maybe," Aly said. "But I don't think they'd take us there. I think it's some kind of religious place."

"Religious places were sacrificial sites," Cass piped up. "Where living things were slaughtered in public!"

"Brother Cass, you are a glass-totally-empty kind of guy," Marco said.

A gust of desert wind brought the smell of fried meat straight down the city road. I could barely keep the drool inside my mouth.

The guards prodded us to move faster. It became clear that the smell was coming from the other side of Wall Number Two, which was looming over the houses now. It was much taller and fancier than the outer wall, maybe four stories high. The bricks were glazed shiny and seemed to be made of a smoother, finer material. "The high-rent district," Marco whispered, as we followed the guards over another moat bridge.

"Where the *awilum* live," Aly remarked.

The guards nodded.

"Show-off," Cass said.

The bridge was jammed with wealthy-looking people. We nearly collided with a Jabba the Hutt lookalike and a lackey who followed him with a platter of food. Chariots creaked to and fro.

On the other side of the gate the delicious smells hit us like a thick slap. We emerged into a circular plaza about three city blocks wide, packed with people—women with urns on their heads, hobbling old men, turbaned young guys arguing fiercely, barefoot kids playing games with pebbles. The *awilum* obviously liked to protect their market by making sure it was inside the wall. The people behind the stalls, the deliverers, even the wealthy patrons were not much taller than I was. Stalls sold every kind of merchandise—food, spices, animal skins, knives, and clothing. Despite the wealth and the abundance of food, a clutch of ragged-looking people begged for money along the edges of the crowd.

Not far from us, a barrel-chested guy cried out to customers as he grilled an entire lamb on a spit. The head guard gestured toward it. "Souk!"

Marco gestured to his belly. "Yes! Hunger definitely souks!"

At Marco's shout, the guards pointed their swords. The crowd fell slowly silent. "Sorry," Marco said, his hands in the air. "I hope I didn't offend."

The head guard grabbed a pile of grilled lamb from a souk stand. Eyeing Marco warily, he grunted toward the other guards, who each helped themselves to food. Then they pushed us forward, not bothering to pay.

"That was cruel," Aly said.

"Corruption always is," Cass said.

"Not that," Aly said. "I meant hogging all the food."

The guards pushed us onward, our stomachs grumbling, down a narrow road past tight-packed houses. We headed up a hill toward the huge central tower, the ziggurat. It seemed to grow as we approached, its many windows whistling eerily as they caught the desert breezes. It may have been ten stories high, but looming over the squat houses the ziggurat looked like the Empire State Building. With windows spiraling up to a tapered top, it was like a giant, finely sculpted sand castle.

It was gated too, and surrounded by lawns and flower beds. As we got closer, I realized it was even wider than I'd thought, maybe a city block across.

"How exactly did they do sacrifices?" Cass said nervously. "Did they carve out the hearts while you were alive, or put you to sleep first?"

"We haven't done anything to make them want to sacrifice us," Aly said. "This city was ruled by the Code of Hammurabi, which was fair and reasonable. Sacrifice was not part of the punishment."

"Just stuff like, you know, selling people into slavery," Marco said. "Cutting off fingers. Like that."

Cass held up his hands, giving them a mournful stare. "G-G-Good-bye, old friends."

The guards pushed us through an entryway into a high-ceilinged room with brightly glazed walls. It was way longer side-to-side than it was deep. The windows let in a soft gray light, and candle flames flickered in wall sconces. We walked on finely detailed carpets past a sculpture of open-mouthed fish spouting water into a marble fountain. Serving maids with braided hair and long gowns carried trays back and forth, and four old men chiseled fine symbols onto stones. We walked into another chamber, where an ancient man sat at a marble table. After giving us a long, shocked look, he tottered off down a long hallway.

"How do you say, 'Where's the boys' room?' in Aramaic?" Marco said.

"Not now, Marco!" Aly said.

Moments later the old man reappeared at the door and said something to the guards. They pushed us forward again.

"Look, Hercules, I'm getting tired of this. I have to pee," Marco said.

The guard moved his face right up close to Marco. Pointing to the room behind the door, he said, "Nabu-na'id."

"Wait," Cass said. "Isn't that the same as King Nabonidus? I thought the Tower of Babel wasn't the palace."

"Guess Nabo did a makeover," Marco said.

We turned toward the jewel-encrusted archway of the inner chamber. The guard smacked the end of his sword on the ground, and it echoed dully. We began to walk forward again.

We were going before the king.

CHAPTER THIRTEEN

PURE AWESOME

FROM INSIDE THE royal chamber came the music of gently plucked strings . . . and something else. Something that sounded at first like an exotic wind instrument, and then like a bird. One instant it dropped so low that the hallway seemed to vibrate. The next it was soaring impossibly high, skipping and flitting so fast that the echoes overlapped until it sounded like a chorus of twelve.

"That's a voice," Aly said in awe, as we stepped inside. "One human voice."

The room glittered with candles in delicately carved metal wall sconces. Wisps of smoke danced up to a ceiling three stories high. Carpets crossed the polished floor, woven with battle scenes. Like the other rooms, this one was longer from side to side. On a platform in the middle sat a massive, unoccupied throne. To its right stood four bearded old men in flowing robes, one of them resting his elbows on a high table. To its left, a veiled woman was playing a flat stringed instrument nestled in her lap, her hands a blur as they hammered out a complex tune. Next to her stood another young woman, also veiled, singing with a voice so impossibly beautiful I could barely move.

"What is that instrument?" Aly asked the head guard. When he returned a blank stare, she pantomimed playing the instrument. "A zither?"

"Santur," he said.

"Beautiful," she remarked.

"Yeah," I said. "Beautiful." I couldn't stop staring at the musician. From under her veil I could see a shock of golden red hair. Her eyes were shut and her head swayed gently as she sang along with the santur.

Aly smacked my arm. "Stop drooling."

Startled, the singer opened her eyes, which bore down on me like headlights. I turned away, my face suddenly feeling hot. When I looked back, I could see a flicker of a smile cross her face.

She was looking at Marco.

"'Sup, dudes?" Marco said. "Nice tune. So, greetings everyone. We don't have too much time. Also, well, to be honest, I have to tinkle. Anyway, I'm Marco, and these guys are—*yeow!*"

The head guard had thumped Marco on the back of the head. The guard and his pals kneeled and gestured for us to get on our knees, too.

The santur player struck up a triumphant-sounding tune. The old men bustled away from us, toward an archway in the rear. A tiny, tottering silhouette appeared there.

It was the withered old king we'd seen on the chariot. He stepped forward into the candlelight, wearing a cape of shimmering reds and golds, and a jeweled crown so big it looked like it might sink over his ears. The men took his arms as he limped toward the throne, his right foot flopping awkwardly. One of his advisers seemed younger than the others, a sour-looking dude with darting gray eyes, whose silver-and-black-streaked hair fell to his shoulders like oiled shoelaces. He took his place at the side of the throne, arms folded.

As he sat, the king cocked his head approvingly at the veiled singer. His pointy beard flicked to one side like the tail of a bird. The song abruptly stopped. Singer, santur player, slaves, and guards all bowed low, and so did we. A slave woman knelt by him, removing his right sandal. As she massaged his shriveled foot with oils, he smiled.

The guards prodded us to our feet and pushed us forward. I had to look away to keep from staring at the king's adviser, whose eyeballs moved wildly like two trapped hornets. "That guy is creeping me out," Aly said under her breath.

"Which one, Bug-Eye or Fish-Foot?" Marco asked.

Sitting forward, the king barked a question in a thin, high-pitched voice. As his words echoed unanswered, the guards began to mutter impatiently.

"No comprendo Babylonish," Marco said.

"Accch," the king said with disgust, gesturing toward the young singer. She nodded politely and stepped toward us.

Smiling at Marco, she said, "'Sup?"

"Whoa. You speak English?" Marco exclaimed.

She pointed at him curiously. "Dudes?"

"Marco, she's just repeating words you said," I told him. "She's a musician. She has a good ear for sounds, I guess. I don't think she knows what they mean."

The king said something to the girl sharply. She bowed and turned, explaining something to him in a soft voice. He nodded and sat back.

"Daria," the girl said, pointing to herself.

"My name is Jack," I said. "His name is Marco, her name is Aly, his is Cass."

"Nyme-iz-Zack . . ." As she spoke, her face puckered as if tasting mango-chili ice cream. Pointing to herself again, she said, "His nyme-iz Daria."

"*Your* name is Daria," I said. "*My* name is Jack. *His* name is Marco . . . Aly . . ." I pointed to the king. "Um, Nabu-na'id?"

"Ahhhhhh, Nabu-na'id!" the king said. As he beamed

with approval, his adviser's eyes bounced like a ball on a roulette wheel. He seemed to have some kind of vision problem, like a jangled nerve that wouldn't let him focus his eyes. He leaned low, whispering into the king's ear. I couldn't understand what he was saying, but I didn't trust his tone of mumble.

Marco grinned at Daria. "Yo, Daria, you're a language person. Maybe you can help us. If you can get us to the Hanging Gardens—Hannnng-inng Garrr-dens—that would be pure awesome."

"Poor . . . ossum," she replied, her face turning slightly pink.

"She's crushing on the Immortal One," Cass whispered.

"No, she's not," I snapped.

"It's obvious," Cass said.

"It is not!" I said, a little louder.

"Will you curb your jealousy?" Aly hissed. "This is a good thing. This could help us. She has the king's ear."

I buttoned my lip, staring at Daria. I felt heat rising upward from my neck into my face and tried desperately not to let myself look embarrassed. Which was about the hardest thing to do at that moment.

Daria wasn't looking at Marco anymore, but at the king and his strange, younger henchman. They were leaning forward, alternately listening to her words, eyeing us suspiciously, and peppering her with questions. I had no idea what they were saying, but she seemed to be calming them down.

Marco was fidgeting. "Yo! King Nabisco! Your Honor! Can I step outside for a minute? I'll be right back—"

Daria whirled around. With a questioning look, she pointed to each of us, then made an abstract, sweeping gesture, as if indicating the great, wide world outside.

"I think she wants to know where we came from," I said.

"America, land of the free," Marco said.

Daria turned toward the king and bowed again. "Meccalandothafee," she said tentatively.

The old king turned to his adviser, who shrugged. Another flurry of words followed between them and Daria. Finally the king sank back into his throne, waving his fingers in a dismissive gesture.

The guards took our arms. They shoved us back through the entryway and down a hallway.

Marco was grimacing. "Let me know if you see a door with a male silhouette on it. I really have to go."

"Hey . . . hey—*Where are you taking me?*" Aly shouted.

I spun around. Two of the guards were forcing her down a side corridor, out of sight. Marco, Cass, and I all braced to run, but our three guards blocked the way. Gripping our arms tight, the pushed us onward with unintelligible grunts, their faces bored and impatient.

Marco was seething. "On the count of three," he said,

"we kick these guys and run."

But before he could start the count, the guards veered through an open door, shoving us into a large room with rough mud-brick walls. Pale white light shone through an open window, illuminating three flat slabs of stone in the center of the room. Each was long enough for one human body, like table in a morgue.

Next to each slab was a bearded court slave, holding a machete. They were avoiding our eyes, looking closely at our necks.

CHAPTER FOURTEEN

LATER, GLADIATOR

"ONE . . ." MARCO SAID.

The servants shoved us closer. They shouted instructions to the slaves, who sharpened their blades on long leather strips that hung from the sides of the slabs.

"Two . . ."

Placing their machetes on the slabs, the three *wardum* walked toward us. One of them carried a pot full of liquid. Each slave dipped his hand in the pot, coating it in some kind of oil. Two of them went toward Marco and Cass, the other to me. He nodded and smiled, reaching toward my head.

"Thr—" Marco began.

"Wait!" I shouted.

Fingers massaged my scalp with warm oil. The servant hummed as he worked, smiling gently. I glanced over to Cass and Marco. They looked as baffled as I felt.

In moments my bewilderment gave way to relaxation. It felt good. Incredibly good. As if my mom were alive again, shampooing my head. As I closed my eyes I saw Marco rushing off to an alcove with a rectangular hole in the floor. And I heard a sigh of great relief.

When my servant was done, he gestured toward the slab. Next to it, the machete gleamed in the light from the open window. Marco and Cass turned, as their slaves finished oiling their hair. "What is going on here?" I asked.

"It's a makeover," Marco said.

"Did we really look that bad?" Cass asked.

"I mean with the knives?" I said.

Now the three *wardum*, finished with their work, were all gesturing toward the slabs.

"Easy, Brother Jack," Marco said. "I'm betting they're not going to hurt us. I'll go first."

He lay faceup on his slab. His servant pulled him toward the top of the slab, so his hair hung over the top edge. Taking the machete, the *wardum* brought it down swiftly. I flinched. A lock of Marco's hair fell to the floor.

Marco smiled, closing his eyes. "Sweet. Can I get a back rub?"

* * *

When they were done, our hair was trim, our feet were washed, and we had fancy new tunics and sandals. The servants gave us over cheerfully to the guards, who grunted with what seemed like admiration at our new look.

"What the heck did we do to deserve this?" said Cass, as we were escorted back into the hallway.

"Either they think we're some kind of visiting gods," Marco said, running his fingers through his hair, "or they're preparing us for slaughter."

Cass gulped. "Thanks for that cheery thought."

The guards quickly ushered us into the hallway, where two female attendants waited patiently with Aly. She was scowling, her own hair oiled and garlanded with flowers, her tunic replaced by a flowing toga-like gown. "If you take a picture, I will kick you," she grumbled.

"You look nice," Marco said.

Aly raised a skeptical eyebrow. "But not as nice as Daria, I'll bet."

Together we were led back through the snaky corridors and out another door into the sunlight. A sweet tang hit us as we marched along a stone pathway, past colorful gardens and birds bursting with song. It was an area of the palace grounds we hadn't seen on the way in. Trellises arched overhead, their purple blossoms tickling our faces. Simply clad *wardum* trudged in and out of a mud hut with bowls, shovels, and gardening equipment.

We stopped at a door, flanked by two windows—an entire two-story house was actually built into the city's inner wall and extended behind it. The guard opened the door and ordered us inside.

Another team of *wardum* bowed to us in the entry room. Two of them carried trays of fruit and flagons of liquid. Two others took us on a brief tour. The first floor had a sun-filled room with a small pool, sleeping quarters, and a locker full of salt-cured meats. The second had simple bedrooms. We ended on a roof deck overlooking the palace grounds. The air was cool and sweet. As the slaves placed the fruit on a table surrounded by cushioned chairs, I stared in disbelief. "Is this where we're staying?"

"I thought goggle-eyes was going to throw us in jail," Marco said, "not paradise!"

As he dug in to the food with two fists, Cass, Aly, and I walked to the waist-high wall around the roof. We scanned the sculpted landscape of gardens and woods. I could see a small cattle pasture, a pig pen, a vegetable garden. "Do you see anything that looks like the Hanging Gardens?" Aly said.

"Evitagen," Cass said, shaking his head.

Over the treetops, I spotted a distant flash of white. Grabbing a chair, I stood on it and caught a glimpse of what looked like the roof of a temple. "Maybe that's the top of it. Looks like a ziggurat."

"Orff onooway fannow," Marco said through a mouthful of food.

"Either that's really bad Backwardish, or you need to swallow," Aly said.

"I said, 'only one way to find out,'" Marco replied. "Let's go see the place."

He headed for the stairs. We all tromped down after him to the bottom floor. As we flung open the front door, two guards turned, gripping their spears. "Later, gladiator," Marco said.

He got about two steps. The guards went shoulder to shoulder, blocking his way.

"Whoa, peace out," Marco said, backing into the house. "Kumbaya. Nice work on the biceps. Who's your trainer?"

"What now?" Aly said.

Marco turned. "We go to Plan B. There's more than one way to escape."

He strode back upstairs, followed by Cass. But Aly was looking at something over the guards' shoulders.

At first I didn't see anything unusual. But I did notice the birds had stopped chirping. Totally. Another sound floated through the gardens, like the trilling of an impossibly beautiful flute. The guards seemed to melt at the sound. Smiling, they turned away from us.

Daria appeared around a bend in the path. She was still wearing a head scarf but no longer a veil. Her face was the picture of bliss as she sang. Now I knew why the birds had stopped. They couldn't compete with a sound like that.

I waved and shouted hello.

"Hello!" Daria replied, as the guards parted, gesturing for her to come inside.

"We can't have her around while we're trying to escape," Aly hissed. "Why is she coming here?"

I shrugged. "She's the language person. The only one who managed to pick up a few words of English. Plus, in case you don't remember, she saved our butts. I don't know what she told the king, but it set us free. I'm guessing they think we're exotic foreigners. He probably sent her to get further info from us."

Aly shook her head. "This is a trap, Jack. Think about the history. Babylon was always under attack from Persia. Nabu-na'id would have hated the Persians. Eventually they defeated him and took over Babylon. When they found out how he'd been ruling the city, they were appalled by what a bad king he was."

"I could have told them that," I said.

"And here we are, four strangers wandering into town," Aly barreled on. "Of course they suspect we're enemies! This girl could be a spy, Jack. The first line of interrogation. They treat us nicely, fill us with food and drink, and then—zap!—they move in for the torture."

"Torture—Daria?" I replied. "How? She sings us into a coma?"

"I'll stall her," Aly said. "You go up and tell the others.

101

Make sure she can't see them planning an escape."

I raced inside. Cass and Marco were at a window in the back of the house, looking down over the outer wall. When I told them about Daria's arrival, neither of them reacted much.

When I leaned out the window and looked down, I realized why. Directly below us, tracing all three sides of the building, was a wide moat.

"Any ideas?" Cass asked.

"It would be pretty easy to swim across that," I said.

"Not so fast," Cass said. From a plate of food, he took a hunk of unidentifiable leathery-brown dried meat and tossed it out. The water roiled with green scales and beady black eyes. A long, crocodilian jaw snapped open and shut.

"Welcome to Paradise," Marco said softly. "Paradise Prison."

CHAPTER FIFTEEN

CALCULATIONS

ELEVEN DAYS.

That was how long we'd been gone. Not in Babylonian time, but real time. Back-home time. In Babylon, it had been just under three hours.

Aly had done the calculation. Now she was sitting with Daria at the rooftop table, running quickly through English words. Whatever paranoid idea Aly had had about torture and spying had faded pretty fast. The two of them had become instant BFFs. Well, BFs. I'm not sure how you could define that second F—forever—in these messed-up time frames.

Cass, Marco, and I paced the floor, waiting. Marco's mouth was full. He'd eaten nearly all the food. Now he was swigging a green fruit liquid. "How can you eat at a time like this?" I demanded.

"Stress makes me hungry," Marco said.

Daria stared at him. "Food. Hungry. Marco eat."

"Good, Daria!" Aly said, furiously scribbling images with a bit of coal on a piece of tree bark.

"She sounds like Torquin," Cass said.

"She's about a million times smarter than Torquin," Aly replied.

And about a trillion times better looking, I thought extremely silently.

"Where'd you find the cool writing tools?" Marco asked.

"Daria brought them," Aly said. "She really wants to learn."

I eyed her warily. "A minute ago, you thought she was a spy."

"Maybe, maybe not," Aly said. "We're bonding."

Daria was looking intently at Marco. "Marco like meb'dala? Tasty good?"

"Aaaah!" Marco said, putting down his flagon. "Tasty good!"

Aly gave Daria an impulsive hug. "This girl is amazing! She picks things up from context. And she doesn't forget anything." Aly quickly drew crude stick figures behind bars in a prison cell, crying. "We—Cass, Marco, Jack, and me— are *prisoners*?"

"Prizz . . . ?" Daria looked closely at the drawing, then shook her head. She pointed to the food, then gestured toward the nice house. Taking the bit of coal, she drew four stick figures standing tall, smiling, with more stick figures around us on their knees with bowed heads.

"Are you saying we're guests?" Aly said, gesturing grandly around the house and giving a happy, thumbs-up gesture. "Guests?"

"Guests . . ." Daria said. "Yest. I mean, yes."

"If we're guests, why the guards?" I said, still pacing.

While I spoke, Daria was drawing an enormous soldier. His teeth were gritted, his sword pointed to a shriveled little man wearing a crown. "Persia," she said, pointing to the soldier. "You? Persia?"

Aly's smile faltered. "No! We are not from Persia! We are from . . ." She gestured into the distance. "Never mind."

"From Nevermind. Ah." Daria nodded. "You are . . . ?"

She drew a stick figure surrounded by stars and mystical symbols, with lightning emerging from its fingers. "What the heck is that?" Marco asked.

"Magic," Cass said. "I guess the king figures we're either Persians or awesome magicians. Process of elimination."

Marco shook his head. "We're not magicians, Dars," he said. "But we do have natural star power."

Daria looked confused. She thought for a minute then struggled for words. "You . . . coming to . . . us. Now."

"Yes, go on," Aly said, leaning forward.

"No . . . other . . . guests . . . comed," she said.

"Came?" Aly said. "No other guests came? No other guests *have come*?"

Daria pulled around the dried bark and began to draw.

"The symbol for ten, three times . . . " Aly said. "Thirty? Thirty what?"

Daria pointed to the sun. She pulled her fists together and shivered as if freezing, then fanned herself as if swelteringly hot. Then freezing again.

"The sun . . . cold hot cold . . . " Aly said.

"I think she means a year," I said. "The sun travels in the sky, and the weather changes from cold to hot and back, in one year."

"Is that what you mean, Daria?" Cass asked. "No visitors—no guests—for *thirty years*?"

"Thirty years is two thousand seven hundred years for us," Aly said. "That would be about the time Ancient Babylon split off from our time frame. They've had no visitors because the rest of the world moved on."

"So no trade?" Cass said. "No goods or food from outside?"

Marco shrugged. "Those farms outside the city are pretty awesome."

"So, wait," I said. "What happens if you go to the next town over? What's there now?"

Daria looked at me blankly.

"Guys, this is all super-interesting but can we cut to the chase?" Marco said. "Daria, can you get us to the Hanging Gardens? *Hanging. Gardens?*"

Daria looked helpless. Not being able to answer everyone's questions seemed to agitate her. She looked pleadingly at Aly. "Teach. I. More. Bel-Sharu-Usur is will here be." Her eyes began to roll wildly.

"I think she's imitating that weird guy behind the throne," Cass said. "He's coming, maybe?"

"Bel-Sharu-Usur . . ." Aly murmured. "That's the same guy as *Belshazzar*—like *Nabonidus* for *Nabu-na'id*. And Belshazzar was the king's evil son!"

"Sun . . . " Daria paused, then gestured toward the eastern sky. "Go up . . . Bel-Sharu-Usur . . . come."

"He's coming *in the morning*?" I asked. "What's he going to do?"

Daria shrugged. She glanced again toward the guards. Seeing that they were out of eyesight, she crossed her eyes and made a disgusted face. "Bel-Sharu-Usur . . . ucccch."

"I don't think she trusts him," I said. "Sounds like he's the one in charge of finding out who we are. If anyone's spying for the king, he'd be my guess. She reports on us now, and Bel-Sharu-Usur comes to check for himself tomorrow."

"Daria . . ." Aly said. "You'll give him a good report?" She did a set of pantomimes—pointing to us, imitating Bel-Sharu-Usur, thumbs-up, and so on.

Daria nodded uncertainly. I could tell she still had a tiny bit of suspicion. "We have to convince her to trust us totally," I murmured. "She doesn't want to be burned."

"Me . . . you . . ." Daria clasped her own two hands together. "Teach."

Aly glanced at me gratefully. "Yes. That's what Jack was saying. I will stick with you, Daria, for as long as it takes."

The two girls started in, batting words around like crazy. Aly was an awesome teacher. But the sun was going down and before I knew it, I had drifted off into a dreamless sleep.

When I awoke, the sun had completely set. I felt as if I'd been asleep for hours. I could hear Marco and Cass in the other room playing some kind of game. Aly and Daria had stood from the table, laughing and chattering.

"It was great to meet you . . ." "Please enjoy food . . ." "I will give a good report, but you must be careful . . ."

I couldn't believe it. Daria was not only beautiful and unbelievably talented, but probably the smartest person I'd ever seen. She'd picked up passable English in just a few hours.

"She's amazing," Aly said as she sent Daria on her way through the front door. "Her vocabulary has grown like crazy—colors, articles of clothing, names of animals and plants. By making faces, I was able to teach her the words for emotions—and she got it all!"

As I listened, I noticed she left a small, leather pouch on the table. I grabbed it and ran for the door.

Daria was already far down the pathway. I burst outside, shouting "Hey! Daria! You forgot—"

I jerked backward as if I'd run into a pole. Mainly because I had.

One of the guards stood over me, his spear still held sideways, where he had blocked my path, like a baseball player bunting for a single. He grumbled something in a language I didn't understand. "What's he saying?" I asked.

Aly was standing in the door, looking stunned. "I don't know," she said. "But at the rate we're going, our kids will be growing up in the twenty-fourth century."

CHAPTER SIXTEEN

THE DREAM

I HAVEN'T HAD the Dream in a long time.

But it's back.

And it's changed.

It does not begin as it always has, with the chase. The woods. The mad swooping of the griffins and the charge of the hose-beaked vromaski. The volcano about to erupt. The woman calling my name. The rift that opens in the ground before me. The fall into the void. The fall, where it always ends.

Not this time. This time, these things are behind me.

This time, it begins at the bottom.

I am outside my own body. I am in a nanosecond frozen in time. I feel no pain. I feel nothing. I see someone below, twisted and motionless. The person is Jack. Jack of the Dream.

But being outside it, I see that the body is not mine. Not the same face. As if, in these Dreams, I have been dwelling inside a stranger. I see small woodland creatures, fallen and motionless, strewn around the body. The earth shakes. High above, griffins cackle.

Water trickles beneath the body now. It pools around the head and hips. And the nanosecond ends.

The scene changes. I am no longer outside the body but in. Deep in. The shock of reentry is white-hot. It paralyzes every molecule, short-circuiting my senses. Sight, touch, hearing—all of them join in one huge barbaric scream of STOP.

The water fills my ear, trickles down my neck and chest. It freezes and pricks. It soothes and heals. It is taking hold of the pain, drawing it away.

Drawing out death and bringing life.

I breathe. My flattened body inflates. I see. Smell. Hear. I am aware of the soil ground into my skin, the carcasses all around, the black clouds lowering overhead. The thunder and shaking of the earth.

I blink the grit from my eyes and struggle to rise.

I have fallen into a crevice. The cracked earth is a vertical wall before me. And the wall contains a hole, a kind of door into the earth. I see dim light within.

I stand on shaking legs. I feel the snap of shattered bones knitting themselves together.

One step. Two.

With each it becomes easier.

Entering the hole, I hear music. The Song of the Heptakiklos. The sound that seems to play my soul like a guitar.

I draw near the light. It is inside a vast, round room, an underground chamber. I enter, lifted on a column of air.

At the other side I see someone hunched over. The white lambda in his hair flashes in the reflected torch fire.

I call to him and he turns. He looks like me. Beside him is an enormous satchel, full to bursting.

Behind him is the Heptakiklos.

Seven round indentations in the earth.

All empty.

CHAPTER SEVENTEEN
THE TEST

"I DON'T GET why he doesn't just fall over," Marco whispered.

Bel-Sharu-Usur walked briskly up the stairs, with Daria tagging along behind him. Behind her was a gaggle of *wardum* with fans made of palm fronds and sacks of food and drink. The entourage for the king's son.

His eyes never rested in one place. He reeked of fish, and something sickly-sweet, like athletic ointment. His hair was dark at the sides and white down the middle, giving him the appearance of a drunken skunk. At the top of the stairs he looked over the city and took a deep breath, blasting us with a gust of foul air.

"Dude, what was on the breakfast menu?" Marco said. "Three-day-old roadkill?"

He gave Marco a twisted expression that could have been a smile or a sneer, then began babbling to Daria.

I eyed a large vase on a wall shelf. From this angle I could see the eyes of a bull and the hindquarters of some other beast. I'd put Daria's pouch inside that vase for safe-keeping. It contained some feathered needles, maybe for knitting. I made a mental note to give it to her at some point when Bel-Sharu-Usur wasn't all over her.

Aly trudged out from her bedroom, looking exhausted. "What's that smell?" she murmured.

As Bel-Sharu-Usur barked questions at Daria, the odor of his tooth decay settled over us like smog. Inches away from him, Daria nodded respectfully and (remarkably) managed not to barf. She seemed to be giving him a long report about us, as we nervously ate fruit that the house *wardum* laid before us on a table.

"Do you understand what she's saying?" I whispered.

"No," she replied. "I was teaching her English. She wasn't teaching me Babylonian."

Daria and Bel-Sharu-Usur went at it for a few minutes in rapid Aramaic. Finally Daria turned to us with an exasperated face and said, "He will walk us."

"Walk us?" Aly said. "Like take us on a tour?" She walked with her fingers out over the rooftop.

"Nice!" Marco said. "Tell him we love gardens. Especially hanging ones."

"Yes, a tour," Daria said, looking at Bel-Sharu-Usur

114

uneasily. "See us Babylon. He does not say, but I think he must watch you."

"He doesn't yet trust us?" I offered.

Daria shrugged. "We must go now. And be careful."

We rushed out. It wasn't until we were walking away from the house that I remembered I'd forgotten Daria's pouch.

* * *

"Chicken . . . clucks," Daria said. "Ox . . . pulls. Pig . . . oinks. Boar . . . snorts. Pine tree . . . grows tall. Sun flower . . . is round. Fence . . . has posts. Temple . . ."

As we walked through the palace grounds, Aly didn't miss an object. And Daria repeated everything perfectly. Bel-Sharu-Usur hung with them, listening intently. It was impossible to tell what he was looking at or listening to. His strangely disabled eyes flitted all over the place, and it was miraculous he could even walk straight. Still, I could sense that he was noticing every movement, every gesture we were making.

His entourage hung behind him closely. Two *wardum* fanned him with gigantic palm-shaped leaves, muttering chants and making sly faces when he wasn't looking. Two others carried buckets of water, stopping to hand him a ladle every few yards. Before us, two trumpeters blew a fanfare at each turn in the road.

All around the entourage, people took a wide berth. Gardeners, workers, wealthy people—all of them dropped into a fearful silence at the sight of Bel-Sharu-Usur.

"He makes me nervous," Cass said softly.

At the whispered words, Bel-Sharu-Usur's ears pricked up.

"Dude, anyone ever tell you that you look like a cross between a warthog and a popcorn machine?" Marco asked him out loud, with a broad smile. "Just sayin'. Peace out."

Bel-Sharu-Usur looked momentarily confused. He glared at Daria, who told him something that made him smile uncertainly.

"I guess she covered for you, Marco," Cass murmured.

"She's hot *and* smart," Marco said.

"So, you think she's hot, too?" Aly said.

Daria turned to Marco with a smile. "Not hot. Is cool in the morning."

I looked at the ground to avoid cracking up.

"What do you call this place, Daria?" Aly asked, gesturing around the palace grounds. "Does it have a name?"

Daria thought a moment. "In language of Sumer people, is Ká-Dingir-rá. In language of Akkad people, is Bab-Ilum. Means great gate of god."

"Bab-Ilum!" Cass said. "Probably where they got the name Babylon. Looc os si taht."

"Can't get a word of Babylonic, but it worries me that I'm beginning to understand you," Marco said.

We walked briskly past a temple whose walls were pitted, cracked, and choked with weeds. A great wood beam along the roof looked about ready to buckle. "This is—*was*—palace," Daria whispered. "King Nabu-Kudurri-Usur. Two."

"Who?" Marco said.

"Nabu-Kudurri-Usur is Aramaic for Nebuchadnezzar," Aly said. "'Two' for 'the Second.'" She turned back to Daria. "That king lived here?"

Daria nodded. "He was good. Then more kings— Amel-Marduk, Nergal-Sharu-Usur, La-Abashi-Marduk. All lived in palace. Kings supposed to live in palace. But Nabu-na'id . . . no. Lives in Etemenanki." Her eyes darted toward Bel-Sharu-Usur uncertainly, and she dropped her voice. "Etemenanki is holy place . . . not king place."

Aly shot me a look. I could feel Cass's and Marco's eyes, too. None of us had expected that statement. I knew her English wasn't perfect, but the tone was unmistakable. Our friend Daria didn't seem to like the king very much.

Any lingering mistrust of her was melting away fast.

Bel-Sharu-Usur was picking up the pace. We jogged after him, entering a grand tiled walkway, its bricks glazed with blindingly bright blues and golds. Inlaid into the tiles was a procession of fierce lions of smaller gold and yellow bricks, so lifelike that they seemed about to jump out. Bel-Sharu-Usur raised his wobbling eyes to a shining fortress of cobalt blue rising at the end of the processional path. It was topped with castle-like towers, the great protective city wall extending from either side. The trumpeters blew again, nearly blasting my eardrums.

"Ishtar!" barked Bel-Sharu-Usur.

"Gesundheit," Marco said, gazing upward.

"It's the *Ishtar Gate*," Cass said. "One of the three most famous structures in Ancient Babylon, along with the Hanging Gardens and the Tower of Babel, aka Etemenanki."

"Thank you, Mr. Geography," Marco said.

"Not bad for someone who thinks he's lost his memory powers," Aly said, a smile growing across her face.

Cass shook his head dismissively. "That was easy stuff. You knew it, too, I'll bet."

If we weren't in a parallel world, I'd be taking a zillion photos. Along with the sculpted lions were other elaborate animals—mostly bulls, but also a hideous-looking creature I'd never seen before. It had a long snout with two horns, the front legs of a lion, rear legs with talons like a raptor, and a tail with scorpion pincers. I ran my hands along it, and the tiles were so sharp they nearly cut my skin.

Daria winced. "Is mushushu. Good for people of Bab-Ilum. Means youth. Health. Also means . . ." Her voice dropped to a respectful whisper. " . . . Marduk."

"What's a Marduk?" Marco asked.

"Not what—*who*," Aly said. "It was the name of the Babylonian god." She turned to Daria. "The mushushu is, like, a symbol of the god? A representation?"

Daria thought a moment. "Representation . . . one thing meaning another. Yes."

"Is it a real animal?" Cass asked.

"Yes," Daria said. "Was in cage. In Ká-Dingir-rá. But escape when Nabu-na'id near. Mushushu bit foot. Bel-Sharu-Usur tried to help father, but mushushu attack face."

"So this creature is the thing that mangled the king's foot?" Aly asked. "And it injured Bel-Sharu-Usur in a way that caused his eyes to move funny?"

"All because they had it in a cage," I said. "But why would they treat the mushushu like that? If it was the symbol of a great revered god—"

"King Nabu-na'id does not honor Marduk," Daria said. "Each year we have celebration—Akitu—for new year. For Marduk. In this celebration, guards slap king, kick king to the ground."

"Sounds like a laugh riot," Marco said. "No offense, Dars, but that's a pretty weird way to celebrate."

"It is to remind king that he is a man," Daria said. "He is not god. People love their king even more after this. But when Nabu-na'id becomes king, he does not come to Akitu. This makes Marduk angry."

As we got closer to the gate, guards bowed to Bel-Sharu-Usur from the two turrets at the top.

As the trumpeters moved into the gate, Bel-Sharu-Usur gave a harsh command. Nodding, the two men reversed course and scampered out of sight. He bustled on through, with the rest of us following behind. We hurried out the other side of the gate and onto another tiled, walled walkway. The walkway soon emptied us into another part of the outer city. This section was less built up, a scattering of buildings among fields, leading to the outer wall in the distance.

To our right was a small field, and just beyond it a temple that was cracked and neglected like Nebuchadnezzar's palace. At the base of the temple wall, a group of *wardum* knelt in worship. Bel-Sharu-Usur stormed toward them.

Immediately Daria sang a high-pitched tune of four notes. Hearing it, the *wardum* leaped up and scattered. Bright potted flowers and bowls of food had been placed on the warped windowsills, and Bel-Sharu-Usur quickly moved in, sweeping them to the ground.

"Whoa," Marco said. "He ditched the trumpeters so he could sneak up on these people? What's he got against them?"

Daria's body shook at the sight. "This place is Esagila. A temple. King Nabu-Kudurri-Usur build Esagila to honor Marduk. But Nabu-na'id . . ." Her voice trailed off.

The crowd was growing, murmuring, looking aghast and angry at what Bel-Sharu-Usur had just done. A giant clay pot came hurtling up from its midst, directly for his head.

"Yo, Twinkle-Eyes—duck!" Marco shouted.

Bel-Sharu-Usur turned abruptly. The pot was dead on target for his face. My reflexes kicked in, and I jumped toward him. But Marco was already in the path of the missile, swatting it away.

The two tumbled to the ground. The king's son sat up, his eyes perfectly still for the first time. His entourage of *wardum* gathered around, closing into a circle that faced outward, preparing to take any further attack.

But the crowd of onlookers stared at Marco with an expression of unmistakable awe.

Guards had appeared upon hearing the commotion. With a shrieking command, Bel-Sharu-Usur pointed to a thin, trembling young man dressed in tatters. The guards seized him, pulling him toward the gate despite his anguished pleas.

"That guy wasn't the one who threw it!" Marco protested.

"It does not matter," Daria said sadly. "Bel-Sharu-Usur will punish who he wants."

Now the king's son put a scaly hand on Marco's shoulder. As he spoke, Marco's face began turning green. "What'd I do now?"

"Bel-Sharu-Usur is thanking you," Daria said. "You saved life. He will do good thing for you now."

"Oh," Marco said, fanning the air between him and Bel-Sharu-Usur. "Make him promise to buy a toothbrush. And tell him to take us to the Hanging Gardens."

As Daria translated, Bel-Sharu-Usur took Marco by the arm and led him to the Ishtar Gate. The king's son shouted a command up toward the turret. In response, the guard unhooked his quiver and tossed it down, along with a long-bow. Marco stepped in and caught them easily. "Thanks, dude," Marco said. "I'll treasure it. Hang it on my mantel. But really, I'd rather see the garden."

Bel-Sharu-Usur spoke to Daria. Her face stiffened. She seemed to be pleading with him, but he turned away, ignoring her.

"The weapon is not for you to keep, Marco," she said. "Bel-Sharu-Usur is grateful you saved his life. He believes you are a man with great power. How do you say . . . ?"

"Superpower?" Marco replied. "Yeah, I've heard that."

"Like a god," Daria continued.

"I've heard that, too," Marco said. "Also hero. But what about my request?"

"He will consider this," Daria said. "But he believes you can help Bab-Ilum with your powers. So you must pass a test."

"Dang . . ." Marco exhaled deeply. "Can't we see the Garden first and do the test later?"

Daria shook her head. "In order to grant your wish, Marco, Bel-Sharu-Usur says you must take this weapon to the king's hunting ground, and kill the mushushu."

CHAPTER EIGHTEEN

THE DARKNESS

IT WASN'T SO much the screeching noises that came from the king's royal hunting grounds. Or the putrid smell of death. Or that we'd had to walk about a zillion miles up the river, far from the borders of Babylon. Or the fact that Bel-Sharu-Usur's guards and *wardum* were all shaking with fright.

It was the darkness that gave me the willies.

We stopped at the tree line. Although the leaves rustled in the breeze and water flowed gently into the forest via dug-out streams and culverts from the Euphrates, a strange pitch-blackness hovered in the distance. A shimmering ribbon over the tree line. We'd seen it from the river, but up close it seemed to make the ground vibrate.

"There it is again," Cass said. "That . . . thing."

"What is that, Daria?" Aly asked.

"King's hunting ground," she said. "Animals inside. When mushushu escape from Ká-Dingir-rá, it went here. Now King Nabu-na'id is afraid. He will not hunt here, for the mushushu is vicious."

"I wasn't talking about the forest," Cass said, pointing above the trees. "The darkness. Over the top."

Daria looked confused. "It is Sippar, of course. You do not recognize?"

"Sippar's a country?" Marco said. "You need to talk to them about their carbon emissions."

"Sippar . . . *was* country," Daria said, her head cocked curiously, as if she were teaching basic arithmetic to a twenty-year-old. She gestured in a wide circle. "Now is name for all . . . around us . . . You must not go near."

"*Everything* around Babylon is called Sippar?" Aly scratched her head. "I think we're missing something in translation."

Bel-Sharu-Usur seemed to be taking an interest in this part of the conversation. He jabbered demandingly at Daria, who obediently answered. "What is he asking?" I said.

"He sees everything," Daria said. "He is surprised you do not know Sippar. Everyone knows Sippar. Thus he wonders if you come from a place of magic."

She looked up to the sky.

"Can we discuss this later?" Marco said, turning toward the woods.

"He's right," I added. "We're on a schedule."

"Please give Mr. Peepers a good-bye kiss from us," Marco said, stepping toward the forest. "Next time he sees us, we'll be with a dead moosh. And he'll owe us a trip to the Hanging Gardens of Babylon."

* * *

Marco and I heard it first.

We had gotten out ahead of Cass and Aly, and the suspicious rustling of branches drew us into a dead run. We lost the trail and ended up in a dense, dark area of thickly knotted trees. "Aly?" I called out. "Cass?"

"Ssssh," Marco said, crouching low, his eyes darting in every direction.

The air filled with screeches. I couldn't see the birds above us, but they were everywhere. And they seemed furious. "Yo, angry birds, chill," Marco said.

"Maybe they sense the mushushu," I said.

"What kind of name is mushushu anyway? Sounds like some old dance craze." Marco stood and began moving his hips and arms awkwardly. *"Come on, come on, do the mushushu . . ."*

"Not funny!" I said. "What if it hears you?"

"That's the point," he said. "We flush it out."

"And Aly and Cass?" I said.

125

"We'll find them afterward," Marco said.

As we moved deeper into the woods, I realized there wasn't a moment in my life when I wished more for a cell phone.

Crack.

"What was that?" I asked.

"You stepped on a twig," Marco replied.

"Sorry." As I moved forward, I thought I saw a shadow skittering through the underbrush.

Marco stiffened. "That's him," he whispered. "Moo shoo pork."

He put a protective hand on my arm. Slowly we inched toward the shadow. The bird noises seemed to be quieting, as if they were watching us. I tried to listen for something mushushu-like—which would be what? Hissing? Snorting? Growling? I heard none of those. But I did hear another sound, a dull roar from deeper in the woods, like a distant engine.

There are streams here, McKinley. That's the sound of running water. Focus.

But the noise was growing louder, deeper, like radio static. Despite the clear sky, the sunlight seemed to be flickering. I glanced away from the shadow toward the noise.

Beyond the trees was the shimmering wall of black, up close. Way closer than I'd expected. It shuddered and shifted, as if someone had pulled a solid curtain behind the hunting grounds.

"It's a lizard," Marco was saying.

I spun around. "What?"

"The shadow? Behind the rock? It's not Munchkin. It's a big old—" Marco's eyes narrowed. "Whoa. Who's playing with the lights out there?"

The ends of his hair rose upward. The air was changing, the temperature dropping. I could hear strange noises, like voices sped up, mechanical roars, stuttering beeps, high-pitched scraping.

"Sounds like we're near a highway," I said.

Marco nodded. "Okay. This is freaky."

Sippar was country. Now is name for all around . . .

Daria's words were stuck in my head. And I began to think their meaning hadn't been lost in translation. "Marco, we know that this place—Babylon—is traveling at the slow time, right?"

"Check," Marco said.

"And according to Daria, they haven't had outside visitors for thirty years," I added.

Marco nodded. "Because everyone else sped ahead. Like us."

"Okay, so say you're a Babylonian and you want to go to, like, Greece," I said. "Or Spain or Africa or Antarctica. What would happen to you if you tried? If the rest of the world sped up, then what's out there—out where those countries are supposed to be?"

Marco fell silent, looking toward the black curtain.

"I'm not sure it matters, dude."

"No? I think we're hearing *us*, Marco," I said. "Sippar—that black thing—may actually be the line between play and fast-forward. We're hearing the twenty-first century racing ahead."

"You have an active imagination, Brother Jack," Marco said.

"After the crack in time," I barged on, "this area was isolated. It became a world by itself. With its own rules of space and time. Like Einstein's spaceship. So that's why they can't travel. There is no next town. The next town is in another century."

Marco sank into thought. "Okay, okay, say you're right. This would be a good thing, no? Maybe we don't have to swim through that dumb portal. We can just walk through the magic curtain!"

As he began jogging toward the darkness, I called out, "*Are you crazy?* Where are you going?"

"A short detour," he shouted back. "Let's see this thing up close!"

In a moment he was out of sight. And I did not want to be alone with a lurking wild mushushu.

I followed the sounds of his footfalls until they became impossible to hear. The eerie sound of Sippar was seeping along the ground like smoke, bouncing off trees. Its frequency was hurting my eardrums, upsetting my balance.

I stumbled over a root and tumbled to the ground.

That was when I caught sight of Marco, crouching by the base of some destroyed mud-brick structure. It looked like it might have once been a wall, a fortress, a gate.

I wanted to yell at him, to tell him never, ever to run away like that again, but the words bottled up in my throat.

Marco was staring at a small plain that stretched out before us. On the horizon, maybe a hundred yards from us, the wall pulsed like a curtain. For a nanosecond I had a flashback to a time in Nantucket with my dad, where we saw the aurora borealis in the northern night sky, a huge ribbon of color waving like a rainbow flag. The blackness was a borealis with the color sucked out, a borealis with evil designs, moving, swallowing up the ground before it, uprooting trees, sweeping dust like a tornado.

Marco turned. "You ready for this, Brother Jack?"

"No!" I said. "I'm *not* ready. Wait. Ready for what?"

With the noise of a freight train, the blackness came hurtling toward us.

CHAPTER NINETEEN

COOPERATION

I COULDN'T FEEL my feet touch the ground. The noise washed over us, seizing our bodies like a river of sound. Marco was yelling. Pulling me away. His fingers were tight around my forearm as we raced back into the forest, but my eyes saw only inches ahead. A bat dropped lifelessly into my path. A tree groaned and fell to my right. I kept focus on the ground, until the earth cracked directly beneath me.

My ankle caught. I hit the ground, face-first. A root dug into my left cheek. I felt a wrenching pain in my back.

And then everything fell silent. Not a cheep from the birds or a babble from the brook.

"Jack?" came Marco's voice. "Are you hurt?"

"Only when I breathe," I said.

Marco emerged from the settling dust to my left. He

helped me up, brushing off my tunic. His face was blackened, the hairs at the back of his head singed. "I think maybe if we'd just taken it at a run . . ."

"You are out of your mind," I said. "But thank you for taking us away. And by the way, you look terrible."

Marco smiled. "You, too."

Slowly his eyes rose upward, focusing on something behind me. I sat up and turned.

The curtain of blackness was receding, kicking up dirt and debris. In its wake, where the forest had just been, was a field of ash with smoldering silhouettes of trees, blackened and bent like rubber. Carcasses of animals and birds lay in states of arrested flight, some burned to the bone. Wisps of smoke rose from a culvert, now cracked and empty.

"You seriously thought we could just run through that, Marco!" I said.

He shrugged. "I thought maybe. You know, us being Selects and all. I was delusional."

The gray field's border lay maybe thirty yards ahead of us, stark and definite. Our side of the border was dusty but untouched. Water gurgled nearby, and a lone bird let out a confused chitter overhead. "What if that thing comes back for us?"

Marco stood and pulled me to my feet. "Let's bag this beast, give it to Ol' Whirly, and find our Loculus. If we keep the black hole to our backs and follow the flow of the water, we'll be going in the right direction."

"Promise not to run off," I said.

"Deal."

We picked a path through the trees, keeping within earshot of the culvert. The air was clearing now, and one by one the birds started to sing again. After a half hour or so, I expected us to be reaching the edge of the preserve. But nothing seemed familiar. "How big *is* this place?" Marco said.

I shrugged. The forest was dank and humid. I wiped the sweat from my forehead. "I don't know."

As I leaned against a tree, catching my breath, Marco paced. "This is nuts. We're never going to find this thing. I say we break off and go to the Hanging Gardens ourselves."

"We're supposed to cooperate with the Babylonians," I reminded him. "Professor Bhegad's orders."

"To heck with P. Beg," Marco said. "We listen to him and we'll be dead by the end of the week. I am so over that guy. That whole lame organization."

I couldn't believe the words leaving his mouth. "So we just go rogue whenever we feel like it—like what you did? Be real, Marco. The KI has been at this for years. They know what they're doing. We can't play around with our own lives."

"Brother Jack, no offense, but I've had some time to think," Marco said, his voice weary and exasperated. "Did you ever think this whole thing just . . . smells funny? Try to imagine yourself as him—Bhegad. You're this old professor who thinks he's discovered Atlantis. You figure out this stuff about G7W, you set up a secret lab. You put your whole life into it, drop your teaching gig at Harvard—"

"Yale," I corrected him.

"Whatever," Marco said. "Now, I've got these special kids. I tell them they're going to be superheroes. But I also know they're going to die soon. So I figure out a way to keep them alive until they bring the seven Loculi back. I don't explain how it's done. It's just some mystical procedure. This scares them. I've got them under my thumb now. I know they'll do my bidding. Then . . . after those seven babies are returned? Bingo—thanks, guys, sayonara! Next stop, Nobel Prize."

I nodded. "Exactly. We go home. We're cured."

"But what if that part—the cure—is a big lie?" Marco said. "What if there is no cure? What if it's all a sham? It's a perfect scheme."

I shrugged. "So what else do we do? If we're going to die either way, there's no difference. At some point you have to trust *somebody*. The KI is our only possible hope. Otherwise there's nothing."

"But I've been thinking about that, too," Marco said with a deep sigh. "You know as well as I do that the KI isn't the only game in town."

I couldn't help laughing. "Right, Marco. Of course! I forgot. The Massa. Those crazy monks who tried to kill us. Let's fly on over there and join up."

Marco fell silent. In a fraction of a second, I could feel a change in the air pressure, like a fist squeezing the last bit of patience from me. "Wait. You're not serious, right?" I snapped. "Because if you are, that is an idea so colossally ridiculous that it redefines ridiculousness."

"Whoa, don't assume, dude," Marco said. "My mom always said, when you *assume* you make an *ass* of *u* and *me*—"

"Not funny," I said. "Not remotely funny. Either you're taking *duh* pills or that dust storm has affected what little was left of your brain."

Marco's brown eyes softened in a way I'd never seen before. "Brother Jack, I wish you wouldn't say stuff like that to me. I'm trying to have a conversation, that's all. You're not even asking questions—like *What do you mean by that, Marco?* The way you would do to someone you respected. I'm not a goofball twenty-four-seven, dude. I wouldn't treat you like that."

I stopped short and took three deep breaths. I could feel Marco's confusion and desperation. He was bigger and stronger than any of us. He could climb rocks and battle beasts, and he'd literally given his life to save us. Marco had more bravery in his fingernail than the rest of us had combined. I never thought a kid like me could bully a Marco Ramsay. I was wrong.

"Sorry," I said, "you didn't deserve that."

"Sssh."

Marco was standing stock-still. Quietly he reached

around for his quiver. I saw a figure moving in the woods. A mass of brown-gray fur, a glint of tooth. A grunt echoed from behind the tree. "Don't move, Jack."

I nodded. I couldn't move even if I wanted to. My knees were locked.

Marco stepped away, closer to the beast. "Peekaboo, mushushu, I see you . . ."

A bloodshot eye, about knee-high, peered from behind the tree.

"*Careful!*" I whispered.

"Careful is my middle name," Marco said.

Without a sound, an impossibly long body leaped toward Marco. Its eyes glinted with a hundred dark segments, and its tongue lashed like a whip. With a high-pitched screech, it lowered its two short, powerful horns. Marco jumped, spinning in the air and bringing the bow down like a club.

He connected with the side of the beast's head. The mushushu roared in pain, sliding into a thorny bush and uprooting it from the soil. Struggling to his feet, the beast turned toward Marco. His back was covered in matted, dirt-choked fur, his belly in scales smeared with slime. Blood dripped from his horns from what must have been an earlier kill. His back leg was tensed, its talons dug into the dry soil. He fixed Marco with red eyes, his thin red tongue whipping in and out of his mouth.

Marco lifted an arrow to eye level. The bow creaked as he pulled back . . . back . . .

With a flick of his finger, Marco released the arrow. It shot through the air with a barely audible whoosh and caught the beast directly in the shoulder. He flung his head back in agony, stumbled to the earth. "Dang, I meant to get his heart," Marco said with disappointment, reaching back for another arrow. "These arrows must be bent. Hang on, Brother Jack. I'm trying again."

The beast's movements were quick and slippery. With a bloodthirsty scream, he leaped again. Marco jumped back, but the mushushu's razor-sharp horn sliced through the side of his leg.

"*Marco!*" I shouted.

I raced toward him, but he staggered away on all fours, scrambling behind a tree. "Stay away, Jack!" he called out. "I'm . . . okay. *Run for help!*"

His leg was gashed deep, spouting blood. The smell of it seemed to excite the mushushu, and he pawed the ground hungrily.

With one hand, Marco clamped down above the wound. He was trying to stanch the bleeding, but it wasn't working. Not by a long shot. I could actually see his face growing paler as the blood gushed out.

With a snarl, the beast lowered its horns and charged Marco head-on.

CHAPTER TWENTY

A TANGLE OF FANGS

MARCO'S ARROWS SPILLED to the ground. All I could see was a flurry of hair, a tangle of fangs, limbs, and an uprooted bush. I ran toward him, scooping an arrow out of the dirt.

The beast was enormous, his body completely obliterating Marco, a mass of ugly gray bristles and bloodstained scales. I drew the arrow back like a spear, aiming for the beast's neck.

I threw as hard as I could. The arrow flew out of my hand and embedded itself into a tree. *"Marco!"* I screamed, running toward him, ready to take on the beast with my bare hands.

Marco's face peered out from under the mass of fur. "Nice aim, Tarzan."

The mushushu lay stock-still. I edged closer. Three tiny, green-feathered darts protruded from the beast's back. "Are you—?"

"Alive?" Marco said, sliding out from underneath the giant body. "I think so. But not that comfy. Fortunately, it looks like Dead-Mouse-Breath lost interest and fell asleep."

Marco's calf was bleeding badly. I ripped a section of hem off my tunic and tied it around his leg to stanch the bleeding. As he sat against a tree, sweat poured down his forehead. "That's a bad cut," I said.

His eyes were flickering open and shut. "It's just . . . a flesh wound."

I looked around for the shooters, but the place seemed empty. "Hello?" I called out. "Anybody there? Aly? Cass? Daria?"

Marco needed care. Immediately. The makeshift tourniquet had stopped the heavy blood flow, but he'd lost a lot. And as brave as he was acting, he was fading in and out of consciousness. "Okay, Marco, I'm going to get you out of the woods," I said gently, hooking my arm around his shoulder and struggling to stand.

From deep in the woods I heard a voice. Then two.

"Hey!" I shouted. "Over here! Help!"

I propped Marco against a tree. He gestured downward, to his stash of spilled arrows. "Take the weapon. Just in case. We don't know who these voices belong to."

"But—" I protested.

"Just do it, Brother Jack!" Marco said.

Carefully I crouched down, reaching for the bow.

With a sharp *thwwwwip*, a dart threaded the space between my fingers and embedded itself in the dirt. As I jumped backward, a face peered out from behind a tree— a woman, her dark hair cropped short and a scar running from ear to ear, circling just below her mouth as though she had a permanent eerie smile. She crept forward, holding a blowpipe in one hand. Behind her was another woman, older, with a broken-looking nose, and a man with a long black beard. They were wearing tunics of the same rough material and design as the other Babylonian *wardum*.

"Look, I—I don't speak your language," I said, "but we have nothing to steal. My friend is hurt."

They looked at us warily. Marco craned his neck to see them and then groaned with the pain.

The woman knelt by him, looked at his leg, and shouted something to the others. As the man disappeared into the woods, she took Marco by the shoulders. Although she was an inch or so shorter than me, maybe just over five feet tall, she easily held his weight.

I lifted his legs. Together we carried him to a flat place, soft with fallen leaves. After we laid him down, she brushed sand and dirt away from the wound. "I don't think they're thieves," I said to Marco.

"They're not MDs, either . . ." Marco said with a grimace.

The man came back with two crude clay pots. One was full of a greenish-gray liquid that smelled something like rotten onions, skunk, and ammonia. The other pot contained hot water, which he poured over the wound. As Marco's leg instinctively kicked upward, the man held it down. Quickly his partner slathered the green-gray goo over three thin strips of bark, then placed them over the wound.

"Geeeeaahhh!" Marco cried out.

The man was sitting on Marco's leg now. Tiny tendrils of smoke rose from the wound. Marco's head lolled to the side, and he went unconscious.

From a distance I heard a sharp, piercing whistle. Three notes. The woman answered identically. A moment later I heard a thrashing through the wood. And a cry.

"Marco!"

I spun around at the sound of Daria's voice. She raced over to the other three. She seemed to know them, talking urgently in a flurry of words. A moment later she knelt by Marco, her eyes brimming with tears. "Is he . . . ?"

"Dead? No," I said. "These people saved him. Who are they?"

Daria took a moment to think. *"Wardum.* But . . . I do not know the word." She pointed to her head.

"Very smart," I guessed. "Um . . . scientists? Is that what you mean?"

"Scientists," Daria said. "Zinn, Shirath, Yassur."

Marco's eyes fluttered open. "Maybe . . . they can invent anesthesia for next time," he said through gritted teeth.

Daria leaned over and gave Marco a hug. "I hear the noise. I run here. Bel-Sharu-Usur not be happy with me. I cannot stay long."

She carefully reached toward his injured leg to lift one of the pieces of protective bark. Underneath, the mushushu's gash had become a raised red-brown welt.

I could barely keep my jaw from dropping open. "That's . . . unbelievable."

"You walk soon," Daria said. "Zinn is best . . . scientist."

"What the—?" Marco tested his leg, bending it. "Thanks, guys."

"Thank you so much!" I said. "But how did they find us, Daria? If they're *wardum*, why are they in the king's forest? Shouldn't they be in the palace?"

Daria looked nervously over her shoulder. "We are . . . how do you say? Push back. Defy the evil Nabu-na'id."

"So you guys are like rebels?" I said.

"King Nabu-na'id maked Marduk to be angry," Daria said. "King not go to Akitu—this is great insult! Marduk caused bad things happen to Bab-Ilum. Many years ago. This one . . ." She waved her fingers frantically in the air, as if they were swarming around her face.

"An attack happened?" I said. "Bats? Birds? Insects? A plague of locusts? Bzzzzz?"

141

"Yes," Daria said. "Also big water. From Tigris."

"Flooding," I said.

"Persians wanted to make Bab-Ilum part of Persia," Daria said carefully. "Maked big army to defeat Nabu-na'id."

"Made," I corrected. "We have to teach you past tense."

"I don't blame the Persians," Marco said through gritted teeth. "I mean, no offense, but your king is kind of a toad."

"Our king is lucky man," Daria said. "Persians no longer. All the bad things gone—after Sippar. Sippar comes all around us." She smiled ruefully. "For King Nabu-na'id, *Sippar* is new god. Is Protector of Bab-Ilum."

"Convenient," Marco said. "Sippar nukes all your neighbors, and now Nabby doesn't have to bother defending his kingdom anymore, like a king is supposed to."

"But Nabu-na'id is afraid of forest, because of mushushu," Daria said. "So we . . . Zinn, Shirath, Yassur, and more . . . we hide here. We meet. Plan."

"But the mushushu's dead," I said. "So there goes your hiding place."

Daria looked nervously behind her. "Mushushu is not dead. Sleeping."

"Whaaat?" Marco said.

We all looked at the beast. Its back was rising and falling very slowly, the feathered darts riding with it. "Those must be tranquilizer darts," I said.

"Anybody got a baseball bat?" Marco asked.

"We leave mushushu here," Daria said. "We say prayer

at Esagila. Ask Marduk for forgiveness. For hurting sacred mushushu. Marduk will listen."

"Wait," Marco said. "Remember what Ol' Follow-the-Bouncing-Pupils promised? We could see the flower show if we nuked Mooshy!"

Daria looked at me curiously. "This is English?"

"Translation: Bel-Sharu-Usur said we could see the Hanging Gardens if we killed the mushushu," I said.

"We think of way to see gardens later." Daria looked again over her shoulder. Quickly she added, "Zinn says you are very brave, Marco. Very strong. And you, too, Jack."

"I didn't really do anything," I said.

"You dragged me to safety," Marco said. "Jack is the definition of awesomesauce."

Daria nodded. "Bel-Sharu-Usur thinks you have magic. The king will want you. For soldiers."

"No," I said. "Absolutely not."

"Good," Daria said. "Because Zinn and her people work for good things. Will use magic for the best future. For fairness in Bab-Ilum . . ."

She was looking at us closely. So were the other three rebels.

"Daria," I said, "are you asking if we'll join you? We can't. We have to return —"

"We'll consider it!" Marco blurted. "Show us the Hanging Gardens, and we'll think about it."

* * *

A rebel. Somehow that label only made Daria seem even more awesome. As if that were possible.

Singer. Freedom fighter. Spy in the king's court. Language genius. She was brilliant wrapped in amazing.

Marco was leaning on her, limping. His white lie—saying we would think of becoming rebels—had made Daria optimistic. It was unfair. You know what else? He was pretending to be more injured than he was, just so he could have his arm around her.

I knew she was nervous about seeing Bel-Sharu-Usur. I was also starting to worry about Cass and Aly. So we went as fast as we could. Daria sang to keep our spirits up, and the birds joined in. The sun seemed to brighten, too, and my spirits lifted. After the song she insisted on learning more English, so over the following few minutes here's a list of what Marco and I taught her:

1. Past tense.
2. The difference between *tree* and *three*. Also *two* and *too*.
3. The basic rules of basketball, demonstrated by Marco with a large rock and an imaginary basket.
4. Two hundred twenty-nine vocabulary words, including *war, layup, peace, peace out, footsteps, body odor, pathway, Cheetos, dilemma, awesomesauce, condition,* and *toilet.*

I will let you guess which of those were Marco's and which were mine.

144

Soon Marco was acting out the rules of basketball, bouncing around, making fake jump shots. "Marco is *recovering*," I said. "He is making a *recovery*. This is another way of saying he is getting better."

Daria quickly repeated those words, but her eyes were riveted on Marco. "Marco, please, I do not understand this three-point play?"

Some guys have all the luck.

"He breaks downcourt . . ." Marco darted among the trees as if they were defenders, pretending to dribble a large rock. "The girls in the stands are crying out, 'Awesomesauce!' He stops at the semicircle exactly twenty-five feet from the basket, and he—"

He froze with his hands in mid–jump shot. "Whoa," he said softly, his eyes fixed on something distant. "Time out."

We ran toward him. As we pulled up alongside, I squinted due to the brightness across the river. The air had changed, from the stink of burned wood and putrid flesh to a blast of cool, sweet air. The aroma was so intoxicating I felt light-headed.

Through slitted eyes I beheld something that took my breath away.

"Is that—?" I stammered.

Daria grinned. "Awesomesauce."

CHAPTER TWENTY-ONE

HEROES

BREATHE, MCKINLEY.

The Hanging Gardens rose on the other side of the Euphrates. They were more like an explosion of greenery than a stately ziggurat. If color were sound, the flowers would be screaming at the sun. They thrust through every columned window, draped the shoulders of every statue, obliterating the fine carvings on the walls. Their vines waved in the breeze like the hands of ballet dancers, and water rushed through marble gullies like distant applause.

"You say—said—Hanging Gardens, yes? We say Mother's Mountain," Daria said. "After Amytis, wife of King Nabu-Kudurri-Usur the Second. Like mother to all *wardum*, so kind and gentle. But always sad. She comed—*came*—from the land of Medea, where are great mountains, big gardens. Nabu-Kudurri-Usur built first Mother's Mountain for her, in Nineveh. To make her happy when she visit."

"Wait," I said. "The *first* Mother's Mountain?"

Daria nodded. "This is second. Built many years later. But Nabu-na'id has closed it. The people may not go there now."

I walked closer, eyeing the surroundings. Beyond the Hanging Gardens, a huge park extended as far as I could see, surrounded by a brick wall. Outside the wall were dry, rubbly roads and small houses, but inside was lush with flowering trees and greenery. "Daria, we need to go there," I said. "As soon as we all can."

"Why?" Daria asked.

"We know about something inside," I replied. "Something important. It—it has something to do with Sippar. With the reason Sippar exists."

Daria's eyes grew distant. "So this is why Nabu-na'id guards Mother's Mountain?"

"I don't know," I said. "But we need to find out."

"What will happen if you take this . . . thing you need?" Daria asked hopefully. "Will Sippar go away?"

Marco eyed me. "Yes!" he said quickly.

Another lie. "Honestly, Daria," I said, "we don't know for sure—"

"Marco! Jack!"

I spun at the sound of Aly's voice. She and Cass were racing toward us through the woods. As Marco waved to them, Daria's friends stiffened. They reached for their blowpipes instinctively, but Daria gave them a reassuring smile.

Cass and Aly practically fell over each other to hug us. Both were drenched in sweat from the run. "We thought you died!" Aly shouted.

"That noise!" Cass said.

Daria looked back the way they came. "Bel-Sharu-Usur? The guards? Where are they?"

But Cass and Aly had spotted the Hanging Gardens. Their jaws were nearly scraping the ground. "That. Is. Utterly. Amazing," Aly said.

"A lot of people say that when they hug me," Marco replied. "Hey, ever seen a mushushu bite?"

Aly turned, eyeing Daria's three friends for the first time. "No, but maybe you can introduce us?"

"I am sorry," Daria said. "These are Zinn, Shirath, and Yassur. *Wardum*, like me. We are rabbles."

"Rebels," I clarified. "Against the king. Loyal to the legacy of Nebuchadnezzar the Second."

A shout rang through the woods, not far behind us. Instantly Daria's friends scattered and disappeared into the underbrush, as if they'd never been there.

"The guards," Aly said. "They're not too happy."

Daria took a deep breath. "You are with us now," she said, linking arms with Marco and me. "We face the guards together."

* * *

Bel-Sharu-Usur knelt by the body of the mushushu.

I don't know what the rebels had done to its metabolism. Daria insisted to us, in English, that it was alive. That the rebels had given it some potion to slow its metabolism. Its chest was now still. It looked deader than dead.

The king's son stood. He swatted away the two *wardum* who were fanning him furiously. Muttering something to Daria, he turned toward his guards.

"He says you are heroes," Daria said. "He thinks you will be of great use to the kingdom."

"True on the first, epic fail on the second," Marco said.

Cass was fidgeting with his tunic. A pair of leathery eyes peered out of one of his pockets, along with a Snickers wrapper and a pack of chewing gum. "Sssssh, it's okay," Cass whispered. "Leonard is spooked by the smell of the mushushu."

"Maybe he thinks it's a relative," Aly said.

"I thought you got rid of that candy and gum!" I said.

"I kept a little . . ." Cass said sheepishly.

As Bel-Sharu-Usur turned, Cass quickly pushed Leonard back into his pocket. I had no idea if the king's son saw the lizard, or if he cared. He nodded toward Marco with a gesture that seemed vaguely admiring, and then he shouted a command to his guards.

Daria's face fell. She began pleading to Bel-Sharu-Usur, gesturing with urgency about something.

Two guards unsheathed their swords. Before we could react, they plunged them into the flank of the mushushu.

I stood helplessly, in shock. The creature oozed blood, its eyes flickering before shutting permanently. Daria raised a hand to her open mouth. Her eyes were wide with horror.

Cass let out a groan. Marco, Aly, and I averted our eyes. "Oh, man . . . why did they do that?"

"I guess . . ." I whispered, trying not to lose the morning's breakfast, " . . . they had to be sure."

Daria was muttering something rhythmic, maybe a prayer. I thought about putting my arm around her, but she turned away. "I—I'm sorry," I said.

Through a mist of tears, Daria's eyes were angry and resolute. "You will go to Mother's Mountain, Jack," she whispered. "I have left you the way to do it."

"You have?" I said.

"Remember . . ." she replied, leaning close to me, " . . . when I came to see you . . ."

I saw the whoosh of metal. Daria let out a cry and fell to the ground. One of Bel-Sharu-Usur's guards stood over her impassively.

"Hey!" Marco shouted, lunging for the goon.

The man pointed his sword to Marco, stopping him cold. Cass, Aly, and I all knelt by Daria. She wasn't bleeding. I quickly realized he must have smacked her with the hilt.

Bel-Sharu-Usur stood over us, yammering.

"Okay, Bobblehead, I've had enough of this," Marco said, turning toward him with fists clenched.

"No, Marco, you must not be so angry all the time!" Daria shouted, her face turned to the ground. "I was punished because *wardum* are not allowed to look upon the faces of the *awilum*—the nobles—without permission. Bel-Sharu-Usur believes you will become nobles. He knows he must convince Nabu-na'id first. But he believes the king will agree."

"I don't care what he thinks," Marco said.

The guard was raising his sword again. Aly grabbed Marco's arm and pulled him away. "Daria cares," she said. "We go wherever he wants to take us. Silently. And we do not talk to Daria."

CHAPTER TWENTY-TWO

IF ONLY . . .

THE GUEST HOUSE was restocked with juices and food, but I wasn't hungry or thirsty. As we moved along the rooftop, the moat crocodiles followed us with their eyes. But I didn't care about them. All I could think about was Daria.

The swoosh of metal. The agony on her face.

Why didn't you do something?

If I'd had Marco's speed, I could have swatted the sword aside. If I'd had Aly's brains I might have figured out in advance that the guard would do that. I could have taken preventative measures.

"Earth to Jack," Aly said. "Your girlfriend is going to be all right. We need you. Escape plans are in order."

"She's not my girlfriend," I said.

"That's encouraging," Aly said under her breath.

"What's that supposed to mean?" I snapped.

"What do you mean, what's that supposed to mean?" Aly looked at me curiously, then sighed. "Never mind, Jack. You are such a boy."

"Will you two knock it off?" Cass said, pacing back and forth along the rooftop. "Think. What do we do now? Wait here under lock and key until Prince Sadist reports to his dad and brings us our guard uniforms?"

Marco drummed his fingers on the edge of the roof's half-wall. "Actually it might not be so bad. As guards, we'll have access to the Hanging Gardens."

"Be real, Marco!" Aly said. "The king will be keeping us close. He'll probably want to train us. He'll want us to prove we can do magic. To earn his trust. By the time we're let off on our own, it'll be the twenty-second century back home!"

"Right," Marco said. "Right. We have to do this fast. I could try to disable the guards downstairs—"

"And if they stab you to death?" Aly said. "Maybe we can think of something else."

"We could drop three pots on their heads," Cass suggested.

"That's the best you can do?" Aly said. "Jack, what do you think?"

But my mind was still on Daria. "'You will go to

153

Mother's Mountain,' Daria said. She told me she left us the way to do it."

Cass, Marco, and Aly all turned in surprise. "Really?" Cass said. "What was it, a key? A secret password?"

"I don't know!" I said. "I don't see anything left behind."

"Big help!" Aly threw up her arms.

"I can focus if I eat," Marco said, bolting toward the stairs. "I always think better on a full stomach."

As Cass scampered after him, Aly's shoulders slumped. We were alone now, and the room's temperature seemed to drop a couple of degrees. "Sorry I snapped at you, Jack," she said.

"We're all tense," I replied.

"I said some things I didn't mean," she said.

I smiled. "I heard some things I didn't understand."

"Yeah. Well." She opened her mouth to continue but seemed to have second thoughts. With a tiny smile, she gestured toward the stairs. "Last one to the fruit bowl is a rotten egg."

* * *

Marco slurped green juice. Cass took tiny bites out of a dried date. Aly played with a bowl of yogurt but didn't seem too interested. I had a plate full of fresh figs but had only managed to finish half of one. Marco kept swiping the rest, one by one, which was fine with me.

The pottery on the wall was decorated with images of

hunters and animals. On one of the vases, a stylized mu-shushu seemed to be growling at me.

I reached over to the vase and turned it around so the mushushu faced the other way. Now a less-accusing bull faced outward. It looked vaguely familiar.

I have left you the way to do it. Remember . . . when I came to see you . . .

I jumped up.

The vase. I had used it the night before. To tuck something out of sight.

"Jack?" Aly said curiously.

I reached into the mouth of the vase and pulled out the leather pouch I'd put there. Daria's pouch. Gently I pulled it open and looked inside.

Three green feathers peeked up at me.

"These aren't knitting needles . . ." I said.

Cass, Aly, and Marco all looked at me as if I'd just grown fins. I held out the pouch so they could see inside.

"She knew," I said. "Somehow she figured we might need some emergency help."

My three best friends began to smile. "May I?" Aly asked.

I handed her the pouch, and she carefully spilled out six tranquilizer darts onto the table.

155

CHAPTER TWENTY-THREE

TO THE GARDEN

WE CROUCHED AT the opening of the *wardum* hut. The sun was just sinking beyond the Ká-Dingir-rá, and I could hear soft, sweet singing inside. "Daria!" I hissed.

The song stopped. Daria peeked out of the hanging cloth, her eyes wide. "Jack! What are you doing here?"

"I just wanted to say thank you," I said. "For the darts. The guards at our house are out for the count."

She nodded. Her eyes radiated fear even in the darkness. "I see. So now you will go to Mother's Mountain. I am glad you came here first. I will go with you—"

"No way!" I replied. "You'll get into trouble. Just tell us the route."

"I will show you," Daria said.

"It's okay, we can do it," Cass chimed in. "I mean, you just leave the Ishtar Gate, circle around the temple, and walk to the edge of the first barley field, right? And then after about fifty-three yards you make a left after the last furrow, where there is this hut and some wood pilings. So if the hut contains some water vehicle, we take it across the river, after which we get out and walk, I don't know, approximately an eighth of a mile to the outer gate of the gardens."

We all stared at him, dumbfounded. "What angle do we go across the water?" Marco asked.

"Maybe sixty-three degrees, give or take," Cass said, "depending on the current? Sorry I can't be more exact. I should be. I saw all of this on our way back from the king's forest. But some of it is pretty fuzzy."

"Dude," Marco said, "what would you be like with a little confidence?"

"Huh?" Cass said.

Aly wrapped him in a hug. "You have not lost one bit of your powers, Cass. You just have to believe in them as much as we do."

Daria had backed away from us and returned with a sack around her shoulder and an armful of shawls. "Wear this clothing. Cover your heads. The king must not know you have gone. I will go with you to the Ishtar Gate. Pul, the child of Nitacris, is very sick. I must help her. We all help each other. My friends, Nico and Frada, will stay with the baby for now, but they have been with Nitacris all day. I will talk to the guards. They know that Pul is ill, and they are kind to *wardum*. I will tell them we are going to the temple of Marduk to pray for help."

"What if they ask us questions?" Aly asked.

"I will talk for you," Daria said. "Bab-Ilum is full of people from many places. It is not unusual for *wardum* to speak languages the guards do not know. I will say that I must return by myself, to sing Pul to sleep. But you will remain for proper prayers. They will understand this. But we will not stop at the temple. Together we will go to the river. You will continue. I will return."

We left right away, walking quickly from the *wardum* compound and across Ká-Dingir-rá to the Ishtar Gate. There, a group of guards were playing a game that involved rolling stones against the base of the blue brick wall. They barely looked up when Daria talked to them.

We scurried through the Gate's long, dark hallway, emerging in front of the temple. Cass and Daria led us to a path that veered around the building. We walked across a broad stretch of farmland, and before long I heard the racing waters of the Euphrates. Daria led us to a hut, where the boats had been stored. Within minutes we were carrying a flat-bottomed boat, and a wooden paddle, to the river.

As we set it in the water, Daria's hand shook. Her face was

taut with concern. "There will be guards at the entrance," she said. "The garden is very big. Mother's Mountain is at the center. Nabu-na'id built a wall around it. He made an inner and outer garden, like the inner and outer city of Bab-Ilum—so now only the king can enter Mother's Mountain. This inner garden is guarded by monsters, who came to Babylon from a foreign land. They are controlled by the garden keeper, Kranag."

"Do you know this guy?" I asked. "Can you get him to let us in?"

Daria's face darkened. "No one knows Kranag. Some say he is an evil god fallen to earth. He came to Bab-Ilum many years ago, around the time of Sippar, with a dark man who had a strange marking on his head. They brought many fierce animals. Great red bird-lions. Small beasts with white swords for teeth. Black birds with skin like bronze. Vizzeet, who kill with their spit."

"Massarym," Aly whispered. "With creatures from Atlantis. That must be when he brought the Loculus here."

"Kranag does not see," Daria said, "yet he is master of the animals. He can talk to the creatures, control them. People say he can become an animal himself. When Nabu-na'id built the wall around Mother's Mountain, he enslaved Kranag there. With a job to protect and defend Mother's Mountain."

"And all those animals—they're in there now?" I said.

159

Daria looked off into the distance. "Perhaps. You must be careful."

Aly shook her head. "*Now* you tell us about this stuff?"

"It's a game changer," Cass squeaked. "Maybe we shouldn't rush into it."

"Hey, it'll be fun!" Marco declared.

"How do you define *fun*?" Aly said.

Daria reached out. She rested one hand on Marco's arm, the other on mine. "I understand if you want to go back."

I looked up toward the Hanging Gardens and took a deep breath. I thought about the griffin and the Loculus. The marauding monks. Back then, if we'd been warned about the dangers in advance, we would have chickened out. But we were forced to go, and we did.

Sometimes you just had to do it.

"We're rebels, like you, Daria," I replied. "We've survived worse than this."

She smiled. From a sack outside her tunic, she drew out a long torch, a small bronze urn with a cork cap, a piece of flint, and a crude metal knife. Last, she gave Marco a blowpipe and set of darts. "The moon is full tonight. Let it guide you. I believe animals are in there, but I do not know how many animals. I hope they are sleeping. I hope you will find what you need quickly. Most of all, I hope you do not see Kranag. If you do, retreat. He has no mercy, no feeling."

"Thanks, Dars," Marco said. He gave her a hug, and

she held tight. When she let go, I moved closer to hug her, too. But she turned and walked away, back toward Ká-Dingir-rá.

One by one, we climbed into the boat. Marco and I dug paddles into the water. On the other side of the river, a light moved along the wall of the Hanging Gardens—a torch held by a guard who had not yet seen us.

We moved slowly, silently. By moonlight I could only make out the outlines of my friends, inches away from me. Cass was holding his pet lizard, comforting it. I looked back toward the shore. Daria had blended in with the night's blackness.

But I could hear her singing.

CHAPTER TWENTY-FOUR

THE TORCH
AND THE VIZZEET

"THEY'RE GONE," CASS whispered.

Stomach down on the river bank, I watched a yellow torchlight wink into blackness. We'd been there for what seemed like an hour, observing two lights, two guards standing still in a long conversation. Now they were moving in opposite directions, checking around the perimeter of the gardens.

"Move," Marco said.

We raced up the embankment and onto the road. In the gravel, our footsteps were impossible to keep silent.

Once through the gate, the ground was covered with cedar chips, trampled to a soft firmness by foot traffic. We followed the arc of a pathway in the moonlight, which led to a thick flowering bush. As we dived behind it, we peered back toward the gate opening. My heart was beating so hard, I was afraid it could be heard clear to the Ishtar Gate.

After a few minutes, a torch passed slowly from left to right and then disappeared.

We moved farther inward. The path drew us to the inner wall, which loomed above us, smooth and impossibly high. To the left was an imposing gate, but this one was a thick wooden door, shut tight.

Another torchlight passed in front of us and stopped. A low, guttural voice barked something in our direction. I thought about running but stayed still.

Behind the guard, from over the wall, came an eerie hooting. *Zoo-kulululu! Cack! Cack! Cack!*

I nearly jumped back. The sound was cold and mocking. The guard muttered something under his breath.

The torchlight moved on.

We rushed to the base of the wall. The only way to do this would be up and over. *Do not think of that sound*, I told myself.

Wordlessly, Marco hooked his hands together to give us a lift upward. Aly climbed first, then Cass. "How are you going to do this yourself?" I whispered as I stepped up. "You were injured."

"Watch me," Marco said.

He boosted me upward. I grabbed the top of the wall and lifted my legs over. The others had jumped down to the inner garden, but I stayed at the top. I didn't want to leave Marco alone.

At first I didn't see him. But he appeared in the moonlight about twenty yards away as a flash of gray. He was rushing the wall like a sprinter, leaping, planting his sole against the wall and using the momentum to jump. His outstretched palm loomed upward toward me, and I grabbed it.

"Piece of cake!" Marco whispered, scrambling to the top. We both leaped to the ground, landing near Cass and Aly. "Now what?" Cass said.

It was a good question. All we could see were the silhouettes of trees, the curve of walkways. The air was sweet and cool, and Aly stopped to pick something off the ground. "A pomegranate," she said. "Big one."

Zoo-kululu! Cack! Cack! Cack! Something enormous swooped down with an oddly metallic clacking of wings. Aly dropped the fruit, and a black bird-shape with bright eyes scooped it up with talons and flew off.

"Sorry, I promise I will not touch your fruit ever again," Aly said.

But my eyes were on a towering structure not far from us. Its upper corner blotted out a section of the moon. "There it is," I said.

Marco was practically shaking with excitement. "Follow me, campers. Let's hope the crow is the worst they throw at us."

He began walking. The Hanging Gardens blotted out the moonlit sky. I could make out long trellises and hear the lapping of water into pools like soft laughter. Along the side of the building was a winding spiral that rose toward the top of the building from a deep pool that was fed by a culvert. It looked like a water slide. "What's that thing?" Marco whispered.

"An Archimedes screw," Aly said. "It was in our lessons from Professor Bhegad. When someone turns it, the motion lifts water out of the well and brings it to the top. That's how the plants are watered."

As we moved closer, I heard rustling. There was movement in the lower levels of the Hanging Gardens. And not just the waving of vines. Shadows were slipping among the trellises.

"Sssh." Marco took out the torch and soaked it with the oil from inside Daria's container. He propped it against a rock and pulled the piece of flint from his pack and struck it against the steel knife. With the first spark, the torch burst into flame.

"Thank you, Daria," Marco murmured, holding the torch aloft. "'Be prepared.' Motto of the US Marines."

"The Boy Scouts," Aly corrected him.

A chorus of screeches rang out from the Hanging Gardens. I heard a sharp hissing sound. Something small and liquid arced high in the air coming swiftly toward us.

Cass recoiled backward. "Yeeeow!"

A swirl of black mist twined upward from a blotch on his forearm. "What was that?" Marco asked.

"I don't know, but it hurts it hurts it hurts it hurts!" Cass said, shaking his arm in pain.

Another tiny liquid missile sailed through the air, heading for Aly. Marco instinctively shoved the torch upward, like a baseball player reaching for a pitch. As the little glob made contact with the flame, it exploded high into the air. "What the—?" Marco murmured.

From all around us, the high-pitched chittering screams came closer. Marco moved the torch quickly left to right. The walls of the Hanging Gardens were black with swiftly moving shadows, long-limbed and monkeylike. As they fell to the ground, they pounded their narrow leathery chests, grinning at us with hairless, long-snouted faces. Their teeth were long and sharp, their tongues bright red. They shot yellow globs of saliva as they approached.

"Watch it!" Marco yelled. We jumped away, and the wet missiles landed in small clouds of smoke. I spun and saw Cass was on the ground, writhing in pain.

Marco charged the creatures with the torch. They screeched, backing away, spitting. The flame erupted again and again, like fireworks. Marco dodged the spit like a dancer, warding them away. Aly was on her knees, hunched over Cass. "Is he all right?" I asked.

"A severe burn," Aly said. "He's in pain."

Vizzeet, who kill with their spit, Daria had said.

166

Marco let out a cry. Smoke rose from the left side of his face near his chin. He staggered, narrowly missing another liquid projectile. I grabbed the torch and charged toward them. They seemed wary of fire, backing away. A spit missile whizzed by my face, and the tips of hair on the side of my face went up in flames.

I dropped the torch and fell. Marco was at my side in a split second, pressing a fistful of sandy dirt into the side of my head, blotting out the fire. He dragged me into the shelter of an archway that led into the center of the building that supported the Hanging Gardens.

"Did I get it in time?" Marco asked.

I nodded, gingerly touching the side of my head. "Thanks. I'm fine."

The ground was cool here. We stayed close to the wall, which made a kind of corridor leading into the structure, about ten feet long. Beyond us was solid blackness. Outside, about fifteen feet from the entrance, the torch lay on the ground, its flames protecting us from the vizzeet. Aly was near us, pouring water from an urn onto Cass's wound.

I eyed the strips of healing medicine, still stuck to Marco's calves. "Hold steady," I said, pulling one of them off. His wound was nearly healed, and I prayed that there was still some of the magic black goo left.

Dropping to my knees, I laid the strip on Cass's forearm, directly over the wound. "Don't take this off!" I replied. "This will make you feel better."

Marco was staring out from the archway. "We have to get out of here," he said. "They hate the flame, but the torch won't last forever."

I peered out, too, looking to our right, where the vizzeet paced and fought, spat and argued.

My head was throbbing. It had nothing to do with the burned hair. In the midst of the shrieking, an eerie but familiar sound was washing over me. I was hearing the strange song again. The one that I'd first heard near the Heptakiklos in Mount Onyx. Near the first Loculus in Rhodes.

It was coming from the left. In the light of Marco's flame I could see the outline of a door, farther down the wall of the Hanging Gardens. Its wood was warped and carpeted with moss. Most of the surface was covered with a great tangled mass of ivy. It looked as if it had not been opened in years.

"Do you hear that?" I asked.

"Hear what?" Marco said.

"The Song," I said. "Coming from our left. I need to go to that door. I think the Loculus is inside."

Marco nodded. "I'll cover you."

With a sudden scream, Marco burst from the entrance. He grabbed the torch from the ground and used it like a fencing sword, swiping it back and forth as he charged toward the vizzeet.

I crept up to the door. Under the ivy was an intricate carving. It was hard to catch the detail. Marco was moving the torch erratically. But as I got closer, I felt my heart pounding. The carved symbols on the door told me we had found what we were looking for.

CHAPTER TWENTY-FIVE

LAMBDA

I RAN BACK to Cass and Aly, dropping to my knees. "Cass, if you can move, we need to get to that door. I think it's where the Loculus is hidden."

They both leaped to their feet. Cass touched the bandage on his arm. "I feel . . . good," he said. "What did you do to me?"

"Rebel painkiller," I replied. "Keep it there. And remember to thank Zinn."

"Yeaaaah!" Marco screamed.

We turned. He was staggering backward. One of the vizzeet had got him in the face. His knees buckled, and a couple of arrows fell from his quiver.

I raced up behind him and grabbed his bow and the

vial of oil, which hung from his belt. Scooping one of the arrows off the ground, I poured oil over the tip, thrust it into the flame, and inserted it in the bow.

I pointed it at one of the vizzeet. With a screech, it spat at me, just missing my eye. The glob of goo landed on the ground behind me with a loud *tsssss*.

I drew the arrow back and released it. The flame arced through the blackness like a comet, directly toward the slavering beast.

I missed. The arrow embedded itself in a tangled thicket of vines that hung from above. Flames shot upward, licking at the feet of the retreating creatures.

The vizzeet were shrieking now, clawing one another to climb higher . . . away from the fire.

Marco stumbled toward me, holding the torch with one hand and his face with the other. "Once on the chin and once above my right eye," he said.

"Hold still." I pulled the other healing strip from his calf, ripped it in half, and pressed each section to a wound. "Can you see?"

"By the dawn's early light," Marco replied.

A sudden *whoosh* made us all turn. An enormous bush, on the second level of the Hanging Gardens, had burst into flames. "This whole thing's about to go up!" Cass cried out. "We have to get out of here."

I was about to destroy one of the Seven Wonders of the

World. And if this thing went up in flames, the entire royal gardens wouldn't be far behind. Our chance to find the Loculus would be lost.

Water.

We needed lots of it. And fast. I took Marco's torch and held it high, lighting the second level of the Hanging Gardens. A grand stone stairway to our right, now overgrown with weeds, led directly upward. "Marco, follow me," I said. "Cass and Aly, get yourselves to the bottom of the Archimedes screw. Find whatever makes it turn, and do it hard. Now!"

Marco and I raced to the stairs and took them two at a time. Already I could hear a deep, metallic cranking sound. Just to the other side of the banister, the Archimedes screw was slowly starting to turn.

I held the torch over the banister and saw Cass and Aly working a huge bronze crank below. Water began flowing upward. Just above our head, on the Hanging Garden's second level, it spilled into a tilted basin that fed a clay gutter that ran through the flowers. "Take a gutter, Marco!" I said to Marco. He looked at me blankly. "Can you shake that gutter loose?"

He put two hands around one of the curved waterways and pulled. At the third pull, the thing came loose in a shower of clay dust.

Around us the flames were catching on to the ivy and

some nearby bushes. "We need to break the screw!" I shouted.

Marco nodded. "Hold this," he said, handing me the gutter.

The thing weighed about a hundred pounds. I nearly dropped it to the ground but balanced it on the stone railing. Marco was kicking the side of a trellis, knocking loose a decorative carved-bronze border from one for the supports. As the mangled hunk of metal fell to the ground, I shouted, "Give it to me—and hold this thing!"

I grabbed the bronze shard and began hitting the screw. Its sides were curved upward, cupping the water on two sides, keeping it in place as it rose. I battered the outer side until the water was spilling out. "Faster, guys!" I shouted down. "Turn it faster!"

The water began spattering outward. I took one end of the gutter and tipped it so that the high end would collect the flowing water and deliver it on the other end to the burning bushes. Marco slid in to help. We moved the gutter back and forth like a fire hose. "This is crazy!" Marco said. "We'll never get enough water!"

"Cass and Aly—turn harder!" I called down.

"Hold tight, Jack," Marco said, letting go of the gutter. "I'll be right back."

I held on as Marco ran downstairs and commandeered the crank.

The screw began gushing now, dousing the bush. The fire was already spreading downward, snaking along the ivy toward the ground. I lifted the gutter up and down, sending a shower far down the railing. Cass and Aly were behind me in a moment, with two wooden buckets they'd found among some garden tools.

They held the buckets under the gutter, collecting water. Racing down the railing, they chased the growing flames, pouring bucket after bucket until the fire was out.

It took a long time. Too long. I couldn't imagine why no one had caught us. Drenched in sweat, Cass came to my side, resting the bucket on the ground and wiping his forehead. He glanced at me in disbelief. "That was awesome, Jack."

"Dudes," Marco called from below. "The vizzeet are getting restless. Come on!"

As I raced down the stairs, I looked into the distance, toward the inner wall. *Where were the guards?* Even this far into the royal gardens, surely they'd seen the flames. "Hurry," I said, racing to the door. "We have to get in here!"

Marco was at my side. He held the torch to the door and smiled at the sight of the carving. "Mary had a little lambda. Amazing. Okay, hold this."

He gave me the torch, then leaned into the metal latch handle. It wouldn't budge. He pounded on the door. After waiting a moment, he drew back and lunged at it. His shoulder collided with a dull, pathetic-sounding thud, and he bounced back with a cry of pain.

From behind the ivy was a dull rattling sound, like knuckles rapping on wood.

I yanked aside the leaves.

CHAPTER TWENTY-SIX

THE NUMBER SEVEN

"LOOKS LIKE THE barrel of an old-time machine gun," Marco said.

"Or a Heptakiklos with a hat," Cass remarked.

"A spinning roulette wheel," Aly said.

My mind was racing. "It could be a code. Think. When we entered the maze at Mount Onyx . . . when we were stuck at the locked door in the underground cavern . . . both times we were able to get in."

"Because of hints," Aly said. "Poems."

"The poems were all about numbers," Cass pointed out. "Mostly about the number seven."

Aly grabbed one of the cubes hanging by twine. "There are seven of these things. They look like doorbells."

She began pulling them, but nothing happened.

"This is a carving, not a poem," Marco said.

"Yeah, but it's the Heptakiklos, Marco," I said. "The Circle of Seven. Seven cubes. Whoever did this knows about the Loculi! It's got to be in there. I hear the Song."

I stepped back. It was impossible to think. My brain was clogged with the sound. My ears were pricked for the screeching of the vizzeet, the guards. Where were the guards?

Numbers . . . the patterns of decimals . . .

"Aly, do you remember that weird thing about fractions and decimals?" I said.

She nodded. "Put any number over seven—one-seventh, two-sevenths, five-sevenths, whatever. Turn that into a decimal, and the numbers repeat. The exact same numbers. Over and over."

"I hate fractions," Marco said.

"Oot em," Cass added. (Which he pronounced *oot eem*—me too.)

I tried to remember the pattern. "Okay, one over seven. That's one divided by seven. We used that pattern to open a lock."

"Torchlight, please. Now." Cass knelt and began scratching in the sand:

"Dude, you remember how to do long division?" Marco said. "You never got a calculator?"

"Point one-four-two-eight-five-seven!" Cass said. "And if you keep going, you get the same numbers. They just keep repeating."

"Okay, I'll do them in order." Aly immediately yanked on the first cube, then kept going. "One . . . four . . . two . . . eight . . . five . . . seven!"

"Voilà!" Marco said, pulling the handle.

Nothing happened.

In the distance I could hear voices. They were faint but clearly angry. "We're not going to get out of this alive," Aly said.

I shook my head. "The guards should have been here already," I said. "I think they're afraid. With luck, that'll give us extra time."

From under a nearby rock, I saw a sudden movement and jumped back. A giant lizard poked its head out, and then came waddling toward us. Leonard, who had been sitting at the bottom of Cass's pocket, now jumped out into the soil. "Hey, get back here!" Cass shouted.

As he bent to scoop his pet off the ground, a shadow swooped down toward us.

Zoo-kulululu! Cack! Cack! Cack! Wings flapping, the giant black bird descended to the ground. It landed in the spot where Leonard had been, its talons digging into Cass's mathematical scratching. With a screech of frustration, it jumped on the Babylonian lizard, missed, and flew away with an echoing cry.

The voices outside the wall stopped. I could hear the guards' footsteps retreating.

"He ruined my equation," Cass said, looking at the talon prints in the sand.

Those, my boy, are not bird prints. They're numbers.

In my mind I saw Bhegad's impatient face, when he was trying to cram us with info. I looked at the top of the Heptakiklos again:

"That's not a hat," I said. "Those are cuneiform numbers. Bhegad tried to get us to study them. But I don't remember—"

"Ones!" Aly blurted out. "Those shapes are number ones."

"Okay, there are two of them," Marco said.

"Two over seven!" I exclaimed. "Two-sevenths!"

Cass quickly wiped away his division and started again:

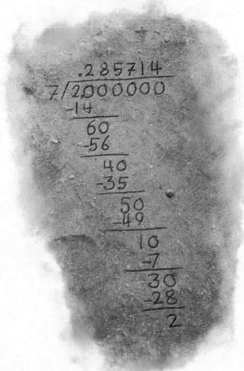

"The same digits," Cass said. "In a different order. Like I said."

Carefully I pulled the second cube. The eighth. The fifth. The seventh. The first. The fourth.

With a loud *clonk*, the handle swung down, and the door opened.

CHAPTER TWENTY-SEVEN

ECHOES OF NOTHING

"HELLO?" I CALLED out.

Marco swung his torch into the room. It was nearly the size of a gymnasium, and totally empty. Bare walls, stretching out on all sides. "Nothing," he said.

Aly leaned in. "All this for *a bare room*?"

I took the torch from Marco and held it to my right. *"Yo! Anyone in here?"*

Cass, Aly, and Marco followed close behind. The echo made our footfalls sound like an army. The Song of the Heptakiklos was pounding in my head now. "It's deafening now," I said. "That song. The thing has got to be near."

"Maybe the Loculus is underground," Aly said.

Marco stomped on the floor. The thumps echoed loudly. "It's hard packed. We'll need tools."

A loud *sssssshish* went from left to right. "Yeow!" Aly screamed. She fell to the ground, cupping her hand over her left ear.

"What happened?" I said.

"I think I've been shot!" she said.

We all dropped beside her. "By what?" Cass asked.

"Let Dr. Ramsay take a look." Marco pulled her hand away from her head. Her palm was covered with blood, but he used the edge of his tunic to wipe gently at her ear. "You're lucky. It just grazed you."

"*What* just grazed me?" Aly said. "Owww!"

I moved the torch to the left. Nothing and no one. I moved it to the right, in the direction the whooshing sound had gone. Floor and wall. I crouched, slowly standing up.

Ssshhhhhish! Ssshhhhhish! Ssshhhhhish!

I felt something whiz by my ear. My shoulder. My chin. "Get down!" Cass shouted.

His voice caromed around the room as I dropped back to the ground. *"What's going on?"* Aly shouted.

I looked at the wall for a hole, some indication of an inner room, where someone could take potshots through a crack in the surface.

But I saw nothing. Whatever was shooting at us was completely invisible.

"Stay low," I said. "The shots happen when we stand up."

"J-Jack, we need to get out of here," Cass said.

"Crawl," I said.

We dragged ourselves slowly toward the door, keeping close to the dusty floor. But the song was boxing my ears, telling me where to go.

In the back . . .

"Guys, we need to head to the rear wall," I said.

"Are you nuts?" Aly snapped. "With you and what armor?"

"Maybe we can do it if we keep low," I said, veering off in that direction.

"Got your back," Marco said.

I held the torch high. As Marco and I pulled ourselves like turtles across the floor, Cass and Aly looked on in silent dismay. The song grew louder. "We're almost there," I said to Marco.

"You mark the place," he said. "Then we'll get some picks and shovels."

My nose began to twitch. I sneezed. Then Marco did, too. My eyes stung and began to tear, and I stopped to wipe them with my sleeve.

That was when I heard a low, persistent hiss . . .

"I—I can't breathe!" Cass cried out. Behind him, Aly was coughing.

Marco collapsed to the floor, his hand over his mouth. "Gas . . ." he said.

I could see the tendrils of smoke now, but my eyes were

swelling. They rose upward, collecting at the ceiling. "Stay low!" I said.

I was losing consciousness. Coughing. I put my hand over my mouth, as close to the floor as I could go without biting it. I tried to suck in something that felt like oxygen.

Now.

With my last burst of strength, I reached out to Marco and yanked him back. Toward the doorway. Toward air.

With the strength remaining in his legs, Marco pushed hard against the floor. We tumbled over each other in a tangle of limbs, bowling into Cass and Aly. Both of them were choking, holding their necks.

I was still positioned farthest into the room. I pushed the other three toward the door. My vision was clouding, and I could feel myself losing consciousness. A breeze from outside wafted in and I gulped it down as best I could.

"Breathe . . ." I said. "Almost . . . there . . ."

An image flashed through my brain, something I'd seen on a flight with Dad to Boston: an airline flight attendant with an oxygen mask, smiling placidly, tying the mask around her mouth. *Secure your own mask first, before attending to children.*

I was losing it. Having ridiculous hallucinations. I ignored this one, preparing to push my friends again.

And then I stopped.

I knew what that image was about. I had to get the fresh

air first. Because I was the one who could. I was one who had some strength left, who had not breathed as much gas as the others. If I could revive myself, just a little, maybe I could save them.

I scrambled around the clutch of bodies, their three backs jerking up and down with racking coughs. Rising upward, I froze.

Stay down.

The bullets—or darts, or arrows, or whatever they were.

I dropped to a crouch. But nothing had been fired. Had the shooter gone away? Or run out of ammo?

Or was he lying in wait, trying to fake me out?

I crab-walked toward the door, gulping in air. Carefully I set the torch down, just outside the door. In that position, it would keep the vizzeet away and also provide light. I would need two hands for what I had to do. I could see Marco struggling to drag Cass and Aly toward the door. Good. He was reviving, too.

My body was cramped, my lungs tight. I breathed again. I had a little more strength, I could feel it. This would have to do.

I turned toward my friends, ready to pull them to safety. But the room began to shake. From above came a heavy metallic sound. The bare ceiling cracked in a couple of places. With a resounding *clang*, the entire floor bounced.

185

I fell backward. As I hit the floor I spun toward them again. I reached forward, focused on their rescue.

But my hand jammed against something hard. Metallic. Something I could feel but not see.

Gripping Cass's tunic in one hand and Aly's in the other, Marco lunged for the door. But his body seemed to freeze in midair and he cried out in agony, abruptly falling to the floor.

I reached forward, grabbed his arm, and pulled. I could only get a few inches before something stopped me. Dropping Marco, I felt around desperately, my hand traveling up and down what felt like metal bars—but looked like thin air.

I held one of the bars and shook. But it was useless.

Cass, Aly, and Marco were trapped in an invisible cage. And I was on the outside.

CHAPTER TWENTY-EIGHT

INVISIBLE BARS

"JACK . . ." ALY MOANED. She flopped onto the floor, her eyes fluttering.

"Get out get out get out!" I cried, shaking the invisible bars. They were stuck solid. Not budging.

Inches from me, Cass was trying to cradle Aly's head, but his hands were twitching. I couldn't keep my eyes from crossing. My lungs screamed at me. I turned and tried to gulp more fresh air. When I turned back, Leonard was crawling groggily out of Cass's tunic pocket. In the light from the torch outside the door, I could see the glint of a tiny silver shard caught in the lizard's claw.

A gum wrapper.

It gave me an idea.

I threaded my arm through the cage's bars and reached inside. Fumbling in the pocket of Cass's tunic, I extracted a pack of Wrigley's spearmint. It took all the concentration I could muster to unwrap one piece and begin to chew it. My mouth was dry, but I worked it, willing the saliva to come. I would need it.

I turned and took another breath of fresh air. Then, against all instincts, I forced myself to hold my breath and walk into the room.

Sshhhish.

This projectile grazed my tunic. I flinched, stepping aside. I was trembling, oxygen-starved.

Move.

I was also standing. But no one was firing at me.

I threw the gum wrapper to my right. Toward the direction I'd come.

Sshhhish.

The wrapper's presence in the air had drawn a shot. There was a zone—an area where the projectiles would be activated. Outside the zone you were safe.

But the gas was still hissing. Although I couldn't see it, I could hear it. As I stepped closer to the wall, to the sound, my eyes began to blur.

There.

I blinked. In a seam between stones, I could see a hole. A dime-sized blackness. I dropped to my knees, avoiding the direct path of the gas trail. And I reached into my mouth.

My fingers shook. I couldn't make my thumb and index finger meet. With my tongue, I thrust the chewed gum to the edge of my teeth.

It fell to the floor.

Steady.

I could see the lump. In fact, I could see two. Three.

My vision was doubling and tripling, and I blinked hard as I reached down. I tried to grab the wet wad but missed, poking it with my index finger.

As I lifted my arm, the gum rose, too, stuck to the pad of my finger.

I fell forward—eyes focused on the hole, finger extended with a feeble burst of energy.

And I went unconscious.

* * *

"Jack!"

Aly's voice stirred me from a dreamless sleep. "Whaaaa—?"

I felt as if my head had been split open with a cast-iron skillet. I sat up, rubbing my head.

"Get down, Jack—you'll be shot at!" Cass screamed.

I ducked. I caught my breath.

To my astonishment, I realized I *had* breath. The tiny, poisonous stream that was closing my windpipe was gone.

Glancing at the wall, I saw the tiny clump of gum, stuck

in the hole. And I no longer heard the hissing of gas.

"That was amazing, Jack," Aly said.

"Thanks," I replied, gathering my thoughts, "Okay, I'm thinking this room has some kind of sensor—some primitive form of electric eye, without the electricity. When we were in one area, it shot at us. In other, we tripped the gas. In each zone, a different trap. All, unfortunately, invisible."

"And we're in the cage district," Cass said.

Marco knelt and began shaking the invisible bars. "We have to lift this thing," he said. "On the count of three! One . . ."

Aly and Cass struggled to their feet. Cass was still coughing.

In the light of the torch, which was still resting on the ground outside the door, the back wall was a long wash of dull yellow. But off to the right, I saw a door opening. In a small rectangle of moonlight, I caught a quick glimpse of what seemed to be a wooden cottage just beyond the Hanging Gardens. But that was quickly blotted out by the silhouette of a cloaked man, filling the doorframe.

"Two . . ." Marco said.

A face peered out of the cloak's hood. From here I couldn't make out any features, just a pale white oval.

"M-M-Marco . . . ?" Cass said, staring at the apparition.

"Thrrrreeee!" Marco shouted. "That means lift!"

Snapping out of our fearful trance, we all crouched

down. The bars might not be visible, but they felt as solid as iron. I quickly dug my fingers along the bottom, to where the cagelike structure met the ground. Crouching, I pulled from my side, they from theirs.

The cage was massively heavy. We raised it maybe two inches.

The apparition moved closer. One eye penetrated the gloom like a flashlight beam—no pupil of any color, just a disk of dull greenish-white. Where his other eye should have been was instead a dark socket. His legs were the shape of parentheses, and his feet dragged across the ground as if he couldn't lift them. A cape hung loosely over his shoulders, which were thin as bamboo.

Aly, Cass, and I stared, stiff with fear.

"I think," Aly said, "this is Kranag."

CHAPTER TWENTY-NINE

KRANAG

"LIFT AGAIN!" MARCO shouted. *"Three!"*

This time we pulled at the same time. I could feel the cage rising . . . maybe six inches. Kranag was walking across the room strangely. And slowly. Zigzagging one way, then the other. He raised his hand, revealing a rusted sword. It took a moment for me to realize he was talking. His voice was like the fluttering of dry wings, all air with a few consonants.

"Keep it . . . up . . . !" Marco grunted.

Knee high . . .

"Go," Marco said. *"Go! Now!"*

Aly ducked first. She slid her body under the cage, not letting her hands leave the bottom. Cass followed. As Marco slid under, the cage dropped with a loud thump.

He grimaced, hopping on one foot. "Out! Out now!"

As we raced out the door and into the night, I heard a sharp clang. Instinctively I spun around. Kranag had struck the side of the invisible cage with his sword. I don't know if he thought someone was still in there or he was frustrated. He stood rigid now, moving his head toward us.

"What's with his eyes?" Marco asked.

"Daria told us he was blind," Aly said.

"He doesn't need to see," Cass said. "His other senses do it for him."

I grabbed the torch and held it high. The night air was surprisingly cool on my skin. The vizzeet had retreated to the second level of the Hanging Gardens, still shrieking and spitting. Their fear of fire kept them far enough away from us, but the torch wasn't going to last forever.

"Let's get out of here!" Aly shouted.

"I say we ambush this guy and snatch the Loculus!" Marco hissed.

I shushed them. Cass was right about Kranag. He was responding to our smallest sound. His hearing was super-sharp. As he moved toward us, he sheathed his sword with one hand. With one uncannily fast motion, his other hand disappeared into his tunic, pulled out a tiny dagger, and threw it.

The shaft spiraled toward my face.

"Down!" Marco shouted, pulling me from behind. I crashed to the ground, nearly letting go of the torch. Above us, the vizzeet cackled and jumped, slavering hungrily.

But I knew how noisy they could be.

Quickly I ran toward them, waving the flame, causing their screeches to become deafening. I gestured toward Cass, Aly, and Marco to move away from the open cavern.

Kranag pulled out another knife and paused. He moved in the direction of the footsteps and threw again. The blade passed harmlessly into the garden.

We huddled at the base of the Hanging Gardens, our ears clanging with the deathly cries of the vizzeet. Kranag stared in their direction and didn't move. The loud shrieks were blotting out all other sounds—including our voices and footfalls.

But he was not moving. He looked like he could stand there for ages.

We had to distract him, and fast.

I looked to the left, away from the open door. If we followed the wall, we could circle around the Hanging Gardens, pass by his little cottage out back, come out on the other side. Maybe we could attack from there, where he wasn't looking.

Right, McKinley. He'll hear you—or the vizzeet will follow you the whole way.

But at least it would confuse him momentarily. He might follow us. Maybe we could hide in that old weed-choked cottage and ambush him.

No. There was a better way. I turned to Cass, Aly, and

Marco and mouthed: *Come on.*

I booked it to the left. A gob of vizzeet spit hit my pinkie finger and I nearly dropped the torch. Holding back a cry of pain, I veered farther from the wall.

We made a right and raced down the long structure. I could see the protective wall, off to our left. From the other side, guards shouted. There were more voices than before. They must have gathered backup. They were too chicken—or too smart—to face the vizzeet without a big crowd.

Our next right put us at the opposite side of the Hanging Gardens from where we'd started. Kranag's hut was illuminated in the moonlight, a shabby rectangle of wood slats with a broken roof and a door that hung off rusted hinges.

"What are we doing, Jack?" Cass asked, speaking for the first time since we'd left Kranag's earshot.

I raced toward a dry, scraggly bush that seemed to be growing from the base of the hut's wall. The whole structure was neglected and overgrown. Dead vines twined up through the wall's slats, threatening to overwhelm the house. To turn it into a tiny mockery of the Hanging Gardens themselves.

As I touched the torch to the bush, it—and the wall—burst instantly into flames.

"I'm distracting him," I said.

CHAPTER THIRTY
TRAPS!

THE AROMA OF burning wood penetrated the night air. When we ran around the Hanging Gardens and reached the door to the cavernous room, Kranag was gone. A massive black shape flapped its wings nearby, from the base of the Archimedes screw. *Zoo-kulululu! Cack! Cack! Cack!*

"Careful!" Aly warned.

We watched in astonishment as the bird used its beak to turn the crank. Water began spilling from the broken mechanism into a wooden bucket. When it was full, the bird grabbed the bucket's handle and flew off in the direction of the cottage.

Marco shook his head, hard. "Am I hallucinating?"

People said he can become an animal himself . . . That was what Daria had said. "It's him," I said. "Kranag."

196

"That bird is Kranag?" Aly whispered.

I nodded. "He's trying to save his home."

"The flames will roast him," Cass said.

I felt the pang of guilt. Setting fires went against everything I had ever been taught. I reminded myself that Kranag had wanted to kill us.

Sometimes you had to make choices.

I watched Cass drop to his knees and start scribbling in the sand. "Okay, Kranag can do some amazing stuff. He knew where all the traps are in that room. To the inch! Did you see how he was walking? Wherever he went—no gas, no arrows, nothing."

"He probably set them up himself," Aly said. "Of course he knows where they are. He doesn't need to see them."

"The point is, *we* can't see them," I said. "We can't see anything."

"Let's go back a step," Aly said. "Daria says he's guarding the Hanging Gardens. But we know different. He's guarding the Loculus. Jack feels it. I can feel it, too—I felt it more the closer we got to the back of the chamber. Marco, you say it might be underground, but I don't believe that."

"Where do think it is?" I asked.

"In plain sight, but invisible," Aly said, a smile inching across her face. "Think about that. The first Loculus gave us the power of flight. I think this one has a whole other power."

Her words hung in the air. I could feel their meaning

seep into our brains. I saw a projectile of vizzeet spit hurtle by and hit the far wall and I almost didn't care.

If what Aly was saying was true, this Loculus could help us unbelievably. "So if we find it and make contact with it," I said, "it may give us its power. . . ."

Aly nodded. "In the words of the Immortal One, bingo."

"Aly, you are the bomb." Cass dropped to his knees and started drawing in the dirt. "Okay, this is how the room is laid out."

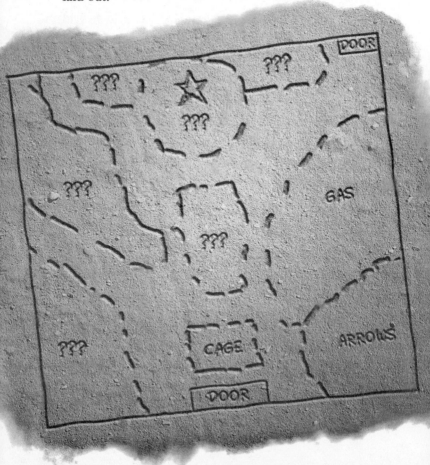

We all looked at him in astonishment. "How do you know this?" Marco asked.

"Don't *you*?" he asked.

"No!" we answered in unison.

"I watched Kranag's walking pattern, that's all," Cass said. "The areas inside the dotted lines—those are the places he wouldn't go. So we need to avoid them. As for that star, he definitely walked a circle around that area. As if there were something inside it. I bet it marks the place with the Loculus."

Marco shook his head in awe. "Brother Cass, you scare me."

Aly put an arm around Cass's shoulder. "Remind me not to worry again when you complain about losing your powers."

"But this was easy," Cass said.

"To you it's all easy," Aly said. "Because you are *good*. That's why we need you. You never lost a thing. Well, confidence, maybe."

I gave Cass the torch. "You ready to be our leader?"

Cass blinked, then nodded. "Okay. Right. Follow me."

He took the torch, casting a wary eye up toward the vizzeet. Stepping over the door jamb, he reached out with his free hand and waved it into the cage area. "The metal bars are still there. Follow me. Walk in my footsteps, exactly. Don't vary left or right. Marco, narrow your shoulders."

"Narrow my shoulders?" Marco said.

"Yeah, you know, hunch up," Cass said. "Don't take up so much space."

The song of the Heptakiklos twanged into my ears. It was so close. I fought the desire to run to it across the room that taunted us with emptiness.

Aly and Marco fell in behind Cass. I brought up the rear. We walked quietly, our sandals shuffling against the hard-packed dirt. The torch flames made our shadows dance on the walls.

"EEEEEEEEE . . . "

Outside, a vizzeet had leaped down from a ledge, landing in front of the open door. Cass swung my torch toward it, trying to scare it away.

I grabbed the torch. Marco and I lunged forward, shouting. "Yaaaaahhh!"

The vizzeet jumped back, but I felt the ground shaking below my feet. A spike broke through the soil, thrusting upward, inches from my foot. I screamed, jumping back.

Marco caught me. He held me off the ground, his arms around my chest.

"Thanks . . ." I said. "But you're choking me . . ."

He didn't answer. His face was rigid. I looked down. There hadn't been only one spike. There had been four. Three of them stood alone, victimless. But one of them had pierced Marco's foot.

"Hhhhh . . . " The only sound Marco could manage was

a shocked gasp. His grip loosened and I slid downward. I positioned my feet to avoid the blades.

"He's hurt!" Aly cried out, moving toward Marco.

"Stay put, Aly!" Cass commanded.

The floor was a bloody mess. I set down the torch, quickly ripped a section from my tunic, and wiped the blood away. Marco's foot was intact. "It came up between your toes," I said.

"Lucky . . . me," Marco said with a clenched jaw. "The edges . . . are sharp."

The spike had four serrated ridges. It had sliced clear through his sandal. Although it hadn't impaled his foot, it had come up between his big toe and second toe and cut them pretty badly. I unfastened the buckle. Gently I pulled Marco's toes apart, away from the blade edges, and lifted his foot out of the sandal. Then I ripped the sandal off the spike and tried to clean it as best I could. "Good as new, sort of," I said, setting the blood-soaked sandal down and picking up the torch.

"Thanks . . ." Marco grunted, slipping his foot back in. "I may wait a few months before I try the marathon. Let's go."

Cass and Aly were staring at him, slack-jawed. Cass pointed off to the right. "I—I think we go this way now . . ."

"I promise not to vary an inch from the path," Marco said.

"I promise not to move my torch away, too," I added.

Cass went slower. Much slower. Our footsteps echoed,

bouncing off the back wall as if there were another set of people there. I could hear my breaths echoing, in rhythm with the strange music.

EEEEEE! Another vizzeet screech was followed by a metallic clang.

I nearly jumped but kept my cool. The creature had tried to jump in but hit the bars of the invisible cage. It was scrambling away on all fours, chattering hysterically.

Cass soon slowed to a stop, not far from the rear wall. "We're here," he announced.

"Where?" Aly said.

"The spot where I drew the star." Cass was trembling. He was moving his ankle along a curved form, tracing a rounded shape. "Okay, this is invisible, but it's some kind of platform. I can feel it. It's raised."

I reached forward, about knee high. I felt a cool, tiled surface that sloped inward toward the top, like a sculpture of a volcano. I slid my hand upward until I reached a rim about three feet high. Slowly I ran my hand to the right and left. "It's a circle," I said. "Some kind of pit."

As I grabbed the rim with both hands, I felt my knees weaken. My entire body shook with the vibrations of the strange music. *Concentrate.*

I reached downward into the invisible pit. The blackness below me turned a muddy gray. I could see floating faces. A beautiful woman with sandy hair, smiling.

Queen Qalani. She was dressed in a fine gown gathered at the waist with a sash. On her head was a ring of bejeweled gold. Her laughter was like the running of water over stones.

But her image instantly pixelated into a confetti of colors, which spread and dulled into a whitish silver that flowed from my outstretched palm downward.

It became a sphere of glowing, pulsing white.

I smiled. I began to laugh. My body felt weightless but I was still on the ground. The song and I were one now. It was the blood flowing through my veins, the snapping of electricity in my brain. For a moment I wasn't aware of any other sound at all.

Until a piercing cry broke the spell.

"Jack!" came Aly's voice. *"Jack, where are you?"*

CHAPTER THIRTY-ONE

NOW YOU SEE IT

I FELT THE back of a hand brushing my arm. "Got him!" Marco said.

Fingers closed around my wrist. I was reeling back now, losing my balance.

The Loculus disappeared. All I could see was the panicked look on Marco's face as he wrenched me away from the pit.

"Don't let him fall backward!" Cass was shouting. "There's a trap behind him!"

Marco held tight, lifting me upward with one arm. I came down hard on my feet and looked into three utterly astonished faces. "What happened?" I said.

"You were gone," Aly said. "You were there one second and gone the next."

"Just—*foop!*" Cass said, practically dancing with excitement. "You found it, Jack—right? You found the invisibility Loculus!"

"I guess I did," I said.

Cass jumped, clapping his hands. From his pocket, Leonard leaped out. He hit the ground and began to run. We all stood gaping as he climbed thin air, up the wall of the pit, and then fell inside.

"Come back here, little yug!" Cass shouted. The scaly creature rolled around the bottom of the pit, looking oddly squashed, panicked by the fact that he was up against something solid that he couldn't see.

As Cass reached down, he seemed to lose color. His outline became a trace line of gray. In a nanosecond he was gone.

And so was Leonard.

For a moment I saw and heard nothing. Then a disembodied "Gotcha!" and a spray of random color, which morphed in a fraction of a second into Cass.

He was standing before us again, grinning, with Leonard in his hand, as if nothing had happened.

"Beam me up, Scotty . . ." Aly mumbled.

Marco pumped his fist. "Epic! Let's snatch that thing and get back home!"

I leaned back over the rim and dug my fingers down under the Loculus. It was cool, smooth to the touch. I couldn't tell how heavy it was, because it seemed to move with my hand, as if powered from within. I didn't know whether I was lifting it or it was lifting itself, guided by my motions. "Got it."

I knew the others couldn't see me. I also knew we had to get the heck out of there. But I couldn't keep my eyes off the sphere. Its insides were a translucent swirl of colors, making patterns like an ocean.

All around us, a low rumbling noise grew. I wasn't fully aware of it until I felt the ground shake and the Loculus itself almost fall from my hand.

"Jack?" came Aly's voice. "Wh-what's going on?"

I heard a cracking sound from above. A piece of the ceiling dislodged and crashed to the floor. Then another.

Was this another booby trap?

Through the thick, rocky roof I could hear the cawing of birds and screeching of vizzeet. I could see black smoke from the fire in Kranag's hut.

I held the Loculus to my chest and stepped backward. I felt Marco's hand on my arm. Aly's. Cass's. With my free arm I guided Aly's hand to the Loculus itself. "You don't need to do that," she said loudly, over the sound of the rumbling. "I can see it. As long as I'm touching you, I can see it. It's like the power passes through us."

The torch was now guttering and weak. A chunk of stone nearly dropped on my head. It crashed to the floor and broke into pieces.

The shaking was going on everywhere, not just in this

room. It wasn't a booby trap. It was an earthquake. The last thing we needed.

"Hurry!" Marco shouted. *"Move!"*

"Be careful of the traps!" Cass warned.

Too late. A door swung open in the floor. My foot sank inside. I let go of the Loculus, windmilling my arms. Marco and Cass both grabbed me and pulled. "Don't let the Loculus go!" I shouted.

Aly caught it. I was able to swing my foot upward. It landed on solid ground.

A boom, like a plane breaking the sound barrier, passed from left to right. I heard a massive crash outside, followed by the cawing of the black bird and the wild keening of the vizzeet. Through the hole in the floor came a river of fur and whisker, undulating, growing . . .

"Rats!" Cass screamed. *"I hate rats!"*

My hair stood on end. The slithery creatures were sliding over my toes, squeaking, chattering, their little legs pumping frantically.

I saw teeth flashing in the light. Cass was swinging the torch downward, trying to scare them away. *"Getoutofhere getoutofhere getoutofhere!"* he shouted.

Aly shrieked. For the first time since I'd known him, Marco was screaming. We stumbled backward. I felt myself falling and willed my body to stay upright. "Run!" Aly's voice called out.

"No, don't!" Cass said. "Follow me! *Force yourselves!*"

Squeals bounced off the walls as a badly trembling Cass walked the correct, trap-free path through a wriggling carpet of rodents. They crawled up his ankles, jumped off his knees. He screamed, brushing away a couple that had run up into his tunic. I could feel their claws dig into my skin. They were too small, too light, too low to set off the traps. But any false move on our part could be lethal.

Cass screamed, tearing rodents from his hair. But he forced one foot in front of the other, tracing a path that no ordinary person would be able to remember. I could feel the squealing in my ears, as if one of them had burrowed inside my head.

The door loomed closer. Rats were scampering up and down the invisible iron bars of the cage. When Cass neared that—our last obstacle—he jumped straight for the entrance.

I flung myself out after him, kicking the nasty creatures away. Aly and Marco landed on top of me. I let go of the torch and it flew away on the ground.

We scrambled to our feet. Standing on a ledge, directly above the door, were four vizzeet.

As I frantically scraped rodents from my tunic, the screaming creatures jumped.

CHAPTER THIRTY-TWO

A WHIP OF BLACKNESS

I LEAPED AWAY, screaming. Marco ran, lifting Aly clear off the ground. Cass was on the ground, scrabbling backward.

The vizzeet landed in the sea of rats, hooting with glee. They spat fountains, nailing rats with pellets of saliva. The rodents screamed and fell, the acid searing their entire bodies, nearly cooking them on the spot. The monkeylike creatures scooped up the rats one by one, gobbling them whole.

Beneath our feet, the ground was still. The vizzeet were beating a retreat around the side of the Hanging Gardens, following the rats. A helix of black smoke rose from behind the structure and I could smell Kranag's hut burning. "The earthquake," I said. "It's gone."

"So are most of the rats," Marco said, his face twisted with disgust. "Hallelujah."

"I can see four of us," Cass said. "Which means the Loculus is not here."

"I dropped it," Aly said, looking back into the room. "Back into the pit."

"You *what*?" Marco snapped. "We have to go in there again?"

"I couldn't hold it with rats nibbling at my toes!" Aly said.

"Okay," Cass said, still trembling. "It's okay. We wait a minute for the last of the rats to disperse. Then Marco goes back in and gets the Loculus—"

"*Marco* goes back in?" Marco sputtered.

"You're the fearless one," Aly said.

Marco swallowed hard. "Yeah. True. Okay. Give me a minute to regain my Marconess."

"Never mind—I'll do it," Cass said. "I'm the one who knows the path best."

Before Marco could protest, Cass was running back inside, threading his way along his own perfectly imagined path. We stood in the doorway, too wise to follow. Minutes later I could see him stopping in the back . . . leaning over . . . disappearing.

A bolt of electricity ripped the sky like a sudden cannon shot. The ground heaved again, and on the second level of the Hanging Gardens, pillars of a marble trellis cracked in two. A thick thatch of vines crashed down, spilling over the sides. At the top, a statue fell from a perch like a shot bird.

The moon disappeared into the swelling curtain of Sippar, which streaked across the sky like a spider's web.

As I fell to the ground, the realization hit me.

It's the Loculus.

Removing it was causing the earthquake and the tightening of Sippar. If we tried to take it, the earthquake would continue. The ground would open, torches in Babylon would tumble, buildings would collapse.

"Put it back!" I screamed.

"What?" echoed Cass's voice from deep inside the room.

"Put it back! We are the ones causing this!" I yelled.

A whip of blackness shot across the sky like lightning, punching a hole in the side of the Hanging Gardens. Dust exploded outward and landed in a loud shower of rock.

"I'm convinced!" Cass called from inside.

I could see him materializing now. Walking the jerky path back to us. Outside the door, he looked upward. "I put it back."

Cass, Aly, Marco, and I watched the blackness slowly recede. The sky rumbled, once, twice, and then fell silent.

I exhaled hard. "Come on, guys, we're going."

"Wait!" Marco said, shaking his head. "Just who elected you captain, Brother Jack?"

211

"The Loculus is Babylon's energy source, Marco," I said. "It's what keeps the area here safe, cut off from our world in this weird time frame."

"We can't go back to the KI without it," Marco said. "You know that!"

I met his glance levelly. "We can't destroy an entire civilization. They need this Loculus, Marco. It's the reason they're here. Their center. The thing that's keeping Sippar at bay."

"How do you know the earthquakes weren't a coincidence?" Marco said. "Taking the other Loculus didn't destroy Greece. That one had the power of flight, this one the power of invisibility. That's it. End of story."

"Invisibility might be a necessary part of the time-rift mechanism, Marco," Cass said. "It may be the ingredient that allows Babylon to actually exist in the same place as our world."

"And if you're wrong?" Marco shot back.

"Do we take the risk to find out?" I said. "Are you willing to be responsible for killing Daria?"

Marco shifted weight from foot to foot. He glanced back toward the chamber.

"Marco," I continued, "we need to talk to Professor Bhegad. If anyone can figure this out, he can. That's why the KI was set up, for problems like this. We can always come back and do this smarter."

Now I could hear a loud clank from the inner-garden gate. Voices.

"The guards are here," Aly said. "I guess Nabu-na'id forced them to go and face the monsters."

"The question is, do those monsters include us?" I asked.

Marco's eyes darted toward the guards' voices. "Come on," he said gruffly, heading for the garden wall. "I'll help you guys over."

CHAPTER THIRTY-THREE

IN THE SHADOWS

THE MOON WAS giving way to the rising sun. As we rushed away, my sandals seemed to get stuck on everything—roots, vines, rocks, salamanders. We were taking a wide berth around farmland. Huts were still shuttered from last night, and we were nearing the copse of woods close to the river, where we'd first come in. My face still hurt, and my feet were battered and bruised.

We'd managed to hide out in the shadows of the garden, while the newly emboldened guards rushed through the inner wall. In the predawn darkness we'd slipped away unseen, but we knew our hours of undetected freedom were numbered.

I wondered about Daria. Had anything happened to her during the earthquake? Where exactly had the fire been?

For a moment I thought about turning back. About staying here instead of returning.

And die here at age fourteen? Stop. Forget that now.

Marco was at the river edge. He was looking back toward the city. I had a hard time reading his face. "Let's do this before I change my mind."

"Marco, wait," I said. "What about the first Loculus? You said you buried it here. At least we can bring that one back. One for two isn't bad."

"Yeah, good thinking," Marco said. "I'll get it. It's right nearby. You guys go ahead before they hunt us down."

"We'll wait," Aly said.

"The guards will be here in a minute!" Marco snapped. "Go! All of you. Now! I can do this in two seconds."

Uncertainly, she and Cass clasped hands and prepared to jump.

I turned to Marco. "Are you all right?"

Marco took a deep breath. "Adjusting. I hate to lose."

"Don't think of it as losing," I said. "We'll be back."

Marco smiled. "Glass half full, right, Brother Jack?"

"Right," I replied.

I heard two splashes in the river. Cass and Aly were on their way. I glanced back toward Babylon and saw four figures running through the entrance gate, clutching spears.

"I see them," Marco said. "They won't touch me. Go ahead."

215

Somehow, I knew he'd be all right. "See you on the other side," I said, turning toward the Euphrates.

* * *

I gasped for breath, breaking through the surface of the river. I felt a pull from above. Over my head, a nylon fishing line waved in the breeze. The hook was attached to my shirt.

I blinked the water out of my eyes. The sun beat overhead, the river was calm. On the shore, a blond woman stood with a fishing rod, looking mortified. A small crowd had gathered around her. "I am so, so sorry!" she cried out.

I looked around for our foursome, Bhegad, Torquin, Fiddle, Nirvana. I didn't see them among the throng of people pouring out of tents down the shore. They were all wearing the familiar white polo shirts with KI symbols. Some of their faces were vaguely familiar from the Comestibule.

I swam for the shore. Aly kept pace beside me. Marco was with us, too, just as promised. I smiled with relief, watching him grab onto Cass's tunic and swimming him toward the shore.

But my strokes felt labored, as if I weighed three hundred pounds. I let my legs drop downward. Luckily we'd reached the shallows and I could stand.

I staggered, as if my knees had been replaced with wet clay. I struggled to stay upright, shaking water from my eyes. Cass and Marco were on their feet, too. Cass looked pale. He was handing Leonard to Marco. "Brother Cass,"

216

Marco said. "Are you okay?"

"Marco . . ." I called out, my voice parched. "Where's the Loculus?"

Marco shook his head disgustedly. "They came after me before I could dig. Guards. I had to book."

I turned. People were slogging through the water toward us. Fritz, the German mechanic with a KI snake tattoo on his face. Brutus, the baker, whose muffins I had botched in the kitchen. Alana, one of Marco's martial arts instructors.

I wanted them to go away. I felt numb. All my aches— tongue, arm, head—throbbed like crazy. My legs felt Gumby-like, and I had to blink to keep my balance.

I felt the shore spinning. The smiles of the Karai people became a collage of floating, chattering teeth. I heard Marco say something, but when I turned he wasn't there. I looked down. Aly had dropped to her knees. Cass fell back into the water, his arms flailing. I could see people rushing over. They had tubes and needles and boxes. They seemed to be floating in midair. Blending into one another and separating.

"Treat . . ." I said, but my jaw was stuck, my tongue thick. " . . . ment."

CHAPTER THIRTY-FOUR

AGAIN

MY BROTHER.

My Dream begins where it last ended, in a chamber under the broken ground. Where the water has given me life from death. Where I float on air made of song. Where I face the empty Heptakiklos and the boy who stole the Loculi.

The boy who looks like me. Who is my brother.

He looks up. He is not surprised to see me.

My eyes are locked on what is behind him. The patch of scorched earth that was once the lifeblood of our land—seven empty bowls carved from the rock, arranged in a circle. A sword in the midst of it all. It sickens me to the core.

I begin to yell. I cannot control myself. He must return what he has taken. He has caused the Dark Times. His recklessness is destroying our world. I see beside him an enormous leather pouch. It has been made from the stomach of a giant horomophorus, a creature that can look over the tops of trees. Even through its thick lining, the seven spheres are visible. Glowing. They contain immense energy.

He smiles. We are brothers, he says. We must understand one another. We can work together.

As he speaks, the dreamscape shifts in the way that dreams do, and I become him. I am now the boy who was my thieving brother. But "thieving" is the wrong word. It is the word of the fallen boy, the one who I am no longer. I know this now: What I'm doing is not theft but salvation.

I look at the agitated, bruised, soil-smeared face that is no longer mine. I look for a sign that he may understand. But whether he does or not no longer matters, because there is no more time.

I take the satchel and I run.

Behind me, my brother leaps toward the Heptakiklos. He grabs the sword in its center and pulls.

It slides out with a loud shiiiiink. *The jolt of light is blinding.*

The earth shakes violently. I fall, and so does he. As he turns to me, his eyes are panicked.

What has he done?

What have we *done?*

He rises to his feet and rushes toward me.

I open the satchel. I reach inside, searching for a sphere of nothing. A space that pushes aside the other six spheres. I see it. I touch it.

I run, as he howls in confusion and anger.

He no longer sees me.

And I know I will never see him again.

CHAPTER THIRTY-FIVE

LAZARUS RISES

"AH, LAZARUS RISES."

"His name not Lazarus. Is Jack."

Voices. I knew them.

"I am referring, dear Torquin, to the biblical story of Lazarus, who rose from the dead."

"Jack not dead, Professor."

"No, and Jack's name is not actually Lazarus. *It is an expression!*"

The room was bright. Too bright. I cracked my eyes open as best I could. The lingering images of my dream floated away.

I focused on a Karai Institute flag hanging in the tent:

Both Professor Bhegad and Torquin were sitting on folding chairs. Torquin was whittling a block of wood into something shapeless.

I smiled. I never thought I'd be so happy to see old Red Beard. "Wow," I said. "You're okay. We thought we lost you in the river."

Torquin scowled. "Almost drowned. Was punished." He violently hacked off about half the block of wood, which shot across the room. "Punishing Torquin, favorite KI pastime."

"The true punishment was what your bodies went through," Bhegad said. "You were gone for almost five months. You did not feel the aging effects in Babylon— but upon your return, G7W kicked in. In other words, your body clocks caught up. You all went far past your scheduled treatment times. I cannot emphasize how close you came to dying, young man. These treatments are temporary, and they do lose effectiveness over time. You are lucky we expanded our camp here to full emergency capacity—under the guise of an archaeological dig, of course. I used my status as a world-renowned archaeologist to get the proper permits."

"Thank you," I said.

From outside, I heard shouts. I tried to sit up, but my head throbbed. The morning sun was orange on the horizon, streaming through the door from the east.

A white-shirted scientist peeked inside. "Marco's gone, sir."

Torquin raced out the tent flap. Bhegad, too. He had been in a wheelchair the last time we'd seen him, and now he was walking on two feet.

I heard a snuffling sound and turned to my right. Aly and Cass were both on cots, eyes closed.

They were unconscious. Marco was missing. I felt flattened. Dazed.

When I closed my eyes, it was hard to open them. So I didn't.

* * *

"Jack?" This time it was Aly's voice that woke me up. She and Cass were both sitting up on their cots, looking groggy. "Hey. Afternoon."

"What time is it?" I asked.

"Three o'clock," Cass said. "Time flies when you're having fun. Professor Bhegad told us he already spoke to you. Sounds like we dodged a tellub."

"Do you have to do that all the time?" I said, clutching the side of my achy head.

"Bullet," Cass said. "Sorry. The good news is they found Marco."

"He ran off," Aly said, shaking her head in disbelief. "He recovered from his treatment before the rest of us. Just before daybreak, he slipped out for a jog. Or so he says. He was gone for hours."

A jog?

I was having a hard time computing this. My mind was still half in dreamland. Memories of our escape were flooding in—the Loculus, Kranag, the near-collapse of the Hanging Gardens . . .

"Actually, when he told us to jump into the Euphrates before him, I thought he might surprise us and stay in Babylon," Aly went on. "That boy hates failure."

"Well, he left the flying Loculus there," I said.

"He tried to get it," Aly said. "He told Professor Bhegad he started digging it up. But when the guards came after him, he had to jump in the river without it. Bhegad was furious."

Cass shrugged. "Imagine how bad Marco must feel. Probably went on a hundred-mile jog to clear his head."

224

I lay back, eyes closed. "Are all seven missions going to be like this?" I said. "I don't know what's harder, finding Loculi or dealing with Marco the Unpredictable. Ever since Rhodes, he's been acting so strange, saying such weird stuff."

Aly raised an eyebrow. "Since Rhodes? He's been like that since the minute I met him."

"I think you guys are being a little harsh," Cass said.

I took a deep breath and shut my mouth. I needed to recover more fully. Then my mind wouldn't be so negative.

I dozed on and off for awhile, and when my eyes flipped open for good, I was alone in the tent with Professor Bhegad, and it was growing dark outside. Bhegad was picking things up, tossing them into suitcases. "Feel well enough to fly, my boy?" he asked. "We're going home to the island."

"Now?" I sat up slowly. "I thought you'd want us to go back to Babylon."

"We have been discussing what happened during your journey," Bhegad said. "And by the way, I must applaud you, Jack, for your unusual discernment at a time of moral crisis. Your decision to leave the Loculus was wise and humane."

"Really?" I said.

"We knew this mission would be hard," he continued, sliding a laptop into his suitcase. "While you were gone, we tried to anticipate every possible scenario. We've had months. Brilliant minds can achieve great things in that time—nanotech engineers, geneticists, metallurgists, biophysicists."

I couldn't believe we were going back to Geek Island. This whole thing was just getting worse and worse. "Funeral directors, too?" I said. "Looks like we'll need those at the rate we're going."

Bhegad leaned in close. "My boy, never forget: saving your lives is the Karai Institute's *raison d'être*."

"'Reason for being,'" grunted Torquin from the far side of the tent. "French."

"So we will not give up on you," Bhegad said. "And believe me, you have not seen the last of Ancient Babylon. We will send you back, by hook or by crook."

Something about that statement made my hair stand on end. Saving lives—was that really their motivation? Marco's words came back to me. *What if there is no cure? What if it's all a sham? After those seven babies are returned? Bingo—thanks, guys, sayonara! Next stop, Nobel Prize.*

If Bhegad was so casual about the lives of the Babylonians, how did he really feel about us?

"We *can't* bring the Loculus back, Professor Bhegad," I said. "We can't kill thousands of people. Even if they're in some kind of weird time limbo, they're still people."

Professor Bhegad smiled. "Yes, and I understand one of them became a bit of a sweetie to you."

226

"She did not—who told you that?" I blurted out. My face burned.

Torquin snorted. "Little bird."

Snapping a suitcase shut, Professor Bhegad headed for the tent flap. "Torquin, commence preparations for takeoff. Wheels up in half an hour. We keep a team here, because I expect to return before long. And this time, when you go to Babylon, Jack, you'll be going with Shelley."

He stepped briskly outside, shouting orders to other people.

"Wait!" I called out. "Who's Shelley?"

Torquin plopped a full suitcase at my feet. "Not a sweetie," he said.

CHAPTER THIRTY-SIX

PINEAPPLE AND GRASSHOPPER

"I HAVE BEEN dreaming of an elppaenip smoothie," Cass said, as we burst through the dorm entrance into the bright tropical morning. He held up a small glass box, in which Leonard was lying on a bed of sand. "And a yummy reppohssarg for you?"

Sometimes, just sometimes, Backwardish just got on my nerves. "You know, Cass, maybe you can spell that stuff in your head, but it's impossible to figure it out by hearing you say it!"

"Pineapple," Aly said. "And grasshopper."

"Thank you, I rest my esac," Cass said.

"*Ee-sack* is not the right way to say *case* backward!" I said.

"You dootsrednu it," Cass replied.

"Aghhhhh!" As I took off after him, Cass ran away, giggling.

Honestly, it felt pretty good being back in the lush lawns and air-conditioned comfort of the KI. We'd all had a day to chill, most of which was spent sleeping. We'd showered and been bandaged up. Bhegad's intelligence committee had debriefed us on every detail of the visit. Even a team of "textile designers" had made patterns of our tunics and sandals.

Today Professor Bhegad was going to treat us to breakfast in his classroom at the House of Wenders and introduce us to Shelley.

"Maybe she's a new Select," Aly remarked.

"Freshly kidnapped," Marco drawled.

"Well, it'll be good to have another girl," Aly said.

"I had a friend named Shelley who was a guy," Cass said, jogging back to us. "Sheldon."

"Guy or girl, I don't know how one more Select is going to make a difference in Babylon," Marco said. He kicked a stone and it rocketed across the campus lawn.

"Easy, Pistol Feet," Aly said. She smiled at Marco, but he didn't notice.

Cass was trilling into the glass box. "Brrrrrr . . . brrrrrr . . ."

"What are you doing?" I said.

"It's my lizard noise," Cass said. "It comforts Leonard. He's very sick. Barely moved since we got back."

"He's homesick," Aly said. "You never should have brought him over from the other side."

Brought him over from the other side.

229

I stopped short. "Guys. Wait a minute. How did that happen? How did Leonard come over from Babylon?"

Aly, Cass, and Marco turned. "Same way we did, Brother Jack," Marco said.

"But Torquin wasn't able to go through the portal—because he's not a Select, and only Selects pass through. *So why Leonard?*" I began pacing across the walkway. "Okay . . . okay, we have to think about this before we see Professor Bhegad. This isn't the first weird thing that's happened with Leonard. Remember, when he fell into the Loculus pit, he didn't disappear—only when Cass reached down to get him! And Cass disappeared, too. Both times—with the Loculus and in the river—Leonard was able to do what a Select did. Not by *being* a Select, but by being in physical contact with one!"

I stopped. The realization was epic. But the others were staring at me weirdly. "Uh, we kind of knew that," Cass said. "Marco figured it out two days ago, back when we were in the water. When I pulled Leonard out of my tunic."

"We talked about it while you were knocked out," Aly said, "in the tent."

I didn't care that they knew. I was thinking about Daria. And the *wardum*. And the farmers and garden strollers and herdspeople. "This could be a game changer," I said. "We can save the Babylonians. They don't have to die. We can bring them through before we take the Loculus."

"All of them?" Aly added. "Evacuate an entire city one by one—and bring them two thousand years into their future? Or . . . another present, that is the future?"

"Well, it's worth thinking about . . ." I said, but the others were looking at me as if I were drooling purple slime. I fell into step as we approached the House of Wenders, a building with columns and wide steps that looked like a museum. The morning clouds had burned away, and Mount Onyx was clear in the distance, rising over the top of the building like a black-hooded sentry.

Professor Bhegad met us in the building's grand lobby, leaning against the statue of the giant dinosaur that had been excavated on the island. "Good morning, cross-dimensional wayfarers," he called out. "Punctuality is a harbinger of future success."

"Listening to him is worse than Backwardish," Marco muttered.

"Right this way," Bhegad said, ushering us toward the elevator in the back. "If I seem a bit distracted, it is because I have had a restless sleep worrying about the possible discovery of the first Loculus by ancient Babylonians."

"Yo, P. Beg, I told you, no one's going to find it," Marco said. "I barely had my hands in the dirt when I saw the guards coming."

"Yes, well . . ." Bhegad sighed. "I am a teacher by trade, and I trust you will take this as a teachable moment.

231

Honestly, there was no need to bring an already-secured Loculus into a parallel world. But—*tempus fugit!*—I cannot dwell on this. All will be right in the fullness of time. As you know, the last few months we have been working very hard. And I think you'll be pleased with the results."

We entered the elevator and the door slid shut. We sank downward so fast I thought my stomach would knock me in the jaw. It was my first time riding this thing, and I couldn't help but notice that Ground Floor was at the top. Underneath it were ten buttons—ten floors going downward. Bhegad pressed SUBBASEMENT SEVEN.

"It's an upside-down skyscraper," Cass said. "A groundscraper."

The door opened into a cavernous room. The air was biting cold. All around us was the low whir and hum of an air conditioner, and the rhythmic clanking of metal. Steam and liquids blasted through clear tubes overhead. Marco nearly tripped over a short, mushroom-shaped robot that whizzed and skittered along the floor. A bat, confused and disoriented, dive-bombed us and then disappeared into the elevator.

"Given the level of emergency, we haven't had a chance to import the best equipment," Professor Bhegad said. "Instead, we've worked with what we have. Sometimes the results are better that way."

We followed Professor Bhegad past a busy workstation.

White-clad KI workers with bloodshot eyes were clacking away at keyboards. They quickly waved before heading back to their calculations. The screens glowed with rotating AutoCAD diagrams, and on each desk was a steaming mug of coffee or tea.

Just beyond them, separated by a floor-to-ceiling wall of clear Plexiglas, was a gigantic machine. It looked as if it had been cobbled out of spare parts—I spotted a Jeep fender, a small jet engine, a window frame, sewer pipes, a table top, and about a hundred patches made from the backs of iPod cases. Facing us was a black-tinted window at about eye level.

We entered through a sliding door in the Plexiglas. The machine made a scraping noise and let off a puff of black steam, which rose up into a vacuum duct overhead.

I backed away, coughing.

"Boys and girls," Professor Bhegad said. "Meet Shelley."

CHAPTER THIRTY-SEVEN

THE LETHARGIC LIZARD

THE MACHINE BARKED a greeting halfway between a *brack* and a *clonk*.

"You lost me, Professor Bhegad," Marco said.

"Wait. We're supposed to go back to Babylon with this thing?" I said.

"Actually, this *thing*, as you say, is not Shelley," Bhegad replied. "Shelley is what it makes."

He pressed a button. A bright light went on behind the black-tinted window. We could see something in a small chamber inside the machine. I moved closer.

Floating in midair was a brownish-gold shard of metal. It was curved like a shield but jagged around the perimeter. Silver-gray wisps puffed into the chamber, clouds of tiny particles that swirled along the surface and then clung to the edges. Turning slowly, the shield seemed to be growing. Curving.

"When it's finished, it will be a perfect sphere," Bhegad said.

Aly's eyes were the size of softballs. "You're making a Loculus?"

"Not a Loculus," Bhegad replied. "A Loculus casing. Something I have long thought about constructing. Using plans drafted long ago by Herman Wenders in his journals. People scoffed at the audacity of his schemes, but the man was a genius, far ahead of his time. The project moved to Priority One upon your return from Rhodes."

"You never saw the Loculus," Marco pointed out. "Neither did Bigfoot. He was in jail. How could you have analyzed the material?"

"Again, Wenders was our guide," Bhegad said. "He had managed to find a piece of a Loculus—at least that was what he claimed. Our metallurgists have analyzed the shard, replicated it, and then treated it with a special alloy made of metal and carbon fiber, organic and inorganic polymers, and silicate derivatives. To give it flexibility and lightness."

"Just stir and bake," Aly said, staring into the black window, "and get instant empty Loculus shell."

"In a manner of speaking, yes," Bhegad said. "You see,

when the Loculi were together in the Heptakiklos, they acted as conduits for the Atlantean energy, which traveled from sphere to sphere. The great Qalani had constructed ingenious skins to allow the free energy flow. We believe we have done the same thing with Shelley. If you put that sphere within a foot or so of a real Loculus, its material will promote a transfer of contents." The Professor's eyes were wild with excitement. "You will be able to leave the real Loculus there. When you bring Shelley back, it will contain what we need for the Heptakiklos!"

"But if this thing works," I said, "and we steal away the energy, how will Babylon survive?"

"My research suggests that the Atlantean energy is like human blood—remove some and over time it will replicate to fill the vessel again," Bhegad said. "All you need is a small threshold of transfer energy. We have configured Shelley to change color when that threshold is reached. After about an hour of exposure, it will become green and may be taken away. Over time, the energy will fill the entire shell."

Marco was taking notes. That sight alone was nearly as shocking as this crazy scheme of Bhegad. "Cool, if it works," Marco said. "A shell for the energy. Is that why you call it Shelley?"

Professor Bhegad smiled. "It is named after Mary Shelley. She wrote a little story about a scientist who created a living thing out of spare parts. Similar to what we're doing."

"It's aliiiive," Aly said.

"Pardon me?" Bhegad said.

"*Frankenstein*," Aly replied.

Bhegad grinned. "Precisely."

* * *

Cass set down Leonard's glass enclosure beside the basketball court. We'd had a few hours since Bhegad's demonstration. We'd eaten lunch, argued, and finally agreed to do recreation time. It had been more than twenty-four hours since we emerged from the Euphrates, and the lizard hadn't perked up a bit. "I'm worried," Cass said. "Professor Bhegad says Leonard hasn't developed the immunities we have. Our air is full of germs that didn't exist in Babylonian times."

A fat dragonfly whizzed by Marco, who grabbed it in midair with quick reflexes that still astonished me. Cass took off the top screen and Marco dropped in the fly. It buzz-bombed the lethargic lizard, who looked up and then went back to sleep.

"Dang, that was almost juicy enough for *me* to eat," Marco said. With a shrug, he began dribbling the basketball onto the court.

Cass sat with Aly and me on the asphalt, watching Marco shoot baskets. As usual he was making shots from a gazillion feet away. With his G7W talents pushed to max, he never missed. Even Serge, a KI computer whiz who had played on an Olympic basketball team, had never beaten Marco.

"Doesn't that ever get boring?" Aly called out. "Making every shot?"

Marco palmed the ball. "Yup. I'll coach you instead, Brother Cass. For free. Right now. That'll be a challenge."

Cass stood up. "Really? You would teach me?"

"If you leave Leonard for a minute." Marco threw the ball directly at Cass. It hit him square in the chest and knocked him over. "First rule, you have to use your hands. It's not soccer."

"Not soccer," Cass said. "Right."

Aly took my arm and led me to the tennis court, about twenty yards away. I looked over my shoulder at Cass. He was dribbling the basketball awkwardly toward the basket. Slapping it, really. But looking incredibly happy. Marco followed, pretending to guard him. "Williams charrrrges the net . . ." Marco called out. "He shoots . . . air ball!"

"Cass looks like he's enjoying this," Aly said.

I nodded. "Maybe he's mapping out the geography of the basketball court."

"Marco is the ultimate cool brother," Aly replied. "It must be tough for Cass. He gets so down on himself, not having a real family. You know, except us."

"Us and Leonard," I said. As I went to my end of the court, Aly opened a fresh canister of tennis balls. "Serve it and swerve it," I said.

"What?" she said.

I felt a sudden tug inside. The last time I'd played tennis was with my dad. When he wasn't overseas on business, we'd play every weekend at the Belleville Rec Center. "Habit," I said. "It's what my dad and I say. He's always trying to teach me how to do spins."

"My mom is a terrible player. She says she loses on purpose, because she likes to be the one who ends the game with perfect love. Which casts out all evil. She has a weird sense of humor." Aly served the ball. "Do you still think of home a lot?"

I hit it back sharply. Too sharply. It sailed just past the line. "Sorry. Yeah, I guess I do. Sometimes."

The truth was, I hadn't been. Not consciously. Not while we were chasing a griffin in Greece and visiting Babylon. But the thoughts of home had built up in a dark corner of my brain. Every once in a while a mental light would flick on. Like when we went to Ohio. And here in the tennis court. I could see Dad hunched over at the base line, wearing his weird tennis hat with drooping white ear flaps. I could picture Mom, too, as if she'd never passed away. She was sneaking up behind him, lifting the flaps as if they were bunny ears . . .

"Wake up, Jack!"

Aly's voice shocked me into reality. The ball whizzed past my ear, landing just inside the line. "Whoa. Can we do that one over?"

"No," Aly said with an *are-you-kidding* laugh. "Fifteen-love."

We volleyed back and forth, the rackets making a sharp *mmmock!* sound on contact.

Mock! "My brother, Josh, is good," Aly said. "He gave me lessons. Maybe you'll meet him someday."

Mock! "Mom is the killer tennis player in our family," I said. "Awesome serve."

Mock! "You never talk about her," Aly said.

Mock! "What?" I replied.

Mock! "Your mom. You always talk about your dad. Did they split?"

The ball sailed over the fence and into the jungle. I twirled my racket and watched it. "My mom died."

Aly looked mortified. "Sorry, Jack. I didn't mean to—"

"It's okay," I said. "I still think about her in the present tense, even though I was pretty little when it happened."

Aly was over on my side of the court now. "When what happened?" she asked gently, quickly adding, "If you don't mind my asking."

"I don't mind," I said. "My mom was a really good athlete. She liked to go on these exotic trips with her geologist friends. Dad didn't like going so much. He'd stay home with me. That was before he had all these long business trips. Anyway, Mom spent months preparing for some hike in Antarctica. She was so excited. Dad and I were following her trek in the cold, through this awesome video feed, when a snowstorm hit . . . It was really bad. We could hear yelling. Then the yelling got drowned out by the wind. Dad says I started screaming, like I knew what was about to happen. The screen turned totally white . . . and then nothing . . ."

As the memory came back, I realized why I never talked about this. It still hurt so much. When the image went black I felt like my entire body had snapped in two.

Aly put a hand on my shoulder. "Oh, Jack . . ."

"We lost the connection," I said, looking away. "Later we found out that the team had wandered off course. They were near this huge, deep crevasse. They'd been warned not to go there, but their equipment failed. They . . . they never found her."

"I'm sorry," Aly said.

Her hand brushed down the side of my arm and touched my hand. I turned toward her. Her face wasn't where I expected it to be. It was so close I could see the contours of a tear flowing down her cheek. Somehow I didn't mind it.

"Yo!" Something hard and rubbery smacked the side of my head and I jerked away. Marco was running toward us, through the gate. "Excuse me. Didn't mean to break up your precious moment."

Aly scooped up the basketball and whipped it toward his face. Marco caught it easily and twirled it on the tip of his index finger. "Can you guys do this?"

I stood there, dumbfounded, not really comprehending Marco's request. Not really comprehending anything. "No," Aly and I both said at the same time.

Marco gave the ball another spin. "It's amazingly easy. I'll teach you. A clinic for G7W geeks! Hey, if Mr. Maps can improve, you can, too. . . ."

"Hellllp!" A shout from Cass made the ball spill off Marco's finger. He whirled around. Cass wasn't on the court.

"Brother Cass?" Marco muttered, taking off like a shot in the direction of Cass's call.

Dropping our rackets, we followed. Together we charged into the underbrush. *"Cass!"* I called out.

We got about thirty feet when I saw Cass's curly brown hair, threaded with leaves. He was stuck in a tangle of vines, thrashing his arms. "Leonard's gone!" he cried.

Marco ripped the vines off him. "Gone? That thing could barely move."

"Here, Leonard!" Cass shouted, looking around desperately.

We fanned out into the jungle. The bushes were thick, the trees dense. Above us, birds cawed loudly. Aly and I gave each other a look. "I say we find another one and pretend it's Leonard," Aly said. "A healthier one."

"Um, we may not need to," I said, gesturing back the way we'd come.

Through the trees was a flash of red hair. Aly and I

tiptoed closer. At the edge of the jungle, not far from where we'd started, was a park bench. It had probably once been in the open, but now it was nestled in the overgrown jungle.

On the bench was a pair of massive shoulders and a hefty frame that made the bench sag in the middle. "Torquin?" I said.

He turned. In one hand was a baby bottle. In the other was Leonard. "He took one ounce," Torquin said.

"What do you think you're doing?" shouted Cass, barreling through the woods.

"Didn't want to bother game," Torquin said. "Made formula."

Cass plopped himself down on the bench. "What kind of formula?"

"Protein. Mashed-up bugs. Some scorpion. Syrup," Torquin said, nuzzling the bottle into Leonard's mouth. "Good stuff. I take every morning."

"I don't believe this," Marco said with a groan.

"Does he like it?" Cass asked, smiling down at Leonard.

"Yummers," Torquin said. "I can keep? When you leave tomorrow?"

We all looked at him blankly.

"Oh. Forgot," Torquin nodded. "Professor says Shelley will be ready tonight. Wheels up at daybreak."

CHAPTER THIRTY-EIGHT

BACK IN BABYLON

"YA . . . HMM-MMM-MMM . . . OHHHH . . ." The chopper was shaking as Torquin bounced along to some tune coming through a set of thick headphones.

"Will you keep it still? We're getting air sick!" Aly shouted from the backseat, where we were sitting.

Torquin pulled one of the phones away. "Sorry. Favorite group. Wu Tang Clan."

In the copilot seat, Marco turned toward him. "Yo, Tork, do you do karaoke?"

Torquin made a face, snapping the headphone back in place. "Japanese food gives heartburn."

Marco was laughing. I wished I could have his attitude. Aly's hands were gripping the rests, her knuckles practically white. Cass looked like he was about to hurl. My eye was

244

on the window, where I could see the distant speck of our second helicopter. That one contained Professor Bhegad, Nirvana, Fiddle—and in the cargo hold, Shelley. It was descending as fast as we were, down toward the camp on the Euphrates.

Calm down, I told myself. I went over all the stuff we'd discussed at the KI:

1. We would not be blamed for the earthquake. No one in Babylon would have a reason to make the connection between it and us.
2. Shelley would be easy to activate. We would have to figure out how to get back into the Hanging Gardens.
3. Our biggest challenges would be the animals and the guards. And Kranag, if he was still alive. Bhegad had given us all kinds of repellents, flashing devices, pepper spray, flammable liquid.

Back at the KI, it had all sounded so optimistic. We'd accepted Numbers One and Two without question. Number Three had seemed like a minor inconvenience.

Now, as we drew closer, I saw everything in a clearer, more realistic light.

We were out of our minds.

"Prepare for landing," Torquin said.

Below us, I could already see the sand being whipped up by our blades. On the banks of the Euphrates, the remaining members of the KI team were swarming out of the tents to greet us. We set down gently. As we climbed down and rushed toward the water, we ran a gauntlet of high fives, shouts of good luck, pats on the back.

Professor Bhegad rushed into the midst of it all, with a tight smile and an impatient wave of the hands. "Let us save the big party for when Shelley returns. This is Journey Number Two. May it be the last."

"Try Journey Number Three for me," Marco reminded him.

"Yes, well," Professor Bhegad said, "to the river, shall we?"

A caravan of KI scientists walked with us to the water's edge. It was all happening so fast. Aly, Cass, Marco, and I caught our breaths. My heart was thumping.

"Be careful," Torquin said.

"Aren't you coming with us?" I asked.

Professor Bhegad answered for him. "We thought about it. It certainly was an option, now that we know it is possible to take along a non-Select. But we decided that you already have relationships with the Babylonians, and the introduction of someone new, with no knowledge of the language or culture, might arouse suspicion."

"In other words, you are on your own," Torquin said. He did not look disappointed.

Nirvana presented a backpack to Marco. "Inside this is a

heavy-duty, ziplocked plastic bag," she said, "with your four slave tunics, sandals, and Shelley."

I peeked inside. Shelley had been folded up into a curved trapezoid.

"Go directly to the Hanging Gardens and deploy Shelley immediately," Bhegad instructed us. "It has been designed so that even a Torquin can activate it."

"Simple tap," Torquin said, poking Professor Bhegad so hard that he stumbled away.

"Perhaps with not so much . . . verve." Bhegad removed his glasses, wiping them on his shirt. "As for the method of approaching the Loculus, I will leave that to you. So if everything is ready . . . Godspeed, my children."

Cass turned to Torquin. "Take good care of Leonard," he said.

"Like he was my own son, but a lizard," Torquin said. He put one of his fleshy hands on my shoulder, another on Cass's. "Have fun. Chisel us a postcard."

He snorted and wheezed in his Torquinian version of a laugh, and I knew he'd been practicing the joke all day.

I turned toward the Euphrates. Aly squeezed my hand briefly. I checked my pocket and felt the outline of a small hand mirror. It was a present I'd made my mom in second grade, lacquered on the back with a photo of her, Dad, and me playing in the snow. Since my conversation with Aly on the tennis court, I'd decided I wanted it with me at all times. Seeing the photo gave me hope and strength.

We ran until the water was too deep. I closed my eyes and jumped.

* * *

"Haaaa!" Marco yelled, tumbling out of the river on the Ancient Babylon side. He reached in and pulled Cass ashore. "Getting better at figuring where to come out!"

Cass was gasping for breath. "I don't know . . . how many more times . . . I will be able to do this."

Aly and I swam to the bank. The trip through the portal had been smooth. Much quicker than the last time. Marco was right. We were getting good at this.

I sat on a rock to catch my breath. It was dark but the moon was bright, and it took me a moment to remember that even though we'd been gone four days, only a little more than an hour had passed in Ancient Babylon.

Marco was running around, collecting rocks the size of his biceps. He pushed each one into the sand until the rocks formed a large lambda shape. "I know Brother Cass can memorize this stuff, but ordinary Immortals like me need a marker." Marco paused to look proudly at his handiwork, then began pulling the uniforms out of his pack. "Okay, campers, remember the drill. We find Daria and tell her how important this mission is. How we are trying to help the rebels by preserving Babylon. We talk her into going to the royal gardens with us. We wear some kind of disguise.

We're her cousins who don't speak Aramaic. If Crag-face is gone, we're in. If he's not, we get him with the darts and then go for the Loculus. Easy-peasy, lemon-squeezy."

"That is such a dumb expression," Aly said.

Cass, Marco, and I walked off behind a dense thicket to change into the tunics. I folded my clothes up and put them in a pile. At the last minute, I fished out the mirror and took a long look at the photo. Carved into the wood below it was my happy birthday message. Dad had inscribed the back of the photo, and over time his message had started to bleed through.

Martin, Anne, and Jack—Happy McKinleys!

Marco was looking off into the bushes. "So. Guys. You get a head start. I'll follow. I—I think I just ate too much for lunch."

"You have got to be kidding," Aly said. "Again? What's with you?"

"What do you mean, *again*?" Marco asked.

"This happened at the palace," Aly said. "The time shift affects your digestive system and no one else's."

"I'm human, all right?" Marco said. "Just go. Now. Trust me, you guys won't want to be downwind of me for about a hundred yards."

"Good point," Cass said.

We bolted. Marco was Marco.

It was a short trek out of the wooded area and onto the side of a large field of grain. The moon had sunk toward the horizon, and the sky had a predawn glow. I caught the comfy whiff of a wood-burning fireplace, which reminded me of home—until I realized it may have been the lingering scent of Kranag's destroyed cottage.

Even in the dim moonlight I could see signs of the earthquake damage we'd caused—gullies running through the field, cracked earth, a wooden hut caved in on one side. People were running in and out of the city via the moat bridge, under the watchful eye of the tower guards.

We fell in with the crowd and snuck through the gate. I'm not sure if the tower guards saw our faces or not, but there was more than enough chaos to keep them busy.

The streets of the outer city were still damp. Some roofs had been blown off, and carts lay broken and abandoned.

In and out of alleyways, people chased animals that had run loose during the storm. We trudged for about a half hour before we reached the higher gate—the one to the inner city and Etemenanki, the Tower of Babel. The air had the silvery glow of early morning now, and I was starting to worry about Marco. "Should we wait here for Superman?" I asked.

"He probably took a shortcut," Cass said. "I bet he's at the cottage already."

Aly nodded. "Any reason to gloat."

The rising sun showed a market in chaos, with people passing buckets of water. The souk stand where the guards had eaten lamb earlier was a smoldering pile of charred wood. I hoped desperately that no one had been hurt. I felt guilty. We'd caused this.

The burning smell hurt my eyes as we walked up the sloped street toward Etemenanki. I thought we might be stopped at the entrance to Ká-Dingir-rá, the palace grounds. But to our relief, the guards nodded politely as we entered. Aly led the way, charging up the street. Cass and I nearly collided with three *wardum* children who ran out of an alleyway chasing some kind of bird that looked like a chicken.

Aly stopped short at the corner to the road that led to our guest house. She held up a finger and mouthed, "Wait!"

We came up beside her carefully. Up the road, a clutch

of soldiers had gathered out front of the guest house, with Daria in their midst. Marco was nowhere to be seen.

Daria caught a glimpse of us and shook her head in a way that meant *stay away*. We backed down the road, out of sight of the house. Quickly I led us into the alley where the little kids had emerged. "I don't like this," Cass said. "Those guards were mad. We're fugitives. We caused mass destruction!"

"They don't know we did it," Aly reminded him.

"Right, but they know we escaped," Cass said.

I spotted a blur coming around the street corner. Daria's face peered out of a shawl. She waved. She ran to us, her features taut with concern. "Where is Marco?" she asked.

"He went to the bathroom," Cass said.

"He is taking bath?" Daria asked.

"Long story," Aly said.

Daria nodded. "But you—why are you here? I left you at Mother's Mountain. Were you caught in the earthquake?"

I glanced at Aly. "Sort of," I said. "We ran away."

"It is bad here," Daria said. "Bab-Ilum needs much fixing. King wants all guards to help. He sent his men to get your house guards. They do not remember the darts that put them to sleep. But they are angry you left. Did you get what you needed?"

"No," I replied. "We have to go back."

"Go back?" Daria said. "This is not possible."

"We have no choice," I said.

"Please, get it another place!" Daria pleaded. "Did the guards at the garden see you? If they know your faces, they will be cruel. They will not let it happen twice."

"Daria, I don't know how to say this," I said. "I know this is hard to believe. But we're sick, and we will die unless we get something from that garden. Something we can't get anywhere else."

Daria's eyes softened. "You are sick?" she asked. "Marco, too?"

"We do not have long to live," I said. "Unless we accomplish our task."

Daria looked away. "Yes, well . . ." she said softly. "The Garden is full of wonders. I, too, have a friend who was once dying. I . . . I stole something from a tree . . . a fruit . . ."

"So you understand," I said. "You'll help us?"

Daria tightened her shawl. She glanced toward the guest house, her face showing a mixture of fear and uncertainty. "Stay here. Do not let the guards at the house see you. I will return."

As she ran off, Aly and Cass sank to the ground, exhaling with relief.

I looked back the way we'd come. I could see through the gate and down a long, sloped path to the city plaza.

Marco was nowhere in sight.

CHAPTER THIRTY-NINE

HIS JACKNESS

"GOOD EVENING FROM WBAB news," Cass whispered. "We have reports of a small stink bomb near the Euphrates that nuked all wildlife within a hundred-yard radius."

"Har . . . har . . . har," Marco drawled, rowing us slowly across the river toward the Hanging Gardens. The sun was now above the horizon, giving us a hint of the sweltering day to come.

"The river reversed course, and the leaves shriveled and fell from trees," Cass continued. "The soil was declared a toxic waste site—"

Marco flipped up the oar and splashed Cass with water. "Whoops."

"Will you two grow up?" Aly hissed.

Cass was trying not to giggle. "Sorry, I just never saw

anyone take so much time to—"

"I got lost, all right?" Marco said. "I wasn't born with a GPS inside me."

"There must not be much of anything left inside you now," Cass said.

But Marco didn't answer back. He was looking intently at the shore. The boat made a gentle *shhhh* as it scraped against the sandy bottom. Cass's smile vanished as he stared up the slope toward the Hanging Gardens. I jumped out in the shallows and pulled us onto the sandy soil.

Daria stood slowly, glancing nervously at us. "I must convince them you are here to help with the earthquake damage. Hide your faces."

She had brought us shawls, and we each pulled them over our heads. Daria scurried up the hill. The gate looked abandoned, but immediately a guard appeared. His face was sweaty, his arms dirty. He'd obviously been working on repairs.

We watched quietly as she spoken to him in a language that didn't sound Aramaic. "How does she pick up so many languages?" Aly whispered. "She's a genius."

"Like you with tech," Cass said. "Not to mention me with directions, and Marco with sports, and Jack with . . . his awesome Jackness."

I ignored the comment. I didn't want to think about how lame my Jackness really was. At the moment I was too scared to start feeling sorry for myself.

"You still have Shelley?" Aly asked.

"Locked and loaded," Marco replied, patting his shoulder bag.

That's when I noticed Marco's tunic was on wrong. "You put that on backward," I said.

"Huh?" Marco answered.

"Wait, you actually removed your tunic?" Aly asked. "You couldn't keep it on while you—?"

"Aly, please . . . TMI!" Cass whispered.

The guard was raising his voice at Daria. He gestured angrily toward the Hanging Gardens. I could see that the upper level had been badly damaged by the quake. Its beautiful stone-columned crown was now rubble. Maybe half of the trellises on all levels were still intact. But Daria was talking calmly, nodding. I could see a tear running down the side of her face.

As she turned and walked toward us, she began singing softly. Beautifully.

The guard's body seemed to sag as he listened.

"She's a good actress, too," Marco said.

"I think the word is *manipulative*," Aly said.

"But it's for a good cause," I pointed out.

Looking exasperated, the guard came stomping toward us. Daria looked levelly at him, then let out a whistle—the three-note rebel signal.

The guard paused as he reached us. He peered curiously at our faces, then reached out and pulled off my hood.

His impassive face grew angry-looking. He muttered something I couldn't understand, then pulled off Cass and Aly's hoods.

As he reached toward Marco, Marco grabbed the guard's hand. "Say 'please.'"

The guard's eyes grew wide. He shouted back to the other guards.

"He recognizes you," Daria called out. "He saw you, when you left during the earthquake. He is angry that you sneaked in, even more angry that you ran away without helping. And Marco—"

"Sorry," Marco said. "That guy bugged me."

At the gate, two guards with long spears stood tensely.

"What do we do now?" Aly said.

"My favorite thing," Marco said, crouching into what looked like a football stance. *"Charge!"*

I couldn't believe it. He was running up to the gate, shouting wildly. He was also unhooking his pack—the pack that contained the emergency weapons Professor Bhegad had given us.

One of the guards chuckled. Both of them raised their spears and threw. The shafts bulleted toward Marco. He let go of the pack. But instead of falling to the ground, he stood, chest out.

"Duck!" I shouted.

I flinched as the spears converged toward Marco's torso.

At the last moment his right hand lashed out. Then his left. He turned, stumbling backward from the impact. I was sure they'd skewered him.

Dropping to one knee, Marco straightened his back and lifted both arms over his head.

He'd snatched the two spears in midair. "Two outs," he announced.

Aly gasped. "That boy is going to give me a heart attack."

The guards' mouths hung open in astonishment. I was too focused on them to notice Daria's guard, who had unsheathed a sword and was rushing Marco from behind.

"Marco!" Daria cried out.

Marco turned quickly. Too quickly. The spears he was holding clacked against each other behind his back. They were pointed in the wrong direction. He dropped one and struggled to turn the other around.

The guard was on him in an instant. He raised his sword and swooped it in a sidearm swing—directly to Marco's neck.

"No-o-o-o!" Aly screamed.

I dived. I wasn't going to make it. A scream ripped from my throat, and my eyes averted instinctively away from the horror. But not before I saw something black hurtling from the left toward the guard. A sharp *clank*. A spark.

In mid-stroke, the sword flew from the guard's hand. It clattered harmlessly to the ground, far from Marco. The man shouted out in shock. He turned toward where the missile had come, the grove of trees by the river.

I saw a flash of green. Then another. Then two more, heading up toward the gate.

The guards all fell to their knees, clutching their necks.

Footsteps crunched over the rocky soil. Zinn emerged from the undergrowth, followed by Shirath, Yassur, and a small group of lean, strong-looking *wardum*. "Whoa," Marco said. "Thanks, guys."

They nodded toward Marco, but their eyes were on Daria. Zinn seemed full of questions. Daria spoke to them quickly. Her voice became tight, as if she were arguing. Finally she turned to us. "They do not understand what you are doing. It is dangerous to try to go to Mother's Mountain. If you are on the side of the rebels, why do you do this alone?"

I took a deep breath. "Zinn has a point, Daria," I said. It didn't make sense to hide the truth anymore. "Okay, there is something inside Mother's Mountain. It's called a Loculus and it was stolen from a place called Atlantis. Its magic cut you off from the rest of the world and created Sippar. But what was stolen must be returned, Daria. Its absence has caused many people to die young. We will be next, if we don't succeed."

"We tried to remove the Loculus," Cass added. "But that's what caused the earthquake. Now we have a new plan. An empty Loculus of our own. We need to get it near yours, to connect the two. We will take some of what's inside. Just enough. That's what we really need. So

259

the Loculus will stay. It will fill with more energy, the way a person makes more blood after they're injured. And Babylon will continue to exist."

Daria contemplated what we'd said. She turned toward the rebels and explained. They listened impassively, skeptically. Zinn especially seemed to have a lot to say.

Finally Daria turned to us and asked, "Zinn would like to know if Sippar is in your world."

"No," I said, shaking my head toward her and toward the rebels. They murmured among each other, and Yassur blurted something out.

"They want to know," Daria said, "if we help you, will you allow us to see your world?"

"I can't promise that—" I began.

"Yes!" Marco chimed in. "Yes, we can. Get us in there, guys. Daria, tell them to help us. And we'll do whatever you want."

Cass, Aly, and I gave him a baffled look, but his eyes were intent on Daria. He smiled as she turned to the others and explained once again.

"How could you say that?" Aly hissed.

Marco shrugged. "How could I not?"

CHAPTER FORTY

MISSILES OF SPIT

I **STOOD AND** followed the others at the entrance gate. Zinn and the rebels ran inside. "Wait here," Daria said. "Zinn must be sure there are no more guards."

"*Arrr . . . !*" came a guttural cry deep in the garden. Then a sharp whistle.

"All clear," Daria said.

We sprinted over the lazy, winding paths. Daria led us to the inner wall, just inside which I could see a giant tree bowed with plump fruit. "When we are inside, Marco, take one of the pomegranates," Daria said. "They are magic and will heal you when you're sick."

Marco boosted us all up and over. He climbed last, snatching a pomegranate off the tree as we began to run.

The screaming of the vizzeet hit us like a fist of sound when we emerged into the plaza of the Hanging Gardens. They spilled from among the fallen columns and the cracked-open walls, arms flailing, teeth gnashing. Missiles of spit hurtled toward us like poison rain.

"Yeeeeah!" cried Yassur, dropping to the ground, his hand clutching his eye.

Zinn and Shirath fell to their knees. With quick, sure movements, they picked darts from pouches and began blowing them into the horde. A vizzeet hurtled backward with a keening scream. It knocked over another three, who panicked and began clawing the first. "They do not like confusion!" Daria shouted, her shawl pulled protectively over her head. "Very nervous!"

"We noticed!" I said.

The darts flew fast, tinting the air with green. As vizzeet fell upon vizzeet, Daria and I crawled over to Yassur. Daria pulled a leather pouch from the sash around his waist, held his head back, and began dripping a clear potion from the pouch into his eye. I grabbed Yassur's blowpipe, loaded it, and put it to my mouth.

The first three shots landed in the dust, but the fourth caught one of the mangy beasts in the shoulder. There were dozens of them now, as if the quake had knocked a whole new tribe of them out of their hiding place. Marco was on his knees beside me, pulling from his tunic pocket a set of matches, a balloon, a string, and a small flask.

"What are you doing?" Aly demanded.

"Kerosene from the KI!" he shouted, first wetting the string and then filling the balloon. He tied the end of the balloon tight and flung it toward the vizzeet. As it landed, just in front of them, he lit a match.

The flame shot along the soaked string. As the balloon exploded, the vizzeet retreated like a tide, rolling in the dirt, tumbling over each other. "Move!" Marco shouted.

We ran around the building. The carved oak doorway was shut fast. Marco reached the cubes first. "What's the combo again?"

I reached around him and pulled: *two . . . eight . . . five . . . seven . . . one . . . four.*

The door opened into blackness. We stood at the threshold, willing our eyes to adjust, glancing at the empty chamber that was not empty.

Shirath and Daria raced toward us. Zinn was right behind them, helping Yassur. Marco turned, holding out his arms. "There are traps," he said. "You cannot see them. We have to follow Cass. Narrow your shoulders."

Cass took a deep breath. He stood before the opening, his eyes scanning the floor.

From the back of the chamber I heard a soft click. The back door slowly opened. *Kranag.*

But the skeletal old man was nowhere to be seen. In his place was a flash of yellow eyes. A low-slung body walking on all fours. A sleek, scaly neck.

"Hello, Mooshy . . ." Marco picked up the spear he had taken from the guards. He reared back with his arm.

"No!" Daria shouted. "One has been killed already. You must not kill this one!"

Its feet blindingly quick and sure, the mushushu ran the jagged pathway around the traps and leaped toward me with its jaw wide.

Marco thrust the spear. Daria screamed.

The point caught the mushushu in its flank and passed right through. With a croaking cry, the beast fell to the ground at my feet. I caught a rush of stinking, warm breath.

Daria, Shirath, and Yassur knelt before the beast. The mushushu convulsed on the ground, its mouth wide open but emitting only a soft hiss.

Its face began to change before my eyes. Below the skin, bones seemed to liquefy, shifting position. The lizard snout contracted, the buggy eyes sank inward. As the face became more human, the body was wriggling into a different shape, too.

"No . . . " Daria said, her face twisted into an expression of such shock that it almost made her unrecognizable.

People said he could become an animal himself . . . Daria's words echoed in my head.

The mushushu was gone. Transformed.

We were staring into the face of Kranag.

CHAPTER FORTY-ONE

FALLING BACK

DARIA AND I knelt by Kranag. His mouth moved without sound, his papery-white face seeming to shrivel as we watched.

"Let's go!" Marco said.

He was looking nervously to our left. I could hear the approach of distant footsteps. Shirath, Zinn, and Yassur were lifting Kranag's body, taking it away from the front of the door.

In a moment I saw why.

Vizzeet began screaming, leaping down from the upper levels of the Hanging Gardens. Black birds swooped down out of nowhere. In a swarm, they descended on the lifeless body of the man who had controlled them.

I turned away. This was a party I did not want to see.

"That is disgusting," Cass said.

"Forget that!" Marco urged. "Get us back to the Loculus, dude."

Cass nodded. He turned and led the way into the chamber, zigging and zagging around the invisible traps. As we made our way to the back, Marco was sweating.

We were as careful as could be this time. This time, nothing shot at us and no gas tried to choke us. We felt our way around the cage and the spikes, which still jutted invisibly up from the ground.

"Okay, now," Cass finally said as we safely reached the rear wall.

Marco unhooked his pack and pulled out Shelley. Setting the trapezoid quickly on the ground, he gave it a sharp slap.

With a clunk, Shelley fell over onto the dirt. "It's not working," Marco said in disbelief. "Bhegad said all we had to do was tap it!"

From the pit, the eerie music washed over me. I could feel all my senses sharpening, my vision focusing. I lifted the metal contraption. It was heavier than I expected, but I held it over my head.

Then I dropped it.

It landed hard on the ground. With a loud *clang*, it popped to full size, bounced up off the stone floor. It hit me square in the nose. Like a rubber ball, only metal and magical.

As I cried out in pain, Marco caught it in midair.

I took it from him and held it high. It was dull and bronze and strangely translucent. As I brought it toward the pit, I could see through to the other side of it. Holding it steady, I leaned in to find the invisible Loculus.

The music intensified. I knew I was disappearing, even though everything around me seemed pretty much the same. I could tell by the looks on my friends' faces.

And by Daria's gasp. "Where is he?"

"Disappeared," Marco said. "But still here."

Daria reached toward me but she stumbled on the invisible lip of the pit. Losing her balance, she fell forward, her hand smacking against the surface of the Loculus. Instinctively I grabbed her arm. Screaming, she lurched away.

We both stumbled back into the room. Marco thrust his arm to keep us from falling back into a potential trap.

Cass and Aly were staring, dumbfounded. "Daria disappeared," Cass said.

"I know," I replied. "I touched her."

"Did you touch her right at the beginning?" Aly asked. "The moment she fell in? Because she vanished the moment she stumbled, Jack."

"She . . . she touched the Loculus," I said. "Are you telling me she vanished on contact? All by herself?"

Daria stared at me, then back at the now-invisible pit.

"What is this thing, Jack? I—I can no longer see it."

"Try to find it, Daria," Cass said intensely. "Show us what you mean."

Daria reached back toward the area and instantly dissolved to nothingness. "It is here!"

My mind was racing. "Daria," I said, "when you told me the story of Kranag's life, you said he came from a strange land. With some other people. A man with a strange mark. What did that look like? Do you know?"

"Nitacris spoke of it," Daria said tentatively, stepping forward and materializing again. "Two lines of gray. Coming to a point at the top. On the back of his head."

"Do you have it, Daria?" I asked.

"Why do you ask?" she said.

"Because we have it," I replied. "All four of us. We are covering it up with dye."

Daria looked at the floor. Slowly she lifted her arm and brought it around to the back of her head.

Then, for the first time since we'd met her, she removed the head scarf.

"I don't believe this . . ." Aly whispered.

On the back of Daria's head, amid the shock of red hair, was a white lambda.

Daria was one of us.

CHAPTER FORTY-TWO

THE MARK

"THAT INSANE LANGUAGE skill," Marco said. "It makes sense now. Daria's got G7W."

"She's also got a pedigree," I said. "Because G7W comes from the royal family of Atlantis. Which means King Uhla'ar and Queen Qalani."

Aly nodded. "Who had only two sons . . ."

"Daria," I said. "Your parents . . . what do you know about them?"

"Nothing," she said quietly. "I was a foundling. For my first years I lived on the streets, until I was taken into slavery. Nabu-na'id and Bel-Sharu-Usur often remind what a great kindness this was."

"It's got to be a lie," Aly said. "She has to be Massarym's

daughter. It's the only way she could have the mark."

"Or Karai's daughter," Cass offered. "Or the daughter of Queen Qalani's sister. Or King Uhla'ar's cousin. Or the brother's fifth cousin twice removed. Royal families can have a lot of people, Aly."

Outside the cavernous room, Zinn and the others were shouting. I could see them sinking to their knees, blow-pipes to their lips. Someone was coming.

"Forget the explanation," Marco said. "Let's go!"

I picked up Shelley. "How close do we need to get?"

But Shelley seemed to be giving me the answer. It began to pulse on its own, lifting upward, out of my palm and into the air. The Song of the Heptakiklos twanged through my body now. Marco, Cass, Aly, and Daria were cringing. They felt it, too.

I could no longer see the pit's smoothly curved bottom. It was covered with a gaseous plasma of light, ebbing and swelling like a living cell. Before my eyes the contours of the Loculus began to form into a translucent sphere, a bright storm cloud of visible energy.

On the shining metallic rim of the pit, a red tile flared like the flash of a camera. Then the next one did, too, and the next and the next, until the light was circling the rim in a spinning pattern that zapped Shelley with electric jolts like lizards' tongues. Inside, the ball of gas swelled steadily to fill the shape of the Loculus.

Shelley's hinged metallic surface was becoming smooth. It changed colors, its dull brown growing silvery, until the two shapes were mirror images. When they were nearly touching, a shadowy bruise grew on the Loculus and another on Shelley—two blue-back shadows facing each other.

The plasma boiled violently as they came closer. It gathered below the bruise, pushing at it, then finally breaking through. The boom rocked the chamber, knocking us off our feet. The Atlantean energy blasted out of the black circle and into Shelley's, with a force so strong I thought the contraption would vaporize.

"It's working!" Cass said.

I could no longer see Zinn and the others outside. But I could hear yelling and a clash of metal. "What's happening out there?"

"Must be more guards," Aly said.

The Loculus was heating up, vibrating like crazy. I heard a bloodcurdling scream outside. A rebel slid across the pathway just outside the door, bloodied and screaming. "How many guards are there?" Cass asked.

Marco was staring at Shelley. "How long before this thing turns green?" he asked.

"An hour," I replied.

Aly looked nervously at the door. "We won't have that long!"

"No," Marco said. "It's not supposed to happen this way. The timing is all wrong."

"What's not supposed to happen?" I asked. "Timing of *what*?"

"Come on, Shelley babe, turn green," Marco said, shaking it roughly. *"Turn green!"*

"Leave it alone, Marco!" Cass shouted.

I grabbed Marco's arm. I was afraid he'd break the mechanical Loculus. "What has gotten into you? Let it do its work!"

Dropping his hands, Marco stepped back. He glanced over his shoulder toward the commotion outside. Behind him, Shelley was starting to make noises. To vibrate jerkily.

"Okay, guys," he said, "you know who brought this Loculus here, right? I mean, the legend is pretty clear. . . ."

"Duh, Massarym, the evil brother of Karai," Aly said. "This is no time for a history lesson, Marco—"

"And what did he do?" Marco demanded.

"Stole the Loculi and hid them in the Seven Wonders!" I shouted.

"He did it because Karai wanted to destroy them!" Marco said. "Karai was mad at his mom, Qalani, for doing what she did. And he had a point. Isolating the Atlantean energy into seven parts was bad. It upset the energy balance. But Karai was too dumb to realize that destroying the Loculi would nuke Atlantis."

273

"Marco, Atlantis was nuked anyway!" I said.

"Why are we talking about this now?" Aly demanded.

"Don't you see?" Marco said. "Karai was wrong. If he'd just left the Loculi alone, he and Massarym could have done something. Repaired them. Adjusted the energy. Whatever. The smartest minds in the history of the world lived in Atlantis. But Massarym couldn't convince his bro, so he *had* to take the Loculi—"

A shadow moved into the light. At the doorway, across the width of the cavern, stood a tall man in a simple brown robe, his face shrouded by a hood, his feet in simple leather sandals.

I had seen a similar outfit before—many of them—on a hillside full of monks on the island of Rhodes in Greece. Monks who were protectors of the relics of the Colossus of Rhodes. Who called themselves Massarene, after the Atlantean prince they worshipped. Who, under the leadership of a guy named Dimitrios, had tried to kill us.

Cass and Aly backed away slowly as the man put his hand on either side of his hood and pulled it down. In the darkness, his salt-and-pepper hair looked mostly black.

It can't be. I stared at him, blinking.

"Brother Dimitrios?" Aly said.

"Well, well," the man replied in a heavily accented voice, "what a pleasure to be sharing such a rousing adventure with old friends."

"What are you doing here?" I demanded. "How can you possibly be here?"

As two other hooded figures moved into the torchlight, Brother Dimitrios said, "I would be rude if I did not introduce my colleagues, Brothers Stavros and Yiorgos. We are here to collect something we have sought for a long time."

Were they Select? Impossible! They were way too old.

He doesn't see the traps—the projectiles, the gas . . .

"Come and get us," I said with a smile.

Brother Dimitrios threw back his head and laughed. "Nice try, my boy. We know what's in here. You see, we have been briefed by one of the best. An expert at both access and intelligence. A young man with his heart and mind finally in the right place."

"You found another Select?" Cass asked.

"I didn't need to." Brother Dimitrios looked into the chamber and smiled. "Good work, Marco."

CHAPTER FORTY-THREE

THE BETRAYAL

"MARCO . . . ?" CASS SAID, his face bone-white.

Marco looked away.

I tried not to see that. I tried to tell myself that he was looking at the Loculus. That he would run safely through the booby-trapped room, lunge at Brother Dimitrios, and punch him in the face for his brazen lie. But he said nothing. No denial at all. Which meant he had betrayed us. The idea clanged around inside my head. It was impossible.

Daria looked utterly baffled. "Marco, who is this man? Is this your father?"

"No, it's a thief, playing a mind game!" Aly said. "Don't listen to him. He thinks we're dumb, gullible kids."

"Am I playing games, Brother Marco?" Dimitrios called from the door.

Marco looked away. "You're early," he mumbled.

"Beg pardon?" Dimitrios asked.

Sweat was pouring down Marco's face. "Remember what we said, dude? By the river? After I brought you here? My peeps were going to put Shelley in place and take the Loculus. I was supposed to have time to talk to them. About . . . the truth and all. Then I would signal you."

"Ah, my apologies," Brother Dimitrios said. "But circumstances have changed. The Babylonian guards are—*were*—more forceful than we'd anticipated. So if you don't mind, the Loculus, please."

My brain wasn't accepting Marco's words. He couldn't be saying them. It sounded like a cruel joke. Like some evil ventriloquist was using him to pull a prank on us.

"I don't believe this . . ." Aly murmured, her eyes hollow. "Marco, *you* brought them here. You've gone over to the Dark Side."

"You can't have the Loculus," I said. "Absolutely not. We need to wait for Shelley to work. If you remove the Loculus too early, all bets are off for Babylon. This place will be sucked up into oblivion. Wiped off the face of the earth. Tell him, Marco!"

Daria stared at her. "Oblivion? What does it mean?"

"It is the place where Babylon is headed, unfortunately," Brother Dimitrios said. "Where it should have gone, centuries ago, in the proper passage of time. This city exists outside of nature. You've had several free millennia, happy and content, while millions of deaths have occurred in the rest of the world." He looked at each of us, one by one. "And as for Shelley, based on the writings of an nineteenth-century crackpot? I hate to disappoint you, but it is a comic-book contraption, nothing more. It cannot possibly work."

Marco was looking guilty and confused, his eyes darting toward the back of the chamber. We all stood speechless, our brains racing to provide some sort of meaning to all of this. "You brainwashed him," Cass said.

"It wasn't *brainwashing*, Brother Cass," Marco said. "I mean, think about it from his point of view. We total his monastery. We destroy the thing the monks had been guarding for years, right? Then we fly away, in full sight. So he tracks us to the hotel. And when I leave with the Loculus, he's there. On the beach."

"So what you told us was a lie!" Cass said.

"I left some things out, that's all," Marco said, "because you guys weren't ready to hear it. Look, at least Brother D didn't kidnap me, dude. Bhegad did that. Brother D didn't take me from my home and stick me on a deserted island. The Karai Institute did that. Dimitrios? He just *talked* to me. About Massarym. About the snow job Bhegad has given us. About what the KI is really up to. He said, hey, go home if you want. He wasn't going to force me to do anything—even after all the bad things we did to the monastery. But hearing the truth really knocked me out. I knew

278

I couldn't go home. Not yet. Because now we have a new job to do."

"But . . . the tracker . . ." Aly said.

"We have ways of controlling those signals," Brother Dimitrios said. "They are blocked by trace amounts of iridium. A patch, placed anywhere on the body, will do the trick."

"Yes . . . iridium . . ." Aly's face was wan. "So you listened to him, Marco, there in Rhodes. You came to Iraq and went looking for the Loculus. You figured out that only Select could pass through the portal. But then, after our discovery, with Leonard, you saw your opportunity to bring these guys through."

"The morning after your treatment," I cut in, "you went for a jog. The KI couldn't find you."

Marco nodded. "I used that iridium patch. Brother Dimitrios was camped about five kilometers north of the KI camp."

"So while Cass, Aly, and I were recovering from our treatments, you had a secret meeting with these guys and told them we'd found the Loculus," I barreled on. "And the extra good news that you could transport them to Ancient Babylon."

Aly's eyes were burning. "You used us, Marco. You lied. When you told us to go on ahead, because you had to relieve yourself—"

"You were bringing these guys over!" Cass blurted out.

Brother Dimitrios chuckled. "This is the excuse you gave them?"

"Okay, it was lame," Marco said. "Hey, it was hard work, guys. I had to move fast. Don't look at me like I'm a serial killer, okay? I can explain everything—"

"And we will, on the way," Brother Dimitrios interrupted.

"On the way *where*?" Aly demanded.

Marco opened his mouth to answer, but nothing came out. Brother Dimitrios was glaring at him. Brother Yiorgos handed him a sturdy metal box. He flipped open the lid. It was empty inside, and just big enough to hold a Loculus. "Bring it to me. It's time."

Marco turned, lunging toward the invisible orb.

I don't remember if I cried out. Or what exactly I did. I only remember a few things about the next few moments. Shock. The weight of Marco's invisible body against mine as he rushed to the door with the Loculus.

He knocked me off my feet. I hit the ground next to Shelley, which had not turned green. Nowhere near.

"Watch it!" Aly screamed, as a shower of bronze knives dropped from the ceiling. I rolled away as they clattered to the ground.

Marco had managed to run straight through, his reflexes quicker than gravity.

"Follow me!" Cass said.

"Wait," I said, looking down at the wheezing bronze sphere known as Shelley. It looked pathetic to me now. *A comic-book contraption.*

Maybe not. Picking it up, I dropped it into the pit. As it clanked sadly to the bottom I turned to go. "Okay, Cass, get us out before the place blows."

He led us back out through the booby-trapped room. We were all so numb with shock we barely paid attention to where we put our feet. It was a wonder we didn't get nailed by a new trap. Or maybe by now we'd sprung them all.

A moment later we were outside. We stared into the faces of several more Masserene monks, at least a half-dozen of them. But Marco and Brothers Dimitrios, Stavros, and Yiorgos were nowhere to be seen. "Where did they go?" I demanded.

The ground shook. An Archimedes screw toppled to the ground in a shower of dust and water. Vizzeet were scattering to the winds, leaving behind the rags and bones that were once Kranag. Black clouds roiled angrily in the sky, lit by flashes of greenish lightning.

The monks stood stock-still. From all sides, the rebels were advancing. Most of them held blowpipes to their lips. Zinn was screaming at Daria, and Daria shouted back to them.

"What are they saying?" I asked.

"They think these men are your people," Daria said. "I explained they are the enemy. Oh, yes—one other thing."

"What was that?" I asked.

"I told them to fire away." Daria pulled me forward with all her strength. I held tight, racing through the garden grounds. Behind us, I could hear the groans of Massarene monks as they fell to the ground. Lightning flared, and a massive ripple ran through the ground, as if a giant beast had passed just underneath our feet.

We scaled the inner wall, dropping to the other side. As we landed, I heard the crack of gunfire.

"No!" Aly cried out. "We have to go back! They're killing the rebels!"

But the wall itself was crumbling now. We had to run away to avoid being crushed.

I looked back through the opening and saw the Hanging Gardens of Babylon collapse into a cloud of black dust.

CHAPTER FORTY-FOUR

YOU HAVE TO LEAVE

WE RAN ACROSS the furrows of grain. A farmer screamed as a team of oxen dropped into the earth, out of sight. We fell to the ground, barely missing the crack that grew across the soil like a grotesque opening zipper.

"Stop here!" Marco's voice cried out.

He materialized at the edge of the farm, not twenty yards in front of us. "Go through the city and directly to the river!" he shouted. "I'll take the old guys and come back for you!"

He grabbed a satchel from Brother Stavros's shoulder and pulled out a glowing Loculus. A visible one. The one we'd taken from Rhodes. Marco must have dug it up when he was bringing the Massa in.

When he was betraying us.

He knelt again and vanished. I saw the satchel bulge and realized he was storing the invisibility Loculus. As he materialized once more, the three Massarene gathered around him and put their hands on the flight Loculus. Together they rose high above the farmland. The men let out frightened shouts, scissoring their legs like little kids. In another circumstance, it might have looked funny. But not now. Not when we'd been betrayed by one of our own.

Not when we were destroying an entire civilization.

"He . . . he is truly a magician . . ." Daria said, looking up at Marco in awe. "Will he be safe?"

"Don't worry about him!" I said. "Let's go!"

Daria and I ran together across the field, with Cass and Aly close behind us. Daria looked bewildered but determined. How little she knew.

The Ishtar Gate was looming closer. One of the moat walls had cracked, and a crocodile was climbing out onto the rubble. It eyed Cass and Aly as they took a wide berth around it. The turrets of the gate were empty. One of them had partially collapsed. As we sprinted through the gate's long passageway, we had to shield our heads from falling pieces of brick. We burst out the other side into utter chaos. The stately paths of Ká-Dingir-rá were now choked with fallen trees. Boars, fowl, and cattle ran wild, followed by guards with bows and arrows. I saw mothers scooping up children and running into houses with broken doors, teams of *wardum* carrying the injured away from harm.

"Daria," I shouted as we ran, "you have to leave this city! It's not safe any longer."

"This is my home, Jack!" she replied. "And besides, I can't—Sippar will stop me."

"The mark on your head—we have it, too," I said. "It gives us special powers. We can take you through Sippar. To safety!"

We were approaching Etemenanki now, the turnoff to the *wardum* houses. I felt Daria let go. "I must help Nitacris and Pul!" she shouted.

"You can bring them with you!" I said, following after her. "And your other friends—Frada, Nico. If they hold on to you and don't let go, they can come, too!"

She stopped. "Go, Jack. You must think of yourself. We will follow if we can."

"You have to come now," I insisted. "Later may be too late!"

She shook her head. "I cannot leave them, Jack. As you can never leave Aly and Cass."

It hurt to hear her leave out Marco's name. And it hurt more to know I could not change her mind.

"You promise you'll follow later?" I asked.

I felt Cass pulling me from behind. *"What are you doing, Jack? Run!"*

"Go out the nearest gate," I shouted to Daria. "Keep going until the trees begin, then head for the river. Look for the rocks arranged like a lambda—the shape on the back of your head. When you dive in, head for a glowing circle and swim through to the other side! Anyone who is touching you can come through with you. Will you remember that?"

A loud boom knocked us to our knees. The top of Etemenanki tilted to one side. A crack ran from the top level downward, slowly widening, spewing dried-mud dust. I could see courtiers racing out of the building.

"Jack! Cass!" Aly's voice cried out.

"You must leave, Jack—now!" Daria shouted.

"Promise me you'll remember what I just said!" I shouted.

"I will," Daria replied. "Yes. Now go!"

Now Aly was pulling me, too. I shook her and Cass loose. Daria was running back to her quarters. For a moment I thought of running after her.

"Jack, they'll be all right!" Aly said. "I don't believe Brother Dimitrios. Either Shelley will work, or Daria will come through the portal."

"How can you be sure?" I said.

She drew me closer. "You and I have a lot to do still. If the Massa gets ahold of the Loculi, there will be more deaths. Us, for example. I will not lose you, Jack. I refuse."

I looked over my shoulder. Daria had disappeared around the corner. "Okay," I said. "Let's book."

We raced through the city streets. By now they were a catalog of damage and destruction—roofs blown off houses, milk cans strewn about, injured animals screaming. I saw an old woman sitting against the side of a house, cradling a man in her arms. I had no idea if he was dead or alive.

When we arrived at the river edge, Brother Dimitrios and the Massarene were already there. They seemed fewer in number, thanks to the actions of the rebels. But as far as I was concerned, one Massa was too many.

The Loculi had been packed in two satchels. The Massa had them now. We had lost, and we would have to deal with it.

"I'm going to bring these guys through, two by two," Marco said. "It'll take a few trips. Or you guys can help me."

Aly, Cass, and I stood on the riverbank with our arms folded.

"I will stay for last," Brother Dimitrios said, giving us a stern glance. "To make sure all goes as planned."

With a shrug, Marco held out his arms. Brothers Yiorgos and Stavros held on tight. Together they ran into the water.

* * *

I don't remember much of the trip, except that I burst through to the other side near one of the monks Marco had apparently just pulled through. He was gasping with panicked high-pitched squeals, like a little kid. "Okay . . . I'm okay . . ." he kept saying.

287

I could see Cass, Aly, and Marco bobbing on the river, not far away. I trod water, catching my breath. Testing my body for symptoms of sickness. What if we were to collapse right now, the way we had last time we came back from Babylon? Where was the KI?

I looked downstream, to where I knew the compound would be. All I saw were piles of blackened canvas and debris.

On the riverbank, Brother Stavros had sidled over to keep an eye on me. "What did you do to the KI compound?" I demanded.

"We had to take action," Brother Yiorgos shouted.

"Action?" My stomach sank. The water temperature seemed to drop twenty degrees. I scanned the shore but saw no signs of life. "Are they alive?"

"Never mind," Yiorgos said. "Come to shore."

Professor Bhegad . . . Torquin . . . Fiddle . . . Nirvana. What had happened to them? Had they escaped? Been taken prisoner?

I didn't want to imagine the worst. I never thought I'd feel so much for the people who'd captured me in the first place. But compared to the Massa, the KI seemed like a bunch of happy aunts and uncles.

We were near a stretch of riverbank, barren but for a dusty, new-model van. "I would advise you to swim with us," Brother Dimitrios called out. "The vehicle is very comfortable on the inside. And quiet. We will have much to discuss."

Yiorgos was swimming toward me, looking suspicious, as if I were going to swim away—to what? No one was there to rescue us now. "I'm coming," I grumbled.

Marco was already near the shore, holding tight to Cass. Aly wasn't far behind. I swam hard against the current. Each time my face lifted out of the water, I noticed the empty, peaceful opposite shore. It was hard to imagine that right now, in a dimension we could not see, a ziggurat was falling in super slow motion. The earth was opening up, fires were spreading, and an entire city was on a crash course with destruction.

After Sippar busted up, what would happen to Babylon? Would it be pulled apart like taffy, exploded like a bomb—or just vanish into space? We knew that time had split almost three millennia ago. But how did time de-rift?

And where was Daria?

I glanced backward. If she took an hour to reach the shore in Babylon, she would show up a week and a half from now. I'd be long gone. She would emerge into a world beyond her most bizarre imaginings.

If she came.

"Brother Jack!" Marco shouted. He and the others were walking in waist-deep water now. As I let my body drop and my feet touch the sand, I could see three more Massarene on

289

the shore. They looked almost laughable in their brown robes and sandals, carrying rifles in hand. But no one was smiling.

"If we run away, what will you do?" I said. "Shoot us? How will you explain that?"

"Dear boy," Brother Dimitrios said, "you do not want to find the answer to that, and neither do we."

"Give these guys a chance, Brother Jack," Marco urged. "You might be surprised."

Cass was staring at the remains of the camp downstream. Tears inched down his cheeks. *"Brother Jack . . ."* he said, practically spitting the words. "What do you know about brotherhood, Marco?"

Aly put her arm around his shoulder. The two of them turned to the van. I was in no hurry. My face felt funny, my chest as if it had expanded a whole other size. I looked back over the water, scanning the surface against all logic for another face. Hoping to hear another voice, accented with Aramaic, calling my name.

But I saw nothing.

Someday, I knew, I would have to forget. But I would never forgive.

CHAPTER FORTY-FIVE

AN EXPLANATION OF SORTS

TRAITOR.

Two-faced liar.

Monster.

The words tumbled through my brain each time I looked at the back of Marco's head. He was in the front seat of the helicopter, sitting between Brother Dimitrios and Stavros, who was the pilot. A sack and a box rested on the ground between Marco's feet, each containing a Loculus. To my right, in the backseat, were Yiorgos, Cass, and Aly. We were flying at breakneck speed. Stavros was a better pilot than Torquin, but not by much.

I was numb. I fiddled with the bracelet Brother Dimitrios had slapped on my wrist, secured with an electronic key. We all had them, bands that contained iridium alloy. The KI—whoever was left of them—would not be able to track us. I didn't really care anymore. All I could think about was the look on Daria's face the last time I saw her. The concern for the sick little boy, Pul. Like nothing else mattered. Like her world was not going to vanish after two thousand seven hundred years.

Marco was talking. Explaining. But his words drifted through the noisy chopper as if they were in some alien language. Now he was looking at us, expecting an answer. "Brother Cass?" he said. "Aly? Jack?"

Cass shook his head. "Didn't hear it, don't want to hear it."

"We trusted you," Aly added. "We risked our lives with you, and you were working for the enemy."

Brother Dimitrios turned to us. "I'm afraid we took you *from* the enemy, children," he said, shaking his head ruefully. "Crazy old Radamanthus and his pointy-headed Karai groupies . . . they have infiltrated your mind, haven't they?"

"Did you tell them about the KI, Marco?" Cass snapped. "Did you give up their secrets? You sold them out, too?"

"We still don't know their location," Brother Yiorgos said. "We can block the tracker signals—that's easy—but decrypting them is beyond our capabilities. Marco couldn't figure the KI location. But he said you might be able to."

"He was wrong," Cass said.

"I knew Bhegad, long ago," Brother Dimitrios said. "He was my professor at Yale. Not a good teacher, I'm afraid. He disappeared in mid-semester, leaving behind an odd note. He was going away to a secret think tank to determine the fate of the world! Genetic and historic consequences! Most scholars deemed it flat-out loony. It seems that while studying the works of Herman Wenders, Professor Bhegad came across the diary of Wenders's son, Burt. A deluded boy, feverish and about to die, who believed his father had found a secret island, the remnant of Atlantis. Legend has it that Wenders and his people set up a permanent base there, which only they could locate. It became the home of a secret Karai cult. The Dark Side." He chuckled. "Until now, I believed it to be a fiction. I thought old Radamanthus was dead."

"If they're the Dark Side, what are you?" Aly grumbled.

"Tell me, what did Bhegad say?" Brother Dimitrios went on, ignoring Aly. "That you will die unless the seven Loculi are returned to the Circle of Seven? Hmm?"

He knew about the Heptakiklos, too! "Did Bhegad leave that info in his note at Yale, or did a little bird tell you?" I asked bitterly.

Marco's face blanched.

"Before you were captured," Brother Dimitrios said, "back in your hometown, you'd begun experiencing tremors—

fainting spells caused by your genetic flaw. Then Bhegad whisked you away to this secret hideout. He keeps you alive, correct? He's devised some . . . *procedure*. Something that keeps you healthy temporarily. But alas, the cure comes only after all seven Loculi are returned. Am I right so far?"

His eyes bore into mine. All I could do was nod.

"And he's told you a story about a fair, golden-haired prince named Karai," Brother Dimitrios continued. "His mother, Queen Qalani, played god by isolating the sacred energy source into seven parts. This upset the balance, creating havoc in the land. So the good prince Karai sought to destroy the seven Loculi. But his evil brother Massarym—a dark young man, of course, because dark is the color of villains, yes?—stole them away, causing the entire continent to implode. Something like that, was it? And you believed this?"

"Think about it, dudes," Marco pleaded. "Think about how we felt when Bhegad told this story. Each of us tried to escape—and then we all tried together. But they were on to us. They brought us back and wore us down. So yeah, of course we came around—but not because we trusted him. For survival. Because we really didn't have a choice."

Cass and Aly were looking at the floor. None of us had a good response.

"Perhaps Prince Karai wasn't such a saint after all," Brother Dimitrios said. "Perhaps he was a foolish young man with a temper. Imagine if the saintly Karai had succeeded. He would have destroyed the Loculi, and the continent would have vaporized in an instant. Massarym took the Loculi away—for their protection."

"Marco already gave us this line," Aly said. "There's one problem with it. Atlantis *was* destroyed!"

"Destroyed?" Brother Dimitrios snapped. "Really? You saw the Heptakiklos, no? Marco took the waters there. He came back from death. You know very well that a part of Atlantis remains today. It was not vaporized. The Karai Institute colonized it. Our rightful home!"

"Massarym saved Atlantis from totally being eighty-sixed," Marco said. "Because he took the Loculi away. He hid them away for the future. For a time when people would know how to use them. Like now."

"Bhegad has lied to you," Brother Dimitrios said. "To him, people are a means to an end, that's all. Like this supposed cure? If he were concerned about a cure, he'd set out to make one. Like our scientists did."

"You have a cure?" I asked skeptically. "You've only known us since we kicked your butts in Rhodes!"

"No, we don't have a cure," Brother Dimitrios said simply. "I will not lie to you. I will always be direct. But we are working on one, and we're very hopeful. And we may indeed have just learned about you in Rhodos, but you must remember that the Massa have been around for a long while. Although we had not met any Select personally before you, we have always known about G7W."

Marco nodded. "These guys are the real deal."

"I don't care if they're Santa Claus and his elves," Aly snapped. "You broke our trust, Marco."

"We were family," Cass said softly. "We were all we had. And now we have nothing."

He was on the verge of tears. Aly was looking out the window in a cloud of funk.

But I was sifting through Brother Dimitrios's words in my brain. I had to admit, against all of my emotions, they made some tiny bit of sense.

I sat back in the chair, my head spinning. Was *I* being brainwashed?

Sleep on it, Jack. A problem that seems unsolvable always looks different in the light of a new day.

Dad's words. I don't have a clue how old I was when he said them. But they were stuck in my brain like a sticky note with superglue.

I glanced out the window. We were flying across the Arabian Peninsula, with the sun at our backs. Underneath us, the desert gave way to a great forked waterway. "There's the Red Sea," Yiorgos said. "We will stop soon to refuel."

"It's the ruins of Petra, to be accurate," Cass muttered. "Passing due west from Jordan to Israel . . . Yotvata . . . An-Nakhl . . . So I guess you're putting us on course for Egypt."

"Very impressive," Brother Dimitrios said. "Egypt is correct. The Karai are not the only ones with a secret headquarters. Theirs, apparently, is where the search for the Loculus ends. Ours is where it begins."

"And ours is actually *in* one of the oldest of the Seven Wonders," Yiorgos said proudly. "The oldest."

"The only one that still exists," Brother Dimitrios added.

Cass, Aly, and I shared a look.

We were heading for Giza, for the site of the Great Pyramid.

CHAPTER FORTY-SIX

HEADQUARTERS

THE GRAY JUNKER of a Toyota pulled to a stop. We had reached a small parking lot at the end of an access road that led from the highway. A sign at the turnoff read CAIRO: 14 KM. Behind us was an old minivan full of Egyptian Massarene. The security detail.

"Home sweet headquarters," Brother Dimitrios said with a smile. "I think you'll like Giza."

Aly, scrunched into the backseat between me and Cass, was drenched with sweat. Some of it was probably mine. Egypt was even hotter than Iraq. Out my window was a cemetery of modest tombstones that stretched to the horizon, disappearing into the desert. We had just passed a village of modern, squarish buildings.

Could we escape there? I sized up the distance. It would be a long run.

Brother Yiorgos opened the passenger door and I stepped out. I'd been so focused on escape I hadn't seen what was on the other side of the car.

The Valley of the Pyramids was nothing like the photos we'd seen in school. The stone structures were mountainous, higher than the Hanging Gardens. Their simple, no-nonsense lines made them somehow more powerful. They looked as if they'd heaved up from the sand by some violent force of nature. It made sense that this was the location of the only remaining Wonder. The pyramids seemed indestructible.

Three main ones towered over the desert landscape, their surfaces seeming to vibrate in the sun's heat. Smaller versions dotted the landscape, along with acres of rubble and ruins. In the distance, three tour buses were pulling into a parking lot, and throngs of camera-toting tourists made their way toward the Big Three. The Sphinx, to the right, sat quietly looking away, content to ignore it all.

"Monuments, like skyscrapers—all built for the pharaohs' corpses!" Brother Dimitrios said, getting out of the car. "Imagine! They make you into a mummy. They load you into an ornate chamber inside the pyramid, filled with treasures. There you stay forever, your spirit properly pampered. Because part of that spirit, the *ka*, was thought to remain

299

behind in the real world. And it needed to be comfortable."

"Kind of like a one *ka* garage," Marco said with a grin.

"That is so not funny," Aly muttered.

Brother Dimitrios began walking across the cemetery, gesturing for us to follow. "Only the Great Pyramid, the one farthest north, is considered to be one of the Seven Wonders. Naturally it's the largest of the three, built for the pharaoh Khufu."

"If it's a Wonder, it has a Loculus," I said. "Have you found it?"

"Alas, no," Brother Dimitrios said, flashing a smile. "But now we have a team of experts. You."

He stopped by a small wooden building, a hut with a rusted lock. Yiorgos began fumbling with keys. As we waited, Stavros's cell phone beeped and he turned away, taking the call. Behind us, several Massarene goons in black jackets were leaning against their minivan, smoking and looking extremely bored.

For the first time since we met the Massarene, we were alone and out of earshot. Aly leaned in to Cass and me. "I say we run," she said, looking toward the village. "We can do it."

"Aly, no," Cass said.

"They're distracted," Aly said. "They can't shoot us because they need us. They don't want to draw attention. The worst that can happen is they chase us. And we're faster than they are."

"This is not only impossible, but insane," Cass said. "I can't believe you're even thinking about it!"

"They won't be, either," Aly said. "That's exactly why it will work."

I sneaked a glance toward the village. Getting there would mean sprinting up the access road, across the main highway, and over an area about the length of three or four football fields. In full view of everyone. Aly was edging away from us, her eyes on the distant road. A loud guffaw erupted from the Massarene. Some dumb joke.

Aly was sweating. Her eyes were red. "I don't trust them," she said. "I don't trust any of them. Especially Marco. Marco is the enemy."

Cass gave me an uncomfortable look. Our friend was losing it. "Aly," I said, "you need some sleep. A problem that seems unsolvable always looks different in the light of a new—"

Aly lunged toward me and Cass and wrapped us both in a quick hug. "I love you guys!"

Before we could react, she bolted across the field, heading toward the main road. Her footfalls made small clouds in the dusty soil. Cass and I stood locked in astonishment.

"Get her!" Brother Dimitrios cried out.

Marco spun around from the wooden hut. "Is this a joke?"

He took off at a sprint. It was effortless for him. He was like a cheetah to Aly's pony.

At the road, the goons jumped into the car. It sputtered, wheezed, and finally coughed to life. Its tires spun, squealing on the blacktop.

Do something. Fast.

The car was to our right. It veered off the road, making a beeline for Aly, coming diagonally across the field. If Marco didn't get her, the goons would.

I ran forward, into the car's path, screaming at the top of my lungs. Waving my arms.

Marco looked back over his shoulder at the commotion. The driver honked, swerving to avoid me. I matched every move, staying in his path. "Jack, watch out!" Marco cried.

The goons were leaning on the horn now. I heard the squeal of the brake pads. I planted my feet, staring into the grille as it came closer. I saw my reflection in the chrome and shut my eyes hard.

The impact came from the left side. Marco knocked me off my feet, wrapping me in his arms. We flew into the air, thumped to the ground, and rolled. I saw the car spinning out of control, its two right wheels lifting off the ground. Brother Dimitrios, Yiorgos, and Stavros ran for cover as the rear bumper plowed into the small wooden hut with a dull boom.

The car came to a stop, impaled in the wall. For a moment nothing happened. Then a welling up of voices from inside the hut. People were flowing out now, examining the wrecked car, crowding around Brother Dimitrios and his two men. I heard his voice shouting "Get her!" People were thronging toward us from the road—Massarene goons, tourists, townspeople.

Marco sprinted away into the crowd, after Aly. But he didn't get far. I could see him stop cold, surrounded by people. I stood, looking into the distance.

Cass ran up beside me. "She did it," he said. "She really did it!"

I looked around. Marco was gone. Brother Dimitrios and his henchmen were lost in the crowd. "Let's go," I said.

We took off, into the chaos. Cass nearly barreled into a thin teen with a backpack. I swerved around a family of five with five cell-phone cameras. As I broke away, a tall man in a white outfit smiled placidly at me.

I barely saw the wooden stick before it made contact with the top of my head.

CHAPTER FORTY-SEVEN

RESURRECTION

I FIGHT THE Dream this time.

I don't want it. I need to wake up.

But it overtakes me with a swirl of gray-black, acrid smoke. I am running as fast as I can. I hear the screech of the griffin, the snarl of the vromaski. I know the end is near.

Who am I this time?

Which brother?

My stride is long, my legs thick. My arms are full. I am carrying papers. No, not paper. Long sheets of tree bark, ripped from the trunk, neatly stacked.

I plunge down a steep hill. My feet slip and I fall, head over heels. I land hard on my back against a bush. Its branches stab me in the neck, and I cry out.

304

Panting, I sit up. I have no time for delay. The thin sheets of bark are strewn about. Seven of them. Each one contains a sketch, made from charcoal. Two are of statues, a fierce warrior straddling a harbor and a Greek god. The other six: A magnificent tower beaming light into the sea. A tapered structure overflowing with flowers. A powerfully simple pyramid. A tribute to a goddess of the harvest. A tomb for the dead.

Seven Atlantean ideals, represented in statuary: Strength. Wisdom. Light. Beauty. Clarity. Rejuvenation. Respect.

They will stand forever, I think. We will die, but they will remind us. They will contain the seeds of hope. Of resurrection.

I gather them up and continue. I hear a sharp crack. The earth shakes. I know this feeling well. I know what happens now. The ground opens. But the crack is not beneath my feet. It's much farther below. At the bottom of the hill. Someone is falling into it.

This is how I know I am Massarym. For I am seeing Karai from above. And I scream at the sight of my brother disappearing.

A face appears before me. A woman I know.

She is floating.

As I look into her eyes, the forest dissolves. The trees fade to a wash of light green, the sounds mute, and nothing matters at all.

I call her name over and over and over.

CHAPTER FORTY-EIGHT

FRAGMENTS

"I DON'T THINK so."

I blinked upward into Cass's face. His hair was haloed by a fluorescent ceiling light. I was in a glaringly bright room with puke-green walls and a tiled floor. My arm was attached to an IV stand, and by the wall was a wheeled table with beeping medical machines. "Huh?" I said.

"You called me Mom. I said, 'I don't think so.'"

"Sorry," I said. "The Dream."

The fragments of images dispersed like fireflies at daybreak.

Cass smiled. He looked like a little kid with a guilty secret. "She made it," he said. "Aly. She disappeared into the crowd."

"Really?" I sat up and immediately regretted it. My head throbbed, and I shot my hand up to feel a bump that was swollen and hard as a handball. "Ow. That's amazing!"

"Yup, their knickers are totally in a twist over it," Cass replied. "Sorry. That's a Marco expression. But there's some hope. Maybe the KI will find her."

I sighed. "Not with that iridium band around her wrist."

"Oh," Cass said. "Right."

The door opened. Brother Dimitrios entered, wearing scrubs. "Welcome, Jack! So sorry about André; he got a little overeager with his stick. We will be sure to set him straight. So good to see you up and about."

"Wish I could say the same," I grumbled.

"I bring good news," he went on. "I know you must be concerned about your friend Aly's well-being. But not to worry. Naturally we know where she's gone, so I'm figuring a half hour . . . an hour, tops."

"You're lying," Cass piped up, then immediately burst into giggles. "I can't believe I just said that. Me, to a figure of authority. Ha! But it's true. I can tell. Your mouth—it's really . . . *thgit*!"

Brother Dimitrios's smile fell. Now I was laughing, too.

Our lives these days were all about traps. Trapped on the island, trapped into going to Greece, to Ohio, to Iraq. Trapped inside some dank underground evil headquarters. Aly had broken the spell. Even if it was for an hour, a few minutes—she had done it. She was free.

"Well, it seems we're in a giddy mood," Brother Dimitrios said. "This is good. You must think we're monsters. We're not. And we're not liars. You'll see. There is much to do, much to show you. Including a surprise or two. Come."

An orderly rolled a wheelchair into the room. Before I could say a thing, he lifted me into it and began rolling me down a hallway, following Brother Dimitrios and Cass.

We headed up a steep incline. The walls were painted with colorful murals depicting the building of the pyramids and the luxurious courts of the pharaohs. My good mood was slipping fast. It was bad enough to have been stolen away to a tropical island. I was just getting used to that. Now what? What were we supposed to do here? The place was clammy and cold and depressing. "Where are we?" I asked. "What happened to Marco?"

"I thought you'd never ask," Brother Dimitrios said. "This is an as-yet unexcavated pyramid. At first our archaeologists thought it would be an early one, a simple mound. These preceded the bench-shaped *mastabas*, which were in turn followed by the so-called step pyramids that looked something like layer cakes. But we have found this discovery to be easily the equal of the wondrous pyramids in this valley—all built to comfortably house the bodies of pharaohs and the queens, who would bless the land forever. And now it houses us!"

"Guess the blessing ran out," I murmured.

As we turned into another corridor, Brother Dimitrios had to duck under an uneven ceiling. "These particular pathways are original, thus a bit cramped. The pyramids seem rock solid from the outside, but they're built with many inner corridors. All the original paths are at an incline. The pharaoh could travel up or down—up toward the sun god, Ra, or down to the ruler of the dead, Osiris." He smiled. "Imagine, if you will, chambers stuffed with gold and jewelry—all designed to pamper the pharaoh!"

"Thanks for the history lesson," I said with a yawn. "But if you expect us to be super-excited about hanging with dead pharaohs or with you, sorry. And if you expect us to be brainwashed like Marco, sorry twice."

"You never told us where Marco is," Cass said.

"You're right, I didn't," Brother Dimitrios replied with a half-smile.

At the top of the incline was a big rotunda. We paused there. It was an impressive place with a polished tile floor. To the left and right were frosted glass doors leading to inner rooms. Straight ahead, at the opposite end of the rotunda, another pathway continued onward. The circular walls were painted with detailed scenes—a baby facing down a fierce griffin, a dark young hunter catching a vromaski with his bare hands, an old man surrounded by admirers on his deathbed. All from the life of Massarym, I figured.

But my eye was drawn to a portrait of a dark, bearded man sitting on a stone block, his fist on his chin as if in deep thought. Around him were images of the Seven Wonders, arranged like the Heptakiklos.

At his feet were seven sheets, each with a crude sketch of one of the Seven Wonders.

The breath caught in my throat. I'd seen those plans in a dream—a dream in which I was Massarym, and I had created them myself.

The orderlies wheeled us to the left, and Brother Dimitrios paused at a frosted glass door.

"Security clearance!" he announced.

A voice, odd and mechanical-sounding, boomed out from unseen speakers. "It's good to . . . see you . . . welcome!" it said in weird, jerky tones that crackled like a bad phone connection. ". . . to have you here . . . Jack and Cass."

Cass and I nodded. What were we supposed to do, thank him? Or her? Or it?

With a whoosh, the door opened into a room much vaster than I'd expected—an underground space the size of a supermarket. Greenish-white stalactite-like formations hung from a ceiling that was maybe twenty feet high. The floor was covered with mats, dividing the room roughly into four sections. In one of them to our left, two soldiers, a man and woman, were slashing at each other with swords.

To the right, deep into the room, four Massa spun and kicked furiously, their limbs churning the air—yet no one seemed to be touching the other. Like a choreographed game of chicken.

The third area, directly to our right, contained an iron cage. In it, a heavily scarred man faced off with a strange, cougarlike black beast. As it roared and charged, the man sprang upward into a flip, kicking his legs out against the bars and landing on the beast's back. In his left hand he held a dagger. I had to look away.

"This is where we train!" Brother Dimitrios had to shout to be heard over the din. "In the great, ancient tradition of the Massa. Because our followers are not Select, they must work extra hard. And they relish new challenges. Behold."

Brother Dimitrios clapped three times.

A sequence of movement began. First, the empty mat sank downward into the floor, like a stage effect, leaving a rectangular hole. Second, a wall of vertical iron bars lowered directly in front of us with a solid thump. It stretched left and right, from wall to wall, as if to separate and protect us from the room. Third, a door in the beast's cage opened.

The entire room stopped and fell silent—swordspeople, kick boxers, animal fighter. Even the beast stood watching, its eyes yellow and fierce.

Slowly, something began to rise up from within the big

rectangular hole. The beast bared its teeth and snarled. The fighters drew back their swords and the kickboxers tensed.

Shoulders . . . back . . . a lone figure, facing away from us, stood in the center of the rising mat. He was dressed in a brocaded uniform, his hair slicked to his skull, a lambda shape showing through.

He turned and smiled. His teeth gleamed, his eyes glowed. Energy poured off him with an intensity I could almost see.

"This place, Brother Jack," he said, "is the bomb."

"Massa," Brother Dimitrios said, "you may attack Marco."

CHAPTER FORTY-NINE

THE BEAST-TAMER

RRRAAAAAAAGGHH! **THE BEAST** leaped out of its cage at Marco. Its teeth glistened, its claws retracted. The sword fighters retreated to the wall.

Marco bent his knees. He sprang from the mat, flipping twice in the air. At the top of the leap, his hand whipped upward and knocked loose three or four stalactites.

They crashed to the floor, breaking into jagged pieces. Marco landed squarely among them. "Here, kitty kitty . . ." he said, scooping a spearlike fragment from the ground.

If he was afraid, he didn't show it. My heart had stopped. Cass had gripped my arm so hard his fingers were raising welts.

313

G7W. It was changing Marco by the day. He was no longer an impossibly amazing basketball player and swimmer. His reflexes, his strength, his confidence—it was all something more than human.

The beast leaped again, and Marco swung. The stalactite pierced the side of the creature and it yowled in pain. As it crumpled to the corner, the two sword fighters attacked.

As the first one struck, Marco lurched back, holding out the bloodstained stalactite. The sword split it with a dull crack. But Marco was directly in the path of the second fighter, who thrust her sword directly at his chest.

"Stop!" Cass yelled. I flinched and turned away.

When I looked back, Marco had arched backward at an angle that should have been impossible. His body was parallel to the floor. His assailant was flying clear over Marco's head, on a collision path with the giant black beast.

Staggering to its feet, the creature opened its mouth.

With astonishing speed, Marco snapped upright and hurled a piece of broken limestone toward the beast. The shard lodged in its mouth, jamming it wide open. As the beast howled in pain, the swordsman bounced off its muzzle and fell to the ground.

"You're welcome," Marco said to his erstwhile attacker.

With a thud, one of the kickers connected squarely with

Marco's jaw. He hadn't seen that coming. Marco stumbled backward, flailing his arms.

"No!" I cried out.

With an outstretched palm, Marco caromed off the wall behind him, jumping high. He hurtled toward the kickers, knocking two of them out cold.

The others whirled toward him like ninjas on steroids, their feet slashing the air like knives. Marco reached his left hand into the air. "Hip!" he said. Then the right hand. "Hop."

I gasped. He had two of them by the ankle. He threw them down to the mat, and they slid headfirst into the blood-spattered cage.

The beast-tamer was still huddled inside. All three hundred pounds of him stared at Marco in fearful silence.

"Amazing . . ." Brother Dimitrios muttered. "Absolutely breathtaking."

Marco stood there, looking around at the chaos. I watched him shake his head as if waking from a dream. "Dang," he said, "did I do *that*?"

* * *

I rolled my wheelchair back. The wall of vertical bars was raised up to the ceiling. Brother Dimitrios was congratulating Marco. Yiorgos commandeered a group of people to mop the floor. A team of burly guys in masks and armor tasered the beast and led it away.

"Extraordinary!" Dimitrios said. "What strength! What promise!"

Marco glanced my way with an amazed grin. He cocked his head and let out a animal-like roar. *"Woooooo–hoooo! I want to do this again!"*

"In due time, my boy," Brother Dimitrios said with a proud smile. "We will have great uses for all of your powers."

Marco was dancing around the room, shadow-boxing, kicking his legs. To him it was all about G7W. Our cool powers. The Massa were letting him loose with it. Turning his genetic skill into a killing game.

To him, this was more than fun. It was an addiction.

What did they have in store for the rest of us?

I stood from the wheelchair. I didn't need it. My head still hurt but I could walk. Cheers rang out from the battle room, which was now full of guards, medical people, animal wranglers. It was Marco Day at the Massa Headquarters. Everyone wanted a piece of the celebrity.

Behind us, the rotunda was empty. Totally empty. No one was minding the store. I quickly scanned the circular room and noticed a corridor to the left that appeared to be empty.

I edged backward. I pictured Aly disappearing into the crowd. She had managed to escape by bucking the odds. By showing courage. She had run when it seemed like a crazy thing to do.

Cass was backing up with me. I could tell we were on the same wavelength. "Ready?" I whispered.

"Ready," Cass said.

"Now!"

We turned and ran. As we sped into the corridor, I noticed a tiny marble-sized contraption on the ceiling. It began blinking red and white. "Hurry!" I called out.

I fought against the pain in my head. One foot in front of the other. The path inclined upward and forked. I chose left.

With a loud thump, a metal gate dropped from the ceiling, blocking my path.

Cass and I whirled around and bolted down the other pathway. We followed it as it curved sharply to the right, ending in a steep flight of stone stairs.

We took them two at a time. At the top, I stopped short.

Before us was a small chamber, lit with candles. In the center was a long wooden sarcophagus, lying on a stone altar. Inside was a tightly wrapped mummy.

"It's a dead end!" Cass said.

"There's got to be a way out," I said, creeping closer to the coffin. These guys were supposed to have free passage to visit the gods."

"Maybe there's a secret passageway," Cass said.

I noticed something glint from inside the mummy's eye slits. I leaned closer. The slits flashed red.

Sensors.

"Go!" I said, pushing Cass toward the door. "Just go!"

Below us, the floor shuddered. Hard. We fell to our knees and struggled to stand. But we were sinking fast. The entire room, mummy and all, was dropping downward into darkness.

CHAPTER FIFTY

A KILLING COMPANY

"HELLO, JACK."

My eyes blinked open. I had no idea where I was. The voice had come at me from all sides. The same kind of scrambled voice we'd heard earlier. I was lying on a sofa in a darkened room, with pillows on the floor and a flat-screen TV showing scenic vistas with soothing music. "You guys really get a kick out of knocking kids unconscious, huh?" I said.

"It is the last thing we want to do," the voice said. "We aim to keep you safe. Pampered, even. Brother Dimitrios asked that you be put into this relaxation room. We have several. Are you comfortable?"

I stood up and looked around for a window, a two-way

mirror, a curtain like the one in *The Wizard of Oz*. "No, I'm not," I said. "As a matter of fact, I'm creeped out beyond belief. Especially by you. Who are you? *Where* are you? *Why are you disguising your voice?*"

"That's a lot of questions," the voice replied. "I'll start with the last one. I have to disguise my voice. My identity must remain a secret to all but the top echelons. A security precaution. I am known as Nancy Emelink Margana, but I confess, that's not real, either. I may not even be female."

"So you're the boss?" I said. "The one Brother Devious reports to?"

"I wouldn't be so harsh with Dimitrios," the voice replied. "He cares deeply about your well-being, and he is a crackerjack manager."

"Crackerjack?" The sound of that term grated against me. The only other person I knew who ever used that expression was my mom. Hearing it from the Massa CEO, or whoever this was, felt like a slap in the face. "Maybe you want to brush up on your slang."

The voice made a strange noise that I took to be a laugh. "Old-fashioned, I suppose. I'm sorry. If you do not like it here, I will arrange for you to be taken to your room. Cass is there already. At any rate, I thought I would personally welcome you from the executive board of the Massa organization. You can be assured that I will be there to help you find the correct path. That's a promise."

I flopped down onto the cushions and stared blankly at the bland images on TV. The Massa organization. She made this sound like some Wall Street company. Which, somehow, didn't surprise me. "Thanks a bunch," I muttered.

* * *

"I'm really, really, really sorry," Marco said, inhaling a pint of Ben & Jerry's Chunky Monkey ice cream by the spoonful. "I know you think I'm this total Arnold Benedict."

The lounge had a full kitchen, a fridge stocked with food, and two giant flat-screen TVs. There were four windowless bedrooms off the lounge, one for each of us. They were actually going to keep all four of us together. Tinker, Tailor, Sailor, Traitor. They'd made us wear these bright yellow jumpsuits that would make us stand out a hundred yards away.

"Benedict Arnold," Cass mumbled. "A world-class turncoat."

"Right, that guy," Marco said. "Hey, I know exactly how you feel. I felt the same way when Brother Dimitrios first found me. I was ready to floor him."

"For about fifteen seconds, before he changed your mind," Cass remarked.

"You'll come around," Marco insisted. "You'll see."

"Why did they put you in here with us?" I blurted out.

"You're not one of us. You're Massa. You should be with them. They're a company, did you know that? A killing company. And it looks like they're training you well."

"That was crazy, right?" he said. "I couldn't believe myself. It's almost like I left my body. Like I was standing outside it and watching all those moves. What did you guys think? Was that awesome or what?"

I wheeled around on him. "Are you kidding us? You think all is forgiven, that it's okay for us to sit here and worship you?"

"Jack," Marco said, leaning forward, "cool stuff is going to happen to you, too. And you, Cass. And Aly, when she gets back. These guys are not like the KI. They don't just do lame exercises—you know, testing us in the garage, in the kitchen, on the mountain. These guys challenge you. That's the only way to strengthen your G7W abilities. Aly will be hacking things you never imagined possible. Cass, you'll be mapping routes all over the world. Jack, you . . . um . . ."

I hated hearing the pause in his voice. The old question in everyone's mind—*What's Jack good for?* "I don't like it," I said. "It smells bad. Like they're trying to brainwash us."

"The food is great, you have to admit," Cass said, pulling another carton of ice cream from the fridge. "Look, they have Chubby Hubby, too, my favorite. And I liked the relaxation room. And the lady with the scrambled voice."

"Nancy," I said. "Morgana. Or whatever her fake name was. Or his. They're just trying to bend our minds. Soften us up."

Marco exhaled deeply. He threw his empty ice cream carton across the room and sank a perfect shot into the trash can. Cass offered him the Chubby Hubby, but Marco just set it down on the counter. "I owe you guys. If I were you, I'd be mad at me. But I'm mad, too. At the KI. They've been on that island forever. What have they done there? They didn't know about the vromaski, which almost killed me. Or the maze, which almost killed Cass. They didn't know enough to warn Jack about the griffin—which almost killed all of us! Then when things get really bad, they send us halfway around the world with some bearded goon who can't keep himself out of jail."

"And then the Massarene tried to kill us in Greece!" I reminded him.

"That's because they didn't know who we were, Brother Jack," Marco said. "They saw us destroying everything they believed in. They didn't know we were Select."

"We all have the lambda," I said. "It's pretty obvious."

Marco nodded. "They thought we painted it on, the way they do. They figured we were trying to fake them out, to blend in. When we tried to steal the Colossus, of course they went ballistic. Then Brother Dimitrios saw us flying—and everything changed. He knew we were the real deal. He's smart, guys. We stay with the KI, we die. Their leadership is bad and they have nineteenth-century ideas. They're like the hard-core nerds in school who make jokes you can't understand and ignore you when you try to talk to them."

"I'm like that," Cass piped up.

"Yeah, but you're cool, Brother Cass," Marco said, giving his head a good-natured push. "You're a real person with feelings. I trust you. That's the thing—I trust these guys, too. They're going to take care of us, *support* us. We will find those Loculi twice as fast."

"And then what?" I said.

"They're close to finding the island," Marco said. "They almost did. A few weeks ago, there were a series of brooches in the KI firewall."

"Breaches," Cass said. "Brooches are things you wear on a blouse. I think they were able to break through when Aly had to disable the firewall briefly. That was because we needed info from the outside. Info about you, Marco."

"Cool," Marco said. "So now when the Massa do locate the island, we'll be able to bring the Loculi back where they belong."

"How is that any different than what Bhegad wants?" I said.

"Bhegad wants to nuke the Loculi," Marco said.

"That's not what he said," I pointed out.

"It's the *Karai Institute*, Brother Jack," Marco said. "Their mission is to do what Karai wanted—which was to destroy the Loculi! Massarym was the one who hid them in the Seven Wonders, so that someday they would be returned permanently. And when that happens, the energy will flow again. Not only will we be cured, but the continent will rise."

"Uh, rise?" Cass repeated. "As in, come up from the bottom of the sea, where it's been for eons?"

Marco smiled. "Can you picture it? A new land mass, dudes. A place with that awesome energy flow. A hangout for the best minds, the best athletes, the best everyone—all picking up that Atlantean vibe. Imagine what they'll do. End all wars, solve the fuel crisis, make the best movies and songs. And we'll all be at the top level. Cass can be Transportation Commissioner, Aly can be Chief Tech Guy. Jack can be something cool, too, because Brother Dimitrios will be choosing. Maybe the chief of staff."

"And what about you?" I asked.

I figured he'd say *Chief Food Taster* or *Sports Czar* or *Babe Magnet*. The whole thing was loony.

But Marco was grinning at me as if he'd just wandered into an ice cream store on a hot August afternoon. "Brother Dimitrios has big plans for the Immortal One. He says I have leadership ability."

"Let me guess," I said. "Head court jester."

325

Marco shook his head. "In the new world, you can keep calling me Marco. But to everyone else, I'll be His Highness King Marco the First."

The words hung in the air. I looked at Cass. He looked at me.

"You're joking," I said.

"Hey, in the old days, thirteen-year-old kings were pretty common," Marco shot back. "Read your history. Also, Atlantis can only be run by descendants of the royal family if it's expected to survive, right? So you learn on the job. And you surround yourself with wise advisers, like Brother Dimitrios. And loyal staff. You attract the best minds from all over the world. The coolest artists and athletes. It will be the most awesome country ever!"

He was beaming. He was also crazy. "Marco, we're friends—or we used to be friends, before you betrayed us all," I said. "So I have to be honest with you. That's the most unbelievably ridiculous thing anyone has ever said. Sorry."

Marco's smile faded. For a moment he just stared down at the table.

Then he looked up, and I flinched from the flat, hard look in his eyes.

"You think I'm ridiculous?" he said, his voice as cold and deadly as his expression. "Fine. I'll do it without you. Go tell Brother Dimitrios. Tell him you want nothing to do with any of this. You'd rather back away from the opportunity of a lifetime. Your loss."

"Marco . . ." Cass pleaded.

Marco stalked into his bedroom. "I'll celebrate my fourteenth birthday without any of you. Because I'll be alive."

CHAPTER FIFTY-ONE

THE PHONE

I DIDN'T FALL asleep until three.

King Marco?

He was serious. And he had gone off to a sound sleep. Me, I didn't think I would ever sleep again. But I did, because an alarm woke me up out of a restless dream.

I looked at the clock on the table: 5:13.

Two hours.

I slapped the snooze button, but the alarm kept chiming. I sat up and shook myself awake. The noise was coming from the bed. I could feel the vibrations. I kicked back the sheets. Nothing. I lifted my pillow.

A smart phone glowed bright blue, beeping, with a screen that announced WAKE UP! in happy yellow letters.

I swiped at the off button. The place fell quiet, except for the mechanical whir of the lounge refrigerator and the whoosh of the air-conditioning ducts. I held the phone and stared at it. It wasn't the same make as mine. Besides, I didn't have a phone anymore. Hadn't had one since the moment I got to the KI.

The alarm app had vanished. In its place was some kind of map. A tiny blue dot pulsed inside a small yellow box. I pinched to zoom out. The box was part of a larger circle.

Dot, box, circle—the phone, this room, the lounge. Outside the lounge was a network of parallel lines leading in different directions—hallways. At the top of the screen, an arrow pointed diagonally to the right. It was labeled "N" for north.

I pushed open the door of my room, stepped warily into the lounge and the hall. No one was there.

But someone *had* been here. While I was asleep. Someone had put the phone under my pillow, knowing I'd find it and see the map.

Who? And why?

Keeping my eye on the screen, I walked. I moved back from the hallway into the lounge. The place smelled like banana peels and orange rinds, and Marco's uneaten container of Chubby Hubby still stood on the counter.

The blue dot moved into the circle as I walked. I slid my fingers around the screen, examining the maze of pathways.

The plan of the Massa hideout revealed itself. The paths ranged much farther afield than I thought. The place was huge, dozens of rooms, a crisscrossing maze of corridors. The map was flat, but if I pressed a button labeled "3D," it tilted to reveal a three-dimensional cross-section of paths on many different levels.

I sneaked into Cass's room and put my hand over his mouth. His eyes popped open in fear, but I quickly put my finger to my lips in a shushing gesture. I flashed the phone's screen to him, and he bolted up out of bed. "Where did you get this?" he whispered.

"Under my pillow," I said. "And I don't think it was the Tooth Fairy. Somebody here is on our side. Follow me."

"Wait," Cass said. "Find out who this is."

I tried to access mail, photos, browser, settings. All of them were locked. "Just the alarm and map are public," I said. "No. Wait . . ."

I'd hit the contacts button. It was showing a list. All the names were in number code.

"Got it," Cass said.

"Got what?" I asked.

"The numbers," Cass said. "Committed to memory."

"Doesn't do us much good," I said. "They look pretty random to me."

Cass scratched his head. "This is where we need Aly."

He was right. This was going to be impossible. "We have to channel our own inner Aly," I said lamely.

"I don't have the brain for this," Cass said, staring at it intently and shifting from foot to foot, as if that would help. "Memorize, yes. Analyze, not so much."

"It's an internal code," I said.

"Duh," Cass replied. "So?"

"So maybe it's not that hard," I replied.

"How does that make sense?" Cass asked.

I was thinking about something my dad and I talked about, when I was studying American history in school. "Back in World War II," I said, "the English stole a code machine from the Germans. If they could figure out how it worked, they could break all the enemy secret codes. They got everything except one part. Every German machine operator had to set each machine by keying in ten letters at the top. If the Brits could figure out those ten letters, they could crack the whole thing."

"Ten letters, twenty-six letters in the alphabet—that's like guessing the winning lottery numbers," Cass said.

"Worse," I said. "But that's when someone realized that it was *German soldiers* who had to pick the letters, not cryptologists. They weren't going to pick anything too sophisticated, or they'd forget it. Well, the English realized *Heil Hitler* was ten letters—and it turns out almost all the soldiers had used that!"

"Really?" Cass said. "You think there are Nazis here? I hate Nazis."

"The point is, everyone in this place has to read internal code," I said. "The leaders and the goons. So think simple. That's what Aly does. She starts with the obvious, then works from there."

Cass and I stared at the numbers on the screen. "They look like email addresses," he said.

"And the last part of each address is the same," I added. "After the dot."

"Either *com*, *net*, or *org*," Cass said.

I nodded. "The first number after the dot is a three. The third letter of the alphabet is c. So I'm thinking that's a *com*."

I grabbed a pencil and paper from a desk drawer and quickly wrote down a key:

```
1  2  3  4  5  6  7  8  9  10 11 12 13 14 15
A  B  C  D  E  F  G  H  I  J  K  L  M  N  O

16 17 18 19 20 21 22 23 24 25 26
P  Q  R  S  T  U  V  W  X  Y  Z
```

"*Com* is three, fifteen, thirteen!" Cass blurted out.

"Give me a minute . . . " I said, trying to match all the numbers to letters. "Aly could probably do this in her head. I mean, you don't know for sure about these double-digit letters. Like a one next to a seven. That could be the first and seventh letters, *AG*. Or it could mean the seventeenth letter, *P*. Hang on . . ."

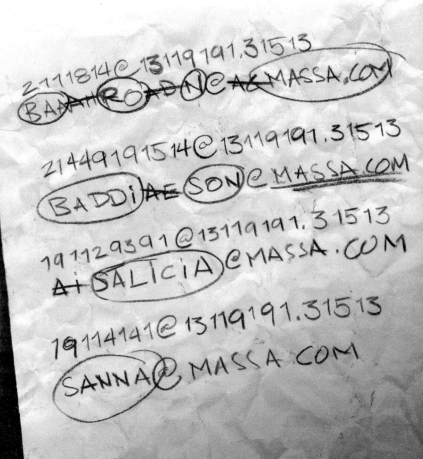

"Baaron . . . Baddison . . . Salicia . . . Sanna?" Cass said.

"I'm thinking the B stands for Brother and the S for Sister—like *Brother Aaron* and *Sister Alicia*," I said. "Monk-ish names."

"Sounds like the way Marco normally speaks," Cass said. "He's made for this place."

"The person who left this wanted us to see it—but why?" I exited out of the app and kept tapping other ones. Each was password-protected. "Great. Can't open any of these."

"Any other great insights from World War Two?" Cass asked.

Finally I tapped an app marked RS. It opened to reveal an image that made us both jump back:

"Whoa," Cass said. "Big Brother is watching."

"I guess someone was trying to take a picture but pressed the button that turns the camera backward," I said, flipping back to the maps app. "Let's use this and see where it leads us."

Cass took the phone, examining the map. "Where do we go if we do escape?"

"We try to find Aly, if she's nearby," I said. "We hack off the iridium arm bands, and hope that the KI finds us before the Massa."

Cass's expression darkened. "You mean, if the KI still exists. . . ."

"We can't think about what happened at the Euphrates camp," I said. "But you heard Brother Dimitrios. He still doesn't know the location of the island. Whatever his people did to the camp, the KI will be fired up. And the geeks will be trying to find us."

"So best-case scenario, we leave this prison and go to a nicer one," Cass said glumly. "I guess I can live with that."

I took a deep breath. "It's all we've got. Think about what Dimitrios did, Cass. He knew what would happen when we took the Loculus. He didn't care about all those people. About Daria. She gave her life for us. At least Professor Bhegad tried to do something. Shelley didn't work, but he spent time and money to create that thing. Both organizations have lied to us. But for all its weirdness, only one cares enough not to kill innocent people. And that's the one I plan to stick with."

Cass's eyes wandered out to the common area. "Okay," he said softly. "I'll go wake Marco."

"What?" I grabbed his arm. "No, Cass. Not Marco. He'll rat us out."

"He won't," Cass said. "Seriously. He brought us here. He knows we're a family. He wants us to stay together."

"Cass, I'm sorry, but you are in a fantasy world—" I said.

Cass jerked his arm away. His face was beet red. "Fantasy? Is that what you'd say if I told you, weeks ago, you'd be trying to find the Seven Wonders? Real is real. We break up and we die. Nothing is more important than staying together, Jack—*nothing*!"

From inside Marco's room, I heard a sudden snort. I leaned in to look. He was fast asleep on his back, snoring.

"Cass, listen to me," I hissed. "When this is over, we will go back to different places. Yeah, maybe when we're old we can move to the same town. But maybe not. Because you make new families when you're old. Real families. This is about survival, Cass. If we tell Marco, we're giving up. Betraying Aly. Deciding to stay here and become the kind of zombie that they're making Marco into. If that's your definition of family, you can have it. But give me a chance to escape on my own."

Cass's eyes burned into mine. The sides of his mouth

curled downward and for a moment I thought he was going to spit, or scream.

Instead, his eyes rose to a small, spherical camera wedged into a corner of the ceiling.

He grabbed the container of Chubby Hubby ice cream that had been sitting out all night. Taking off the top, he heaved the container toward the glass.

A lump of brownish goop flew through the air, saturating the camera. "Promise me that if we get out, we'll come back for him," Cass said.

"Promise," I replied.

Without looking at me, he headed for the door. I grabbed the first things I could get my hands on and threw them into a plastic bag: a knife, a flashlight, a canister of pepper, a bottle of vegetable oil, and another tub of ice cream from the freezer.

I glanced back into Marco's room one last time. His back rose and fell.

Silently, I slipped out after Cass.

CHAPTER FIFTY-TWO

HACK ATTACK

"I DON'T LIKE this," Cass whispered. "It's too quiet."

"We're in an enclosed stairwell," I said. "Stairwells are quiet."

I jammed the kitchen knife into a small, square metal door on the wall, about eye level. The lock wouldn't give, but the door bent outward enough for me to peer under it with the flashlight. "Circuit breakers," I said.

Cass nodded. "Aly might be able to hack into their system," he said, "but you're MacGruber."

I slipped the knife into the box, said a prayer, and began sliding it right to left. The angle was bad, the torque was weak, but I managed to flip most of the switches from on to off. "Either I just shut off some lights," I said, "or I disabled the washing machines."

We pushed open the door from the stairwell to the hallway. It was pitch dark. "Hallelujah," I said. "The security cameras won't pick us up. I think we'll be okay if we stick to the light of the phone."

Cass eyed the map app, staring down the long hallway. "At least I know the dimensions of this hallway. I memorized them. The map is showing a lot of closets in this area of the compound. Small rooms. Mostly supplies, I'm guessing. We're far away from the main corridors—the control rooms and all. That's also where the exits are. I'm thinking we can wind around back, where it looks like there's a delivery exit."

Cass led the way. We felt our way through darkened hallways, zigging right and then left twice. The reach of the circuit breakers ended there. We were entering an area lit by fluorescent lights above. I looked around for overhead cameras and saw nothing here. "We go right next, and we'll be close," Cass said.

But as we neared the next hallway, I heard footsteps.

We plastered ourselves against the wall. At the end of the corridor, where it came to a T, voices were talking in Arabic.

My back was against a door. At eye level was a sign labeled in several languages. The third line read SUPPLIES in English. Under it was a simple keypad with numbers from one to nine.

In these bright yellow uniforms, there was no hiding.

We looked like two giant bananas. Cass turned to me, his eyes wide with fear. *Run*, he mouthed.

But I was thinking about the workers who had to get in and out of this supply closet. And about the German soldiers who had to code the secret-message machines.

I turned toward the door. I thought fast.

Massa.

That equaled 13-1-19-19-1.

I pressed each digit. Nothing happened.

Cass was pulling me away. *Simplicity*, I thought. *Something easily remembered. A number they would all know.*

On a hunch, I keyed in five digits.

Click.

The door opened. We hustled inside and pulled it shut behind us.

I willed my heart not to fly out of my chest. We listened for the guards. Their conversation was growing more animated. But they were staying put. They hadn't heard a thing.

Cass flicked on an overhead light. "How did you do that?" he whispered.

"Smart guessing," I whispered back. "Remember the code for 'com'—three-one-five-one-three? It's a number palindrome, the same back and forward. Easy to recall. Something they probably all see on their cell phones. So I tried it."

"I don't believe this," Cass said. "I can't wait to tell Aly."

I glanced around. The shelves contained all kinds of caustic liquids. I jammed small bottles of bleach and ammonia into my bag.

Cass was eagerly taking down a pile of neatly folded uniforms from the top shelf. Massa uniforms. Brown and institutional. They looked exactly like the things Brother Dimitrios and his goons were wearing here.

Cass's eyes were saying exactly what I was thinking. We would be much less noticeable wearing these.

We each took one that seemed about the right size and changed into them. Another shelf was stocked with matching baseball-type caps, each embroidered with a lambda.

Perfect. With these outfits, especially with the hat brims pulled low, we could pass for employees. Well, from a distance. A long distance, where no one would notice that we were thirteen.

"I have another route," Cass whispered, staring at the phone. "Left at the intersection, then right at the fork. There's a big room we have to go through. On the other side of that room, we're pretty close to the exit."

Slowly, silently, we opened the door and stepped out. We stepped quickly down the hallway, passing a lounge arrangement like the one we'd just been sleeping in. Then an intersection.

"What fork?" I said. "This is a four-way!"

Cass was fingering the screen like crazy. "Sorry. There are all these levels. They overlap. Maybe the fork is on the level above us. Or—or below . . ."

"Pick one!" I said.

"Straight," Cass shot back.

We headed down a long passageway toward a big, domed room. Some kind of control center. No door, just an archway. We could hear humming, beeps, shouts, an occasional burst of something in English—but even that was gibberish. *Sector Five atmospheric control . . . waste systems redirecting to path 17B . . . clearing air traffic . . .*

A man burst through the opening, tapping furiously on a tablet. He was heading right for us. If he looked up, we were toast. Two kids who happen to exactly match the descriptions of the recently captured Select.

I pulled Cass toward me, pretending to show him something on the phone. We hunched over the screen, our backs to the guy.

The guy rushed past us without even looking up.

"We are so close," Cass whispered. "But this room—it's huge. Like some kind of command center."

"Keep your head down," I said. "Pretend you have something important to do. Don't run. Walk like a grown-up. When we get to the other side—"

"Wait," Cass said. "You want us to walk straight through *there*? We can't do that!"

"They don't know we're missing yet," I said. "This is the

342

last place they'd expect to see us."

"But—"

"Think about Aly," I insisted. "She did the exact thing no one expected. It takes guts. Which is what we need right now."

Cass looked into the room and swallowed hard. "I hope you're right."

We barged inside, keeping our heads down. The place was crawling with people. Most of them looked like they'd just awakened. From the walls, enormous monitors glared down at us like the schedule boards from airports. They showed hallways and rooms, lounges and storage spaces, satellite maps, cross-sections of pyramids. An enormous Jumbotron-type screen loomed over everything, tiled with all the different views of the compound, inside and out. This place was their security center.

I scanned the room quickly. Best to stick to the shadows as much as possible. I pulled Cass to the wall, where the traffic was lightest. We made our way around, hugging the wall as close as we could. I could see an archway at the other end. It led into another corridor that looked no different from the one we came from. I let Cass lead. Cass knew the route.

He was picking up the pace. As long as no one was looking for us, we would be fine. We were just about to reach the archway.

Boooweep! Booooweep! Booooweep!

The sound was more like a whack to the head than an alarm. It shrieked through the room, pounding our ears, blotting out all other sound. Cass jumped nearly three feet. Startled workers turned from their screens to look up at a huge Jumbotron-type screen. It blared two words in bright red letters against a white background:

SECURITY BREACH!

Under it were photos of Cass and me.

CHAPTER FIFTY-THREE

THE EXIT AT THE END OF THE HALL

"GO!" I SHOUTED. *"Just go!"*

We bolted through the archway, out of the room and into a wide, modern corridor. Workers were hurrying curiously toward the control room. Some of them were checking their phones.

We ducked into a restroom and hid in two adjoining stalls. A guy raced out from the stall next to ours, muttering under his breath. We waited until the footfalls died down, then sneaked out.

"Second left!" Cass said, eyes on the phone. "Looks like there's an exit at the end of the hallway there."

"I'll scope it out first!" I sprinted ahead to the second corner. Before making the turn I stopped, back against

345

the wall, and peered around.

Cass was right. The corridor just around the corner from us ended in a doorway, about fifty feet away. But standing in front of it were Brothers Dimitrios and Yiorgos. They were yelling in Egyptian at two hapless-looking guards.

I sprang back. "We're busted."

"What are they saying?" Cass whispered.

"How should I know?" I replied.

It wasn't until then that I realized my head was buzzing. And not just because of the chase.

It was the Song of the Heptakiklos. Near us. Very near.

"Do you—?" Cass said.

I nodded. Cass peeked at our phone. Then he looked across the hall at a door on the wall across from us. A door like a bank vault, thick and ornately carved.

"Jack?" he whispered. "How much room do you have in that sack?"

He held out the phone to show me our GPS location. The room opposite us, behind the vault door, showed as a rectangle.

In that rectangle were two glowing white circles. "This person who owns the phone," I said, "is definitely trying to tell us something."

We walked closer. "Where's the handle?" Cass hissed. "Vault doors are supposed to have big old-timey handles, like in the movies."

"Ssh," I said.

346

Dimitrios was still talking. I focused on a smooth black panel, where a doorknob might once have been. It glowed black and red. "It's a reader," I said.

"Fingerprint, like at the KI?" Cass said, his face tense. "Or maybe a retinal scan."

"RS" was the name of the app—it meant Retinal Scan.

"Cass, you are a genius!" I said.

I snatched the phone from him, and he flinched. Both of our hands were way too sweaty. The phone slipped out, clattering to the floor.

Dimitrios's voice stopped. We froze.

I scooped up the phone, fumbling with the controls. I pressed the control button to get the app grid. I swiped too hard, scrolling past three screens.

"Who's there?"

Dimitrios.

I scrolled back until I found the one I was looking for. *RS*.

I pressed. The eye filled the screen. I could see myself reflected in it. My chest contracted.

There was something about this eye, something that seemed familiar.

Do it. Now!

"Jack, they're coming!" Cass shouted.

I turned the phone and held the eye up to the black sensor.

Beep.

CHAPTER FIFTY-FOUR

DEAFENING SILENCE

THE DOOR CLICKED open. We pushed it hard and slipped inside. The thing weighed a ton.

"Stavros? Is that you—finally?" Dimitrios's impatient voice bellowed.

Click.

The door made an oddly delicate sound as it shut.

We held our breath. A different voice shouted from the right, the direction we had just come from. "Nowhere, Brother Dimitrios! Vanished from their rooms. Both of them. But they can't go far."

Brother Yiorgos.

Now the voices met, directly in front of us. "The trackers?" Dimitrios demanded. "If they escape—"

"They're wearing the bracelets," Yiorgos said. "The KI

will not be able to find them if they escape. Which they will not do."

Dimitrios made a sound of disgust. "I want every exit out of this place sealed," he said.

I could hear his footsteps thumping away from us. We stood still in the ensuing silence, not daring to move. The room was pitch black. A string, connected to an overhead lightbulb, tickled the top of my head. My chest felt like a rabid hamster had been let loose inside.

I knew a Loculus was in here. Maybe both Loculi. The Song was deafening. I stared at the sliver of light under the door. It flickered as guards raced past. Now random shouts were echoing loud and fast. Voices I didn't recognize. Languages I didn't know.

When this wave of sounds was gone, I reached upward and pulled the string. The bulb clicked on, flooding the room with greenish-white light.

The rear side of the door was a slab of metal, undecorated. At the spot opposite the sensor was a thick iron latch, which had opened when we'd used the retina.

I turned into the room. It was empty, save for an old, sturdy-looking wall safe with a rusted panel:

"Try the pattern!" I said.

Cass started with 142857, then went on to 428571 and 285714. "They're not working!" he said.

"Stop," I said, staring at the panel.

Simplify.

The number keys looked old. Some of them were faded. If people had been opening this safe for years, their fingers would wear off the numbers.

The wear and tear showed a pattern.

I lifted my finger toward the one. Then I tapped out a pattern that resembled the shape of a seven—left to right across the top, then diagonally down to the left-hand corner.

1, 2, 3, 5, and 7.

With a dull click, the door swung open.

Inside, embedded in the wall, was a deep rectangular hole that contained two wooden boxes. "Eureka," I whispered.

Cass opened one, to see a familiar glow—the flying Loculus. As he reached inside, it levitated to meet his fingers. "Good to see this again . . ."

I opened the other box, which seemed to contain nothing. As I thrust my hand inside, my knuckles hit something solid. I grinned. "Two for two."

Attached to the wall, to the right of the safe, was a table containing a couple of sturdy sacks—big ones, which had obviously been used to carry the boxed Loculi here.

I placed the flying Loculus, in its box, inside one sack.

The other Loculus I would need to have in hand. Quietly I sidled to the doorway and put my ear against it. Silence.

Looking at Cass, I mouthed *Let's go.*

As we turned back to the Loculus, the door beeped. I looked over my shoulder.

The inner latch was turning downward, slowly. I reached up, pulling the lightbulb string. The light went out.

And the door began to swing open.

CHAPTER FIFTY-FIVE

PUSH HARDER

THE LIGHT BLINKED on. A man with thick stubble looked straight at me. He muttered something extremely nasty-sounding in another language.

Then he looked away.

Behind him, a woman wearing a Massa cap peered inside. Her eyes circled the closet.

My back was jammed against the wall, my palm firmly on the Loculus. I held my breath. Cass was clutching my arm so tightly I wanted to scream. I wanted to remind him that invisibility depended on contact, not grip strength.

The two began to argue. The woman reached up and shut the light. Slowly the door swung back.

We waited for the click. Even then, neither of us dared

take a breath for a few seconds. Until the footfalls had faded into the distance.

"That was close," Cass said. "I owe you, Jack."

"Stay alive," I replied. "That will be the best payback. Now let's get out of here. Hang on to my arm."

I held on to the invisibility Loculus, and Cass took the flying one. No one would be able to see us. I carefully thrust the handle down, pushed the door open, and stepped into the hallway.

It felt great. Too great. You have no idea what your body feels like when you're invisible. Solid but weightless. It's the opposite of being underwater. There you have to adjust to the resistance. You push harder. Every motion is exaggerated. With invisibility, it's the opposite. You feel like your arm will fling off with every swing, your feet will slip and thrust you into the air. You have to pull back. It makes you want to giggle.

And I could hardly imagine a less giggle-worthy moment.

I turned left. At the corner I peered around to see the exit. At the end of the long hallway, in front of the exit door where we'd seen Dimitrios minutes before, three burly men stood guard.

Cass's grip tightened on my arm. We lifted off the floor, only a few inches, to avoid having to make footsteps. I sucked in a lungful of the dry desert air that blew in through the open door. It felt liberating.

Unfortunately the ceiling was too low for us to fly over the guards' heads. So we hovered, waiting.

The sound of a truck stopped the men's conversation. Through the door I could see uniformed men piling out, rifles and ammo belts across their chests. We shrank against the walls as the small militia ran inside, shouting.

I shivered. Cass stared wide-mouthed.

The soldiers were fitted out for war. They were here to find us.

As the guys spread out to the different hallways, the three guards turned back toward the open door. They were looking outside again, shoulder to shoulder.

What do we do now? Cass mouthed.

With my free hand, I reached for the pouch on my belt and mouthed back, *Call MacGruber.*

By now, the container of ice cream was melted and gooey. I tossed it, and it landed about three feet behind us with a dull thud. It was totally visible, totally a mess. For good measure, I threw the bottle of vegetable oil after it.

The guards turned. Their faces scrunched in bewilderment, and they began walking toward it curiously. Leaving the door. Heading directly in front of us.

We backed away, flattening ourselves even more.

One of the guards bumped against my shoulder. Solid. I nearly dropped the Loculus.

He staggered back with a gasp. In his eyes I could see

two and two coming together reluctantly. These guys must have been taught about us. About what we had found.

The man called sharply to the others. All three reached into holsters, pulling out pistols.

Two of them walked slowly toward us, their eyes unfocused but intent. The third moved to the door, blocking escape.

The guard closest to us grinned. "We know you are there. Exactly where, you cannot get away. I will be proud to be the one to bring you in. So. You have to the count of three to appear, or I will shoot. One . . ."

I looked at Cass. My fingers were sweaty and slippery on the Loculus. I wedged it under my arm.

The guard poked me with his rifle butt and laughed. "Three!"

CHAPTER FIFTY-SIX

MUSTACHES EVERYWHERE

I HEARD THE click of a safety catch. I wrapped my fingers around the pepper container, screwing off the top—and I tossed the contents.

Moving fast, I wriggled out of the gun's way. And I tossed the contents.

"Yeeeeeaaaa-CHOO!"

The guards and his ally sprang back. The other guard, the one at the door, faltered, just in time for me to throw another fistful of pepper.

"Let's go!" I shouted.

We tore out of the building to a chorus of sneezing, and a new vocabulary of very bad words.

We kept to the outer wall, staying in the shadows.

356

Not far away, we sped by the soldiers' truck. As I passed, I noticed a set of keys flung into the cup compartment. "Have you ever tried driving?" I asked.

"Yup," Cass piped up. "On the farm."

We jumped in. Cass put the truck in gear, and we lurched away in a cloud of foul odor.

* * *

The streets of Nazlet el-Samman were a relief. They smelled of cinnamon and frying meat. We had ditched the truck just off the highway, far away from here, and jogged the rest of the way.

"Police?" I asked whoever would listen. "Do you know where the police are?"

"How about a girl, about our age?" Cass said. "Really smart?"

We looked around desperately for cops and for Aly, but it was hard to see. The street was packed shoulder to shoulder. On the one hand, this might help shield us from the Massa, but on the other hand, we could barely move. I had to grab Cass's arm to keep from being separated. Every hat looked like a Massa lambda cap to me. Every person looked like a Massa. I saw at least seven men who were dead ringers for Brother Dimitrios. Mustaches were everywhere.

It was getting close to lunchtime and vendors stirred up food in great big pots. A kid in a striped T-shirt raced in and out of slow-moving tourists. "Hahahaha!" he cackled, easily evading a pursuer who must have been his younger brother. A girl walked purposefully by us, pulling two goats on tethers. Voices rang out loudly in all kinds of languages: "Over here . . . *ella tho . . . kommen sie hier bitte . . . bienvenue . . .* the best!"

"Jack, I'm starving," Cass said.

"No," I said. "Just no. We have to get out of here."

"This is fast food," he said. "We can eat and run."

"No!"

We wound our way past tables full of plastic pyramids in Day-Glo colors; arrays of T-shirts that said MY PARENTS TOOK ME TO EGYPT AND ALL I GOT WAS THIS DUMB T-SHIRT; and an artist with a beret who was painting a portrait of a patiently smiling grandfather on a canvas labeled PYRAMID OF GEEZER.

I pulled Cass into a narrow side street. Even in full sunlight, the alley was dark. An angry-looking chicken stood in a doorway, scolded us, and then lost interest and went back in.

"What do we do now?" Cass asked.

"I say we get away from this place," I said. "The farther the better. They'll come after us. They'll see the truck and cover the whole area. We can stay invisible but that's not going to help us in the long run. We'll keep an eye out for a hardware store so we can wrench these iridium bracelets off, and hope the KI picks us up."

"What about calling home?" Cass asked.

I thought about Aly's disastrous phone conversation with her mom in Rhodes. But I knew the sound of Dad's voice would be pretty amazing. It was tempting. "I'll think about it."

Cass gazed back into the street. "It's easier to think on a full stomach."

I rubbed my forehead. It ached. And not the weird, G7W kind of pain that meant I needed a treatment. It was pure hunger.

I looked left and right. The alley was empty. No one watching. Quickly I placed the invisibility Loculus in the empty box, closed it, and put that into the empty sack. "Keep your eyes open," I said.

We walked out the alleyway and into the bustling street. In the shadows of the nearest building, a skinny cat and two skinnier kittens eyed us warily. I stepped on an errant chunk of pita bread and kicked it toward them. As they pounced, a fat guy with a thick mustache grinned at us from behind a long, hissing grill. "*Bueno! Bon! Primo! Ausgezeichnet! Oraio!* The best!"

He held out a chunk of shish-kebab meat on a toothpick, which Cass scarfed right down. "Ohhhhh, he's right," Cass said with a blissful smile. "It's amazing. I'll have a full one, sir."

I pointed to a delicious-looking hunk of meat, roasting

on a stick. "Whatever that is."

"Ahmed! Shish-kebab, shwarma!" the guy called out. His partner, a tall guy with a darker mustache and chiseled arms, doled out Cass's dishes first. Then he cut five slices of the shwarma meat and laid them on a fluffy piece of pita bread with onions, peppers, and steaming rice.

I could barely control my drool before biting in. "Ah, hungry boys!" the man said. "American dollars? Only six!" He smiled. "Okay, for you—only two-fifty!"

Money.

In the preparation for the time-rift, I hadn't thought to bring any. "Um . . . Cass?"

"I left home without my American Express card," Cass said.

I peered up at the food vendor. He was tending to another customer, a fat guy with an Indiana Jones hat, plaid shorts, white socks and sandals, and a family of four.

Invisibility could come in very handy. I swung my bag around and pulled open the box.

"Hahahahaha!" With a piercing laugh, the kid in the striped T-shirt sped past. He knocked my arm hard. The box toppled onto the street.

"The Loculus!" Cass cried.

I dove for the box, scooping it up off the pavement. I felt inside, praying the Loculus was still there.

Nothing. I could hear the music. I knew it was around

somewhere. But I couldn't see it. "It's gone," I said.

Cass was on his knees, feeling around for it. I dropped down to join him. People screamed in surprise as we pushed them away.

"Hey!" the shish-kebab guy shouted.

I turned. Ahmed, his partner, was catapulting over the counter. "You thief!" he said. "You pay!"

Tourists were turning to stare. A gray-haired guy with an ice-cream cone snapped a photo. A little girl began to cry.

"Stop them!" Ahmed shouted.

No time to think. I sprinted into the crowd. I knocked over a basket, upsetting a snake charmer who tried to smack me with his oboe. As people gathered around to look, I tripped over a pair of baby goats who were lapping water from a puddle. They bahhed angrily as I tumbled onto the stones. I landed in front of a trio of break-dancers in flowing white garb. "Excuse me," I said, ducking into an alleyway.

My back to a dark wall, I caught my breath. I looked around frantically for Cass.

Where was Cass?

I stepped back toward the street. "Cass!" I called out. "Cass, where are you?"

"You!" I spun around at the sound of the gruff voice.

Ahmed was approaching from behind, his fists clenched.

I ran back into the crowd. Ahmed's partner was waiting,

361

a grin on his face and his arms wide.

The two baby goats stared up from the puddle and scolded me. I knelt down, scooped up one of them, and flung it toward the man.

He looked startled. Instinctively he caught it. I swerved around his stand and into the thick of the crowd. I ducked low, threading my way through the people, hoping against hope I'd run into Cass.

I ducked under an archway that led into a courtyard. Sprinting across to the other side, I came into a wider, less touristy street, with boxy buildings, a bus stop, and a gas station. "Cass?" I called out.

A car screeched to a halt at the curb. The driver called out, "Taxi? Taxi?"

"No!" I said.

The cab door opened hard, as if kicked. I backed away, nearly falling to the pavement. I saw a mass of white fabric, a huge pair of sunglasses, and a beard. A red beard.

A beefy hand clapped the back of my neck and shoved me into the backseat, headfirst.

CHAPTER FIFTY-SEVEN

THE CHILLING

"HAVE ONE. NEED the other."

I unfolded my twisted body from the floor of the taxi. I knew the voice. *"Torquin?"*

My captor pulled a white hood from his bush of red curly hair. "Better if you sit," he said.

I stared at him in numb disbelief. "How—?"

To my left, another voice chimed in. "He's here because I got a hardware store guy to cut off my iridium bracelet."

I spun around. I'd been so stunned to see Torquin, I hadn't noticed who was sitting with me in the backseat. Aly grinned. "You can hug me. It's okay."

I threw my arms around her, squeezing her hard. "I was worried about you!"

"You were?" Aly said.

"Yes!" I exclaimed, pulling away. "Look, we can talk more later. Listen, Aly. Marco is lost to us. He's with the Massa and I don't think he's coming back. Cass is somewhere back there, on the main drag. We got separated. Let me run back and see if I can find him."

"Massa coming," Torquin said, reaching for the door. "Can't let you go. Torquin find him."

In the distance I could hear sirens. I turned to see a police car screech to a halt beside a public bus. Out of the car walked a man in a police uniform, along with Brother Dimitrios.

"Drive!" Torquin said.

I sank out of sight. The taxi driver put the car in gear. "Englees?" he said. "Where we go?"

Before anyone could answer, the door next to me flew open. I felt something smack against me, and I fell against Aly.

As the door shut again, Cass materialized out of thin air on the seat next to me. "All present and accounted for," he said, dropping two sacks onto the floor of the taxi. "Including Loculi."

Aly screamed. She reached across me toward Cass, and I felt myself scrunched up into a big hug sandwich. "Are you okay?" she said.

"The shish-kebab gave me gas," Cass said. "Otherwise, I'm gnileef doog."

"Airport," Torquin snapped.

I could see the driver's eyes in the rearview mirror, like two white lanterns, as he slammed on the gas pedal.

* * *

"Well, well, the mad bomber returns!" Fiddle called out as we stepped from the jet onto the KI tarmac.

A woman with a shaved head ran toward us and wrapped me in a hug. It took me a moment to realize it was Nirvana. "Long time," she said. "Longer than you know."

Professor Bhegad was walking toward the ladder with only the slightest limp. His tweed coat looked a little more ragged, his hair grayer and more sparse. "Where are the Loculi?" he called out.

I stepped down the ladder, pulling the bags around to my front. "They're in here, Professor," I said.

He snatched them away with a big grin. "Marvelous! Marvelous!"

"Uh, we're fine, too," Aly said. "Thanks for asking."

Professor Bhegad set down the bags, then turned sheepishly toward us. He thrust his hand toward mine and I shook it. "Well, Jack, you don't look a week older. Which makes perfect sense. Aly . . . Cass . . . so good to have you all back."

"We—we lost Marco," I said softly. "He's with the Massa."

Bhegad's shoulders slumped. "Yes, well, I was afraid

of this. We will deal with it. But let's not dwell on the negative now. We have you, we have the Loculi. Only five to go." He leaned down, investigating the contents of the bags. Then he pulled open the top box, the one with the invisible Loculus. "This second one has nothing in it. . . ."

"Its power is invisibility," I said.

"Extraordinary . . ." he said, peering closer. "The boxes appear to be lined with iridium . . . it shields the Loculi from transmitting powers. How would they know that?"

"They know a lot," Aly said.

Bhegad nodded. "And they will know more, now that they have Marco. We will have to act fast." He wiped his brow and smiled wearily. "But first, a little celebration at the Comestibule. Everyone has missed you. Come. Your rooms are waiting. Take a shower, settle in, freeze up . . ."

"The term is *chill out*, Professor," Nirvana said.

"Ah, well, impossible to keep up with the hep lingo," Bhegad said, walking briskly toward campus. "Dinner begins at seven. A Seven Wonders theme meal. Colossal beef stew, pyramid flan, hanging garden salad, and such. So, my children, we will see you after your chilling."

I glanced and Aly and Cass.

I wanted so badly to feel good about being back.

I almost did.

* * *

366

"What the heck is pyramid flan?" Cass asked, plopping down on my bed. His hair was still wet from the shower, his KI clothes crisp and bright white.

Aly walked in behind him. "Flan is like custard. My mom always orders it at restaurants."

I was still getting dressed and hadn't yet pulled up my pants. "Will you *please*?"

"I won't look," Aly said, turning away.

I zipped up and belted. From my dresser I grabbed the cell phone, which I had transferred out of my Massa custodial outfit.

Cass was staring at it. "Wait. You still have the phone?"

I nodded. I wondered if it still worked. Pressing the button at the bottom, I saw a warning flash on the screen: LOW BATTERY.

I pressed okay and the giant eye stared up out of the screen. "Who the heck is that?" Aly asked.

"The reason we got out," I said.

"We had a helper," Cass added. "A elom. Or, I guess technically, *an* elom."

"Wait. There's a *mole* inside the Massa?" Aly asked.

My brain was kicking in now. Going back over our capture. The rescue had been thrilling, and I hadn't wanted to think about the bad stuff. Marco. Daria.

Even thinking about them now gave me a sudden pang in the chest.

But the eye seemed to be staring into me, as if it were alive. As if it knew me. "Yeah," I said. "A mole."

"Do you know who she is?" Aly asked.

"No," I said. "How do you know it's a she?"

"The lashes," Aly replied. "They have mascara on them. Looks like there's some eyeliner underneath, too."

I thumbed away from it and brought up the contacts app. "There's a name at the top of this list," I said. "Probably hers. I mean, they're *her* contacts. It's in code like the rest of the names."

We stared at the number: 19141325 61361291411.

I grabbed a pencil, then found the sheet where I'd written the number-substitution code.

Then, slowly, I matched the numbers to letters:

"Sister Nancy . . . " I said. "Nancy Emelink. The person whose voice we heard in that room with all the pillows. The boss of the Massa."

"That was a woman?" Cass asked.

"And she told you her name?" Aly added.

"She didn't tell me," Cass said.

I thought back to that day. To what the woman had said. The words were so strange. "There was another name, though. Morgana . . . Margana? It's not here in these numbers, but she mentioned it to me."

"Huh," Cass said, his head cocked. "Which, by the way, is 'huh' backward. But here's the weird thing. *Margana?* Did she really say that? Because that's *anagram* spelled backward!"

An anagram.

The person—the weird voice—had added the word to the end of her name. Why?

I wrote out the name NANCY EMELINK in big, block letters. Immediately Aly went to work. I could see her writing AMY CLENKINEN, LYNN MCANIKEE, and a bunch of others.

But I could not bring myself to pick up a pencil. The letters seemed to be dancing on the paper, rearranging themselves in my own mind.

I felt a sharp sting of cold at the base of my spine, running up to my neck.

"Stop," I said.

Aly looked up. "Say what?"

"I said, *stop*!"

I grabbed the pencil from her. My hand shook as I separated out the letters that I was seeing.

MCKINLEY

"What?" Aly said. "Is this some kind of joke?"

Cass peered over my shoulder. "There are some letters left," he said. "N, A, N, E . . . "

They danced around in my head, too. And as they did, I felt the blood draining from my body to my toes. "Give me the phone," I said, my voice dry and parched.

"Jack . . . ?" Aly said.

"Just give it to me!" As she handed it to me, I tapped the screen. The big eye was still staring up at me. The iris that got us into the secret room. The reason we were here, safe and sound.

I put my thumb and index finger on the screen and pinched in. A forehead and nose appeared. I pinched again—the eye zoomed downward and became part of an entire person. A woman in a uniform. She was standing in a group, with Brother Dimitrios, Yiorgos, and Stavros.

She was smiling. I knew the smile.

It can't be.

I pinched outward again, slowly, enlarging the woman until only she filled the screen.

Welcome to have you back.

The head of the Massa had said that. She had used those very words. It hadn't been easy to understand, and I'd been so angry I hadn't really listened closely.

It was a phrase I'd heard only one person use.

My fingers slackened. The phone slipped out, falling to the floor. I tried to move my mouth to talk, but I couldn't. The eye had belonged to the person in the photo. A person who couldn't have been there. Someone who died many years ago.

"It's *Anne*—the letters spell Anne McKinley . . ." I said.

I couldn't bring myself to continue. But Cass and Aly were staring at me in total bafflement. The words needed to be said aloud. I swallowed hard.

"The head of the Massa," I said, "is my mom."

ABOUT
THE
AUTHOR

PETER LERANGIS

is the author of more than one hundred and sixty books, which have sold more than five million copies and been translated into thirty different languages. These Include *The Colossus Rises*, book one in the *New York Times* bestselling series Seven Wonders, and two books in The 39 Clues series (*The Sword Thief* and *The Viper's Nest*). Peter is a Harvard graduate with a degree in biochemistry and has run a marathon and gone rock climbing during an earthquake – though not on the same day. He lives in New York with his wife, musician Tina deVaron, and their two sons, Nick and Joe. In his spare time, he likes to eat chocolate. Lots of it. Seriously, he loves chocolate.

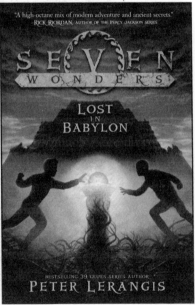